The Drift Latitudes

BY THE SAME AUTHOR

Navigation of a Rainmaker
Wings of Dust
In the Hour of Signs
The Carrier
Travelling with Djinns

Published in French

Nubian Indigo

JAMAL MAHJOUB

The Drift Latitudes

Chatto & Windus
LONDON

Published by Chatto & Windus 2006

2 4 6 8 10 9 7 5 3 1

© Jamal Mahjoub 2006

Jamal Mahjoub has asserted his right under the
Copyright, Designs and Patents Act 1988 to
be identified as the author of this work

First published in Great Britain in 2006 by
Chatto & Windus
Random House, 20 Vauxhall Bridge Road,
London SW1V 2SA

Random House Australia (Pty) Limited
20 Alfred Street, Milsons Point, Sydney,
New South Wales 2061, Australia

Random House New Zealand Limited
18 Poland Road, Glenfield,
Auckland 10, New Zealand

Random House (Pty) Limited
Isle of Houghton, Corner of Boundary Road & Carse O'Gowrie,
Houghton 2198, South Africa

The Random House Group Limited Reg. No. 954009
www.randomhouse.co.uk

A CIP catalogue record for this book
is available from the British Library

ISBN 978 0 7011 7822 2 (from January 2007)
ISBN 0 7011 7822 1

Papers used by Random House are natural,
recyclable products made from wood grown in sustainable forests.
The manufacturing processes conform to the environmental
regulations of the country of origin

Printed and bound in Great Britain by
Mackays of Chatham PLC, Chatham, Kent

Contents

For Judith Marie Mahjoub (*née* Gerlach)
1929–1998

I

Revenant Kin

'Time is the metre, memory the only plot.'
Derek Walcott, *Omeros*

Prologue

Ernst Frager, 1957

Time was air. Seconds transformed into tiny magical orbs that glinted like mercury as they wriggled past the glass inspection windows in the brass tubes that snaked through the control room. The silver spheres were the only indication of what was happening in the ballast tanks. It was his job to keep an eye on them, to see how fast they moved, in which direction, and when they stopped.

Beyond fifty fathoms, 'racking' sounds could be heard as the hull reached the limits of its designed range. At one hundred fathoms the vessel would simply fold like a punctured lung collapsing in on itself. In between, there was the silence of twenty-seven men listening as the sea drew them ever more tightly into her embrace.

In his mind's eye, the ship was a fragile egg trailing air as it fell through water that was not boiling, was not even luke-warm, but cold, dark and icy; a man's heart would seize up after only a few minutes in it. The first thing he learned in basic training was how the escape drill was redundant: if the frozen water did not kill you the instant it hit you, then the downward draught made it impossible to escape the pull of the sinking vessel. 'When you join the U-boats you pledge your life to your ship,' his crewmates had told him. 'No one escapes from one of these things. Either she lives, or you perish with her.'

Like children listening to the anguish of an ailing mother, they plunged deeper, faces tilted upwards in awe as they continued to sink through the viscous brine. Down, down, down, endlessly, as though the firm substance of the world had given way. As though the very parameters of existence had dissolved, leaving them to slide to the bottomless void of the soul. All around them the strange wail of the sea brushed against the hull as she plummeted.

As the car slipped over the crest in the road and the sea came into view once more, resplendent in the sunlight, the colours skidding off the surface in vivid flashes, Ernst pulled over onto the grass verge and climbed out with a sigh.

It was four decades since he had been trapped down there beneath the waves, but Ernst Frager still recalled the feeling of the ship contracting as every millimetre of pliancy was slowly expelled. His nerve endings raw against the taut skin of the hull. What was supple and yielding became a brittle shell sliding through water. The vessel juddering and shivering. Rivets rattling like loose teeth.

There were key moments in his life, tangential notes, when he lost all sense of balance and found himself nudged in a new direction. Such nodes of transition were announced by a mixture of fear and childish excitement, his stomach tumbling over and over as if he was standing on the edge of a high cliff, trying to talk himself out of it and knowing he would jump anyway.

The way he felt now; the way he had felt in the little village in the mountains above Munich just after the war; the day he decided to ask Edith to marry him, knowing she would never leave England and realising that he was prepared never to go home again; in Uncle Rudi's fishing boat when he had seen his first submarine, which began a fascination that ended that night on the bed of the Irish Sea in 1918, out there where the sun was now spinning its golden tales on the water.

The way he felt now.

After a time he got back into the car. He let in the clutch and felt the Jaguar begin to glide silently down towards the battered bronze shield. The sea rippled below. It felt as though he were flying. Through space, across time. Away from the past and far far into the future.

4

I

She stood on the waterfront and looked to the sea. The wind blew in gusts, kicking spume from the grey Mersey. A hard wind that blew straight into her, as though prodding at the emptiness within.

She always found it difficult coming home. She had spent most of her adult life trying to get away, to purge this city from her. An instinctive urge which sent her scurrying to new places, picking up new accents, languages, habits along the way, alibis: a life story that would have been unrecognisable to those who knew her. She remembered how she used to make her mother cry. Calling from another place, city, country, saying, not this weekend, Mum, too busy with one thing and another. The feeling of guilt mixed with pleasure – knowing this was a price she was ready to pay for her independence. They cried to each other on the telephone, but never in person.

The frail, unfamiliar figure was waiting for her on a hospital sofa the colour of burnt toast. It had been too long, Jade realised; her visits had dwindled to a trickle, to a drought in recent years. She hardly recognised her own mother. Perhaps it was the setting. A slurry of tattered magazines slumped in exhaustion beside her. The television set laughed and applauded. Her mother sat in silence, alongside a catatonic woman with huge eyes who sat rooted to the game show, picking at her nails.

'Hello, Mum.'

Miranda stared blankly at her daughter for a moment, not recognising her. It wasn't the first time. Ben had called in his usual fog of confusion, talking about another turn. Miranda had been found wandering around a shopping mall, unable to remember her name or address.

'She could have vanished, just like that.' Ben's voice had

faltered. Miranda was the linchpin holding them all together.

'You needn't have bothered. I feel a lot better today. Can't imagine what was wrong with me.' Miranda was fidgeting, straightening the line of her pale blue dressing gown.

'If you behave yourself they might let you out today.'

Miranda leaned her head close to Jade's and nodded in the direction of the silent woman glued to the television. 'She only comes here because her husband hits her,' she scowled.

'Let's go home, shall we?' said Jade.

Home was a semi-detached house on Brodie Avenue, set back from the busy road. The longest part of her childhood had been spent here, just the two of them. The residents had changed. She recalled shopkeepers, hairdressers, retired servicemen, car mechanics, people who stopped to say hello when you were on your tricycle in the street, people who waved to your mother up there on the porch. There used to be front lawns and a mixed bag of people who were neither on their way up nor down, but wedged like molluscs tucked into a rocky crevice. There were Irish names, English, Jewish, West Indian, African, Caribbean, Hindus, Bengalis, Sikhs. People spoke of 'back home' as though it were accepted that part of everyone belonged elsewhere.

This was the house her father (not Ben) had bought for them, in preparation for the day when he would come to live with them. He never did. Instead, mother and daughter grew up together in that place, learning how to take care of one another in the shadow of his absence. The house was always full of neighbours, noisy children, lodgers, a steady stream of visitors passing through, standing on the back doorstep waiting for a cup of sugar they had come to borrow. Going home was like stepping back inside the box she had taken so long to get out of. The pebbledash walls seemed to shrink each time.

Maya was waiting outside when the taxi pulled up, just as Jade had once done.

'She looks less and less like you, bless her.'

'Thanks, Mum, I always think she looks like herself.'

The black and white squares on the front porch were worn soft with memory. Once they had reminded her of a chess set. The two of them, her mother and her, like the last two pieces

6

left on the board, waving to the stranger climbing back into a taxi.

'You remember so many things, my goodness. You were just a little child.'

'We were there together, Mum.'

Nowadays everything seemed to be growing smaller: the house, the memories, even her mother, physically smaller. Miranda seemed to be floating away into the distance, like a kite on a string. The three of them laughed together as they made their way up the path to the house, Maya the glue between them.

'Home again,' clucked Ben. 'Back to the roost.' Dependable old Ben, awkwardly clutching a newspaper, his old trousers shiny from where a briefcase once swung against them, a smudge of chalk still faint around the right pocket. They all ignored him, passed him by, left him standing out there like laundry drying on a line, until he remembered that he might as well go in.

Together, crammed into the kitchen, improvising a meal, Maya was keen to learn about the time when her mother was her own age.

'Mrs Murdock,' Miranda offered, stroking her grandchild's hair.

'She sounds terrible!' squealed Maya. She was. Mrs Murder they used to call her. 'The equator,' Mrs Murdock once declared, 'divides the world into two equal halves. These are called hemispheres.' It was simple. Jade was in one hemisphere and her father was in another. 'People used to be afraid of crossing the equator because they thought terrible things would happen to them.'

'Please, Miss, what kind of terrible things?'

Sea monsters, and your skin turning black, that kind of thing. They sat at their desks and drank milk from cartons shaped like pyramids and tried to make sense of what awaited them out there in the world. Then there was Aunt Lillie and the hair salon on Hardiman Street, above the skeleton of St Luke's Church.

'Why don't they fix it?' Jade would ask, pressing her forehead to the iron railings. Aunt Lillie would drag her away up the hill. Six and a half years old, wearing a bright red raincoat with matching sou'wester and she's already asking damnfool questions. Sunlight bobbing in minuscule globes on the yellow tips of daffodils and the frail tendrils of her hair.

'That's so people remember.'

'Remember what?'

'Remember not to forget is what.'

Sometimes it was easier to talk like this, about a past that neither of them could summon except in fragments. The afternoons spent in Auntie Lillie's salon while her mother was at work. Part of her grew up there, giddy with the smell of hair dye and lacquer and the warm electric air of the dryers that were fixed to the wall like a row of enormous mauve eggs. Moving from leather chair to window, punching the buttons on the green adding machine and then pulling down the handle just to hear the mysterious sound of the ratchet spinning, the tongue of white paper curling out of the top. She knew that the machine was her father's. A part of him permanently lodged among them. An adding machine.

'You mean he gave it to Auntie Lillie?'

'No, I mean he made it.'

It had struck Jade early on that her whole life was a random collection of fragments that made no sense whichever way you arranged them. Miranda's parents had arrived from Trinidad, children hand in hand, in 1948, convinced that a warm welcome awaited them in the motherland – a coming home of sorts. England was looking for new hands to build her up after the war. To put the great back into Great Britain. And on first sight it surely looked like it needed it. The grey buildings, the heaps of bombed-out rubble, even the sky looked drab and down in the mouth. Reality was a step down from the rainbows their imagination had held out for them to walk over. Why, they didn't even have food in the shops, still used rationing in those days. You couldn't buy a pound of beef, not for love or money if you didn't have your ration book with you. And these English were not the educated gentlemen they had seen back home in Port of Spain. Miranda's mother once told Jade how they had imagined all Englishmen to be like colonial officers, with their fine manners and their plummy voices. Well, who would have expected that the entire damn country would talk like they was royalty, she used to say. Stands to reason that there was a whole lot of other English people who were, well, as plain as plain could be. We all equal subjects under the eyes of the King, her father maintained. Look to me like he's squinting awful hard trying not to see us, replied her grandmother, holding up a stamp with George VI on it for him to examine. But Jade's grandfather maintained the firm conviction that the British had changed their ways. The war had shown them they just could not get along without help. How do you think they would have beaten that wicked Hitler if it wasn't for us, he would say. They needed every hand they could get and mark my words a lot of them hands was black. No, in this brave new world everyone was equal. You could get anywhere you wanted to through respect, hard work and diligence. We got to *strive* our way up to the top. And her grandmother, on her knees scrubbing the front step, would say, from where I'm looking I can't see the top, but there's not an awful long way to the bottom.

The old stories came back to Jade on Sunday afternoon, standing on the porch as they were about to leave for the station.

Ben thrust a bundle of papers into her hands as she was getting out of the car.

'I've been meaning to give these to you. Thought I would send them down.' He clicked his tongue and stared straight off into space, hands twisting the steering wheel. 'Never got round to it, though.'

'What are they?'

'Letters. Don't know who they're from. Haven't read them.'

Blue envelopes with the red chevrons around the borders. Why would anyone be writing to her at her old address? The most recent was dated three months ago, the oldest had been posted more than a year ago.

'Ben . . .'

'I know. I'm sorry. Just kept slipping my mind.'

She was late. Maya was tugging her arm. She pushed the bundle into her bag and forgot about them until they were on the train.

9

Rachel

I watch them in the late afternoons, when the sun has worn itself blunt and the light is so gentle and fine-spun that the world takes on the aspect of a faded charcoal sketch. The scene has a petrified, timeless character, as if the clock has stopped. Nothing moves along the streets at that hour save for the odd straggler. A boy sent on an errand, say, or a milkman hurrying by, perched side-saddle on a sorry-looking donkey, both of them making their knock-kneed way home.

This is my time, my own private moment when the world halts its rumble and fuss and I am reminded that this is the way things are when we are not engaged in the burning pursuit of satisfying one appetite or another. It only lasts a short while, this interlude, this tranquil moment of lucidity. The clay of the earth slides from the leached colour of dusty tombs to a livid red that grows deeper still until it all turns gracefully on its head and the stars emerge, blinking like startled silverfish in a pool of nocturnal dye. And then the radios come on, of course, and the shouting takes up where it left off a couple of hours ago, and car ignitions sputter, and the whole mad whirligig starts up again.

They always come walking through our neighbourhood at that particular time of day, just when I am watering the plants. I haven't a clue where they come from or where they are going. I have never asked, you see, because I never mention it to anyone. Perhaps I am afraid of losing the solace I derive from my afternoon vigils.

Secretly, a part of me worries they might just disperse or evaporate like sprites if I were to speak their existence aloud. I cherish their presence, I don't want to dispel them, not just yet.

They walk in single file, silently, never appearing to speak to one another, their silence a sign of unspoken communion with nature. All the more ironic because they are no longer within their own landscape, with the cattle kraals, smoky dung fires, and grass huts of the unbound tracts from where they hail, far away to the south in those vast muddy swamplands of theirs. They have been plucked out and set down here like spindly butterflies pinned to a sheet of vellum. Here in a sleepy suburban side street in a run-down quarter on the outskirts of the capital city of a backwater nation of the world. Not a nation at all, really, but a collection of disparate peoples herded together by the muddle-headed rulers of a bygone imperial age. We live in the wake of history like a new picture that sits badly in an old frame.

Amin, who is my husband, would think I was mad if he caught me standing here alone watching them walk by. He already thinks me half-cracked, so this would simply be grist to the mill, as we used to say. Added to the fact that, like most of the sophisticated urbanites of this city, he considers people from the south, from the remote regions of the country in general, as primitives, animists, pagans, idol worshippers and ulti- mately, of course, what their ancestors used to be – slaves.

I suppose that I am drawn to them because I see something of myself in their predicament. Not that I would ever describe myself as being either a pagan or the descendant of slaves even, far from it. But we are bound together by the fact of our displacement.

All of this would be lost on Amin, I am afraid. Perhaps one day you will meet him. He is not the man I married thirty years ago. Oh, perhaps I am being too harsh, the poor dear is still in there somewhere, but time and circumstance have taken their toll. He is kind to me, can still be endearingly consid- erate at times, and I cannot begin to imagine what I would do if he were no longer around. I used to think it was habit rather than need which kept us together, but now I am not so sure. Sometimes I think of us as two separate planets with thousands of leagues of darkness between us. Both vaguely aware of one another's existence across the numb void, but unable to draw nearer, or pull away.

So the afternoon vigil is mine alone. In those silent figures slipping through the antique light, I see the echo of my absent son. A time of mourning, then, of communion with the dead.

I go out there when the heat has burned itself down and there is an hour or so for me to water the plants. I wander through the garden spraying them all. The oleander, bougainvillea, and the big lime tree whose leaves are flecked with dust. They turn a virulent green the instant water strikes them, giving off an invigorating scent. In my own quiet way, I suppose I am quite proud of my garden, which is crammed full of all manner of herbaceous life: tamarind, papaya and hyacinth, cassia, guava, even grapes (although these have not been very successful). It is a small garden, and for most of the time it seems dust-bound and immobile, but in the afternoons when I walk through it seems to stir, filling the air with the most delightful blend of fragrances, and all the colours become vivid and alive again.

It is there, standing in the midst of that window box of an orchard, my own private little Eden, that I spy them furtively through the iron grille of the back gate. Off in the distance. Frail, desiccated figures slipping across the periphery of my world, hinting at distant perturbation. It takes a moment to place them, like a hazy memory – almost gone, but not quite.

Why do they come by here exactly during my time, for me to witness alone? I wonder. Is it merely coincidence, or something more?

I have never been a great believer in astrology and predestination and whatnot, but recently I have been unable to help myself wondering. I am actually quite a pragmatic type of person by nature, with little time for histrionics of one ilk or another.

This won't do. I am wandering about in circles. The point is that I have never believed that things happen according to a preordained scheme of rhyme or reason, until now, that is. Religion, for me, is associated with memories of my childhood, not a constellation that bodes well. In particular, with the stern education drummed into me at St Joseph's Convent school in Hendon. More than a world away.

While standing there in silence watching the procession file offstage, I wonder if perhaps they have always been there, and it is I who have simply been unable to see them. I have been blind to so many things; your existence, for one. It is almost as though all the lost moments of one's life – time squandered, opportunities wasted – all of those things which one thought consigned to the past were in fact hidden among the leaves, like fine spiderwebs stretched between the branches which you miss until you happen to look more closely.

2

Her immediate impulse on reading the first letter on the train was to reach for her phone and call her mother. But then she wondered if Miranda even knew about them, if perhaps Ben had not kept the letters from her. She put the matter aside, thinking she would give herself time to think, but then everything was overtaken by other events.

The man called Thursday died at 19.57 on Sunday evening, about twelve hours before he was discovered, and at almost the exact moment when Jade and Maya stepped off the train in Paddington station. Time of death given by the shattered wristwatch on his arm. He drowned in a pool of muddy water, held down by a tubular arch of brass-titanium alloy that measured thirty-seven metres in length and two and a half metres in diameter. It protruded from the mud like a palaeontological relic, a dinosaur wishbone.

When Jade arrived they were still trying to cut through the debris that had collapsed on top of him: the iron gridwork for pouring the mezzanine gallery, along with assorted timber and metal supports, iron rods, plates. When the arch fell the whole central structure had given way. It had been poised on the delicate crux where all the hidden threads that go towards creating the illusion of free suspension were meant to come together. Covered in an oily film, the arch now shone like a fallen rainbow in the foggy cold.

Startled pulses of blue and red from the emergency vehicles hurt her eyes. An air of melancholy hung over the scene: firemen kneeling to cut through a tangle of steel hawsers, a livid fan of sparks sputtering into the air; the bloodless white light from inside the ambulance. Desultory figures stood around in the rain, reluctant witnesses.

Her building. It was like waking up in the middle of a bad dream and finding it to be real.

'Does anyone know how it happened?' she asked Verne as he wandered back over holding two styrofoam cups. Where had he managed to find tea in the midst of all this?

'Seems not. They are all pretty pissed off. Time is money and all that. He wasn't supposed to be here anyway. It looks like he had made a little bivouac for himself under one of the Portakabins. Sleeping rough.'

They were lifting his body now, the ambulance crew, their sterile rubber gloves unable to get a grip in the wet, the mud dragging him back.

An arch which began life in her head, a simple stroke of pencil across paper, had ended falling from the sky, divested of all magic, demanding a sacrifice.

They stood sheltering from the downpour under the unfinished cupola. An orange plastic safety net fluttered in the damp breeze. The pools of rainwater merged across the broken, muddy ground forming a *mappa mundi* – the little inlets expanding, connecting into oceans, dissecting the continents of a world. The foundations here dug down into the Cretaceous bedrock, 140 million years old.

'They found a bomb here once,' Verne said. 'A big one – German V-2, I think. It didn't go off. Had to be dismantled.'

'Who told you that?' she sipped the tea she didn't really want.

'They dug up a fin or something.'

She poured her tea into the mud as Verne spoke, wondering why he was talking so much.

'Makes you wonder, though.' He lit a cigarette and breathed smoke in the direction of the river.

Jade tapped her watch. 'I have an eleven-thirty conference with Mason Chalmers. I need to be getting back.'

Verne snorted. 'You go ahead. I don't mind waiting.'

Jade sighed and looked over at the gang of labourers gathered out in the open like lost sheep. Superstitious people, builders. It put her in mind of that play by Ibsen, *The Master Builder*, where the architect falls from the top of a church spire for defying God.

'Does anybody know who he was? I mean what about family?'

Verne's dismissive tone suggested he was annoyed. 'They have procedures for that kind of thing.' He was guessing. He too was watching the group of labourers, who seemed to be waiting for something.

'They must have left the arch suspended with cable braces over the weekend,' he mused. He paused, a cigarette halfway to his mouth, as one of the ambulance crew slipped and went down on one knee in the mud, causing the stretcher to lurch sideways. One leg swung downwards. The black shinbone looked all too frail and human. The boot swung lightly in the air. 'I thought they were supposed to strap them into place?' Verne murmured.

Thick weals marked the soft mud where earth movers and bulldozers had passed. It was cold. The rain had stopped but the pallid sun made little impact. She could feel the chill eating its way through the thin soles of her rubber boots, up into her bones. She swung away and walked towards the edge of the site. There was a glimpse of the Thames visible. It looked old and grubby, and seemed to slink by rather than flow. There was nothing particularly graceful about its motion. Simply a dull fact. Like a dead man.

On paper the mezzanine gallery was a jutting lip that reared outwards over the shallow ornamental pond that was to occupy the front lobby of the building. It was high enough for a double-decker bus to pass under at the centre point. It was to be secured in place by leaning arches, high-tensile alloy ribs and pins so that it looked rather like a series of rings, one inside the other, opening upwards towards the sky.

There was a discreet burring against her hip which turned out to be Kyle, sounding agitated:

'Where are you? Regan tells me there was an accident at the PharmaKorp site . . .'

Jade did her best to try and sum up her thoughts coherently: 'Some confusion as to what happened exactly. It's possible that they had not finished securing part of the overhead frame they were putting up inside the cupola. The central ramp, I think.' She looked over towards Verne who was chatting with one of the foremen. It looked like they were telling jokes. What about? she wondered. Death? Football? Women?

'Look, you shouldn't really be there,' Kyle was saying into her ear.

'It looks like a series of errors, a sequence failure. They must have left it unsecured over the weekend. The rain may have had something to do with it. Could be the suspension system.' They would have knocked off early on Friday. It had rained without let-up for seventy-two hours. The entire weekend. The lime-rich clay was so deep-set it threatened to suck her rubber boots off with every step. She was aware she wasn't making much sense.

'Is there any way you can reschedule the meeting?'

Kyle made noises. He wasn't happy. The Mason Chalmers project was by no means in the bag. To cancel a meeting at this point might jeopardise their chances of winning the contract. Kyle seemed to make up his mind.

'I'll call Mason Chalmers and see what I can do. He won't be happy. Come and see me as soon as you get back.'

She wanted it over and done with. She felt as though this accident was pulling her back, stopping her from moving on. Ridiculous. She folded the telephone into her pocket as a bulky man in a luminous yellow site-jacket came towards her. The name Hal was written in black marker on his hard hat.

'Looks like the gods have got it in for us,' he muttered, wiping a hand over his face. 'I mean, I've seen my share of accidents. It always has a bad effect on morale.'

'Do you have any idea what happened?'

A firm shake of the head. 'Too soon to tell. The weather could have something to do with it. Shouldn't have. That support should have been able to stand up by itself.'

'It was certainly designed that way.'

Hal gave her a wary glance as he turned to watch the ambulance making its way up out of the crater in the earth.

'Is it going to slow down the work?' she asked.

'No worries,' he said, rocking back on his heels. His eyes were blank and emotionless under the wet rim of his safety helmet; 'We'll give them a couple of hours to secure the site and then we'll be back to work. I'll have a chat to the lads.

Things like this happen. Occupational hazard.' He tried a grin and it failed.

'And the police?'

'They usually work fast on this kind of thing. Shouldn't take long. After lunch, should be back to normal. But there might be trouble with this one.'

'How so?'

'Insurance people could turn sticky. He was sleeping on the site over the weekend which he was not supposed to do. I had my suspicions, and I warned him, of course, for all the good it did. Goes against all regulations. But some of these people just don't listen.'

'Why would he be sleeping on the site?' asked Jade.

Hal shrugged as though the answer was obvious: why would anyone sleep on a building site? He had nowhere better to go.

'Bit of a mystery, our man Thursday. Nobody really knew him.' Hal had long furry eyebrows that emphasised the drooping lines of his face, fleshy jowls. The more concerned he tried to look the sadder he appeared. 'Everything is subcontracted these days. Anyway, there will be questions asked.' He thrust his hands into the pockets of his jeans for a packet of mints. 'It's all a fucking mess if you want my personal opinion. Company brings in new work gangs from one week to the next and nobody really knows what's going on. Least of all me. All fine until something like this happens, then a ton of shit falls from a great height, usually on yours truly.' He was worried about his job. 'Perhaps you shouldn't be telling me this,' she ventured. Hal's eyes met hers but he said nothing. They both watched as two policemen climbed out of an umarked car that had just pulled through the gate. Hal took a deep breath and pushed his shoulders back; 'Here we go,' he said. Jade watched him walking over to the police officers.

'Christ!' muttered Verne as she came up to him. 'It's like everything else, nobody cares. Just leave it to someone else to pick up the pieces. Shall we go and find somewhere warm?'

As they made their way back across the site, Jade allowed herself a moment of disbelief. 'Everything was running smoothly. We were going to finish ahead of schedule, and now this.' She glanced at Verne, walking alongside her, tall, rangy stride, hands in his trouser pockets.

They crossed out of the building site, up the narrow side street to the car where they changed out of their muddy boots and then she led the way to a small pub she had spotted as they had arrived. They had to wait for the bartender to finish setting out the ashtrays.

'A large glass of white wine, please, and . . .'

'Just a tonic water,' Verne said. 'Some of us have to drive.'

'Quite right.' Jade nodded. 'Do you ever get the feeling that someone has it in for you?' she asked.

'Well, it's not that bad, surely?'

'This project means a lot to me, Verne.'

'One accident doesn't make this a disaster.'

Jade closed her eyes for a moment, wishing herself somewhere else, someone else. It struck her that something was deeply awry, but she couldn't say what exactly. Thursday, if that was his real name, belonged to that species of fleeting spirit that had been engaged in building this city for centuries. They used to be Irish in the old days. Now they were from anywhere and everywhere. They lifted the walls into place, put up the towers of concrete and steel. They left those shimmering edifices hanging in mid-air, and then, like a sleight of hand, they vanished, not to be found on any wage slips, or social security forms. No papers, numbers, tax returns, National Insurance premiums, nothing. Just an empty building, soon to be filled with voices, light, urgency, life, none of which had any inkling of their existence. Where had he started out? Where did he come from? Sleeping rough underneath the Portakabin on a heap of cartons and plastic sheeting. It was April, for God's sake.

Verne was flicking through the pictures he had taken on the digital machine he had with him.

'It looks to me as though it was caused either by a failure in the metal, or in the calculations of what load it had to bear.'

'Or else someone was not following the correct construction sequence.'

'I don't like the sound of this,' said Verne.

'That's what they say in the movies.' She got to her feet and held her hand out for his glass. 'One for the road?'

3

The stamp had a picture of a camel rider racing full tilt across the desert. Sitting on the tube, rummaging through her bag for a pen, the letter surfaced again. She refolded the flimsy blue airmail paper carefully and sat with it in her hand for the rest of the journey home, trying to imagine the woman who had sent it to her.

This home was a quiet, tree-lined street in Maida Vale. An avenue of slowly decaying houses from another age. The value of property had soared in the decade since Jade and Etienne had put down a deposit on the place. Most of the houses on this street had since been converted into flats for young professional singles, couples, people who planned to stay for just long enough to move on up into a higher income bracket. No one could afford an entire house to themselves, nor could they afford to remain here indefinitely. Jade was the same. After Etienne had gone she divided the house in two. The upstairs flat had been rented out, for the last two years to Alice, an Australian chef who worked in a Thai restaurant nearby.

The shared front hallway was cluttered with bicycles, boots and coats. She could hear music coming from within as she pushed her key into the door.

If Etienne walked in today he wouldn't recognise it as the home they had once shared. Was that conscious on her part, eliminating all trace of the stage upon which their marriage had played itself out? Much of the interior of the house had been ripped away to let in more light, more open space. The builders had dug down to the core and put in iron stanchions to transform the load-bearing structure. The only thing that remained unchanged was the brass knocker on the front door, and the façade which had been restored without resorting to aluminium or plastic. From the outside it still looked part of an ordinary Victorian terrace. Alice had the front upper half of the house and the converted attic. The old staircase was gone, replaced by a new set of floating stairs that freed up more space. Alice had her own front door around the side of the house. The original dining and living rooms and most of the hall were knocked into one big area. At the back of this were wide steps that dropped down into the large open-plan kitchen and dining room. The floor of the kitchen was alternate blocks of lacquered cherrytree wood and terracotta tiles, with Andalusian ceramics at the corners to add a touch of colour. The rear wall of the house had been replaced with a large sliding window that took you into the garden, which was overgrown and in serious need of attention: Jade's efforts had come to a bird bath underneath the drooping boughs of an old willow tree, and a row of desolate plant pots. Below the kitchen she had excavated a basement area to make a room for herself.

Jade put the kettle on to make herself a cup of coffee. But then she pulled open the refrigerator and her eye fell on a chilled green bottle of Chardonnay so she poured herself a glass. A wisp of steam rose from the forgotten kettle on the counter.

Maya was sitting on a high stool at the little island table in the middle of the room. At thirteen she seemed to be getting taller and thinner every day, her face growing more distinct. She was becoming independent. Jade put a cutting board and three carrots in front of her.

'Here, try and chop these up.'

'Julie was after me again today.'

'Which one is Julie?'

'She's the English teacher, remember?'

'We used to call teachers Miss, or Mister. When did it all become so informal?'

'When we came out of the last ice age and you Neolithics were left to die out.'

'That would explain it.' Jade sipped her wine, listened to her daughter and tried not to think about work. She pulled tuna steaks out of the refrigerator.

'Did you know that ninety per cent of the world's marine

stocks of megafauna, large fish to you, have vanished in the last fifty years?' declared Maya.

'Really.'

'That's right. Think of it. No swordfish, no tuna. Even the dolphins in the Yangtze river are in danger of extinction.'

'The Yangtze river. Right.' Jade fixed her daughter with a look of disapproval. 'I hope this isn't the early onset of some sort of eating disorder.'

'Just think about it. No tuna left in the sea. Isn't that sad?'

'Oh, God.' Jade gazed at the two fillets on the plate. 'Well, I promise not to buy them again. How about that?'

'You want me to contribute to the destruction of our ecosystem by eating that poor thing?' Maya's face was a picture of incredulity.

'What do you suggest, then?'

'*Rosti*. That's made of potatoes. You don't have to kill a potato to eat it. Nobody ever tells you about potatoes going extinct.'

'Right. Well, I can make that. I have a recipe somewhere.'

'Mum, you buy them ready-made at the supermarket.'

'Aha, but that's terribly wasteful.' She turned the tuna steaks on the frying pan and squeezed lemon juice over them. If Maya didn't eat hers she would take it to lunch tomorrow in a salad. 'All the resources that go into preparing what is basically just potato, it's all very wasteful.'

'Good point,' mused Maya, knotting her fingers in her hair. 'But it does keep people in employment. Further down the food chain, I mean.'

'Further down the food chain?' Jade scowled. 'Where did you get that?'

Maya cocked her head. 'Do you like smoked tuna, or is this one of your experiments?'

Jade managed to burn her hand in her haste, and the fish slid out to land on the floor. 'Bugger!' she cried as she threw the pan into the sink.

'So, it's toasted cheese sandwiches, I guess,' said Maya quietly, sliding off her stool to take a roll of kitchen paper and start cleaning up. Jade gazed at the floor, at the greasy mess, the broken chunks of fish.

'I'm sorry,' she apologised. 'I've had a bad day. I so wanted us to have nice quiet supper together.'

'I can do the toasted cheese. I am a genius, the maestro of toasted cheese. Why don't you go and sit down for a minute?'

Jade began to say something and then thought better of it. Instead, she nodded her agreement and, lifting her wine glass off the counter, walked out without another word, leaving the kitchen to Maya.

Against one wall of her studio there was a wide teak specimen cabinet purchased from an antique dealer on the Fulham Road. A beautifully made piece. 'They don't do work like that in this country any more,' nodded the dealer sagely. 'Have to go to Indonesia, or Thailand. Not the same, though. Belonged to a biologist or something, used to keep insects in it.'

'Lepidoptera,' Jade read off the little plaque. 'Butterflies. It was full of butterflies?'

'Yeah, them too,' he rubbed his bristly chin. Heavy grey eyes. The look of a man who lost something a long time ago and has never found it. 'Butterflies and bugs,' he muttered. It wasn't hard to knock the price down.

Jade didn't tell him what she was going to do with it, but suspected that he might not have been too happy to see his little cabinet stuffed with old bones: the small skeletons of squirrels, mice, birds. She was fascinated by the delicate power built into these minuscule anatomical wonders. Ribcages, backbones, hips, flared shoulder blades, fluted femurs, the tiny intersections of a bat's wings. Such a frail frame on which to hang one's life. She wanted to understand the mechanical link between strength and motion. With modern materials you could forget about the old geometries, imitate the way a spine distributed weight, how the load was distributed along the web of bone and cartilage.

On the bookshelf facing her desk was the skeleton of a large monitor lizard, *Varanus Niloticus*, which measured over a metre from tip to tail. She used to spend hours sketching sections of the tail, measuring the curve of the spine. She wanted to capture that flying grace, the poised energy of a leaping cat caught in mid-flight, and turn it into a building.

'It's ready,' said Maya from behind her.

23

'Give me a second. I just want to check something.'

Maya wrinkled her nose and walked back down to the kitchen. Jade switched on the desk light and pulled out her original sketches for the PharmaKorp building. Some of her best ideas had come to her at this old desk. The raw stages of conception. Earthy charcoal smears across vast sheets of rough foolscap; the strange creature taking form in her mind spilling into the world thus, in heavy carbon splashes. The refinements came later; the calculations and adjustments, load-bearing design, distributing weight into strings. A three-dimensional tectonic landscape gradually emerged from amorphous abstraction. The early sketches came as raw, malleable forms. She let them emerge at their own pace. They would harden like a crystal emerging from a desiccating solution. As the water evaporates the lattice-work grows stronger. She had settled on the idea of a crucible of light, a cradle of inventive alchemy. She sold them the idea. The great brass bands that circled the central sphere were meant to evoke some kind of scientific instrument. The directors of the PharmaKorp company were a conservative lot but they eventually came round.

The arch which had collapsed would eventually have been countered by a twin on the opposite side. It supported itself, once it was in place. That was always the trick, wasn't it? How to get it all to stay up with no strings attached, and also, more important, without falling down.

'It's getting cold.'

'I'll be right there.'

Was it possible that somewhere in the process of turning charcoal into steel she had made a mistake, an error in her calculations which caused the whole fragile structure, suspended in her imagination, to come crashing down. Thursday. A nobody – he didn't even have a proper name. A non-person. A ghost. Her ghost. Was it her fault? Was there a flaw?

Maya chatted animatedly while they ate their meal, about how much fun it would be to go somewhere special this summer instead of the usual routine, which involved Maya being sent off to Hendaye on the French Atlantic coast to spend time with her father and her half-brother, Luc. Etienne had settled down after the break-up and was now knee-deep in nappies again. This time around he seemed to be ready for it.

'Your father would not be happy if you missed your time with him.'

'Oh.' Maya pulled a face. 'You know how busy he is with Sophie. Just the two of us. Please. We can travel to South America. I'd love to go to Peru. How about that? Or what about Australia?'

'Let's wait and see. That's quite an ambitious plan you've cooked up. I'm not sure how much holiday I'll have this year.'

'Life is not just work, you know,' insisted Maya. 'I mean I'll be grown up soon and then it will be too late.'

Jade stared at her daughter for a long time, looking for some kind of clue as to what was going on inside her. 'OK. I promise we will go somewhere. Now go and finish your homework and tidy up your room – laundry in the basket, please, not all over the floor.'

Maya wasn't messy, just easily distracted; always something else coming along to draw her attention elsewhere. While she disappeared upstairs, Jade cleared away the dishes.

Once the specifications package had been passed, reponsibility shifted to the engineers and constructors responsible for putting the damn thing up. The architect's presence was not really required, except to witness it happening, to make sure things were going according to plan, to be on hand for any queries about material, last-minute changes that had to be made. She wondered vaguely about the possibility of seismic activity and then realised she was clutching at straws. The faint tapping of rap music came from Maya's room. When Jade looked in to see how she was doing she found her lying in bed reading a book. It was easy to see her as a young woman.

'Not too long now.'

'Just one more chapter. I promise.'

As she was pulling the door to behind her, Jade remembered; 'What was it you wanted to tell me about Julie, your teacher?'

'Oh, it doesn't matter, Mum, really.'

When she returned to her desk Jade realised she was suddenly tired. She stared at the heaps of paper and the diagrams and sketches and saw only a hatched blur. Her mind was exhausted. So she sat there for a long while in the silent room. Then, finally, she admitted to herself that she was getting nowhere. She went upstairs to switch off the lights and finish tidying up the kitchen. She looked in on her daughter to find her sound asleep, sprawled across the bed, book on the floor and light still on. Jade cleared up the worst of the torrent of clothes on the floor and switched off the light. She went through the house, checking windows and doors. Back in her room she undressed quickly and got ready for bed. One wall was adorned with a collection of masks; porcelain white Kabuki shells, heavy wooden African masks from Cameroon, huge jagged headpieces from Sumatra. When she woke up at night it was as though she were surrounded by faces staring down at her. She felt alone and wondered if this was how things would always be. Some people have lives, she thought, they have husbands and lovers and they do reckless, frivolous things together. As she was dropping off to sleep she felt her mind suddenly clear and in that space she saw a person she did not know. A woman calling to her, only the words were silent. She was speaking but Jade could not understand her. She did not recognise her, but she knew who she was.

4

The offices of Giles, Stock & Waverley hummed with their usual confident efficiency. Jade nodded a few hellos here and there as she crossed the floor, shrugging off her coat. She liked the feeling of walking in here in the mornings. The thrill that came from knowing that plans were in progress, projects were developing, turning from the ether of her imagination into hard reality. 'Turning light into dreams' ran the studio's logo, printed on the glass panes of the forty-foot window that looked out over the Thames. She climbed the brushed-steel staircase in the centre of the room at a half-run. The Crow's-nest, as it was known, was one of the more drastic structural innovations introduced two years ago when the waterfront building was renovated. It was all part of the changes introduced when Kyle took over in the wake of his father's death. He wanted a new image, he said. It impressed visitors to walk in through the studio entrance on the seventh floor of the building and see the way the roof seemed to lift off above their heads.

The lower floor was packed with concentric rows of tables, banks of computers, printers, light boxes, photocopiers. Beyond that, a ring of doors, storage cabinets, shelves. Designers, graphics, computer people, technical and administrative staff, and all the rest of them, almost thirty people occupied this space. A large oval table in the middle formed the iris – the central meeting point. The stairs wound around the periphery of this work area, rising to a suspended circular ring of polished steel from which conference rooms and individual offices fanned out. Jade had dreamed it up and Kyle approved it. The circular upper deck was covered by a dome of interleaved mirrored glass sheets that opened and closed like the aperture of a camera, according to light and temperature. Seen from the air, the whole thing was meant to resemble a human eye. A new way of seeing the world. They even had a helicopter fly over to take a picture of the building from the air to provide an image for their new logo.

When Edmund Waverley had passed away three years ago Kyle was unanimously voted studio director. There was some logic to this. It gave a sense of continuity: the father was gone but the son would carry on ensuring the firm's reli-ability and characteristic verve. The other two original partners, Giles and Stock, had retired years ago. The only problem was that Kyle had little of his father's grasp of architecture. Malicious tongues would say that technically he would never have made it anywhere else but his father's studio. Kyle was fundamentally an idle slacker, he lacked judgement, was keen on short cuts, tended to think you could cajole a client into submission. He enjoyed inviting prospective clients to lavish lunches, was good at flattery. Ultimately, however, this meant that the kind of contracts they won began to change. Kyle's party act tended to attract people who were looking for a bargain, ways to cut corners. It was difficult to say exactly when things started to slip, but at some stage they started to lose the reputation they once had. GSW were no longer taking the lead. They lost the initiative, along with some of the more promising members of the team. Jade hung on, finding herself taking on greater responsibility, more decisions. Here was an opportunity, she felt. There was a chance, she believed, that she could turn the firm around. It was an established studio with a good reputa-tion, all it needed was a good person at the helm, and that person, she knew, could be her. And it was true, Kyle couldn't do anything without her. They were virtually run-ning the company between them. He had come to depend on her – up until recently, that is. Up until Regan made her appearance.

The sunlit Thames flooded into view behind Kyle. All of the rooms had windows reaching to the floor. Kyle's had the most spectacular view. The idea for the circular dome came from the concept of the Greek agora – the cradle of democ-racy; a meeting place, a market, a sharing of ideas. All of the employees were supposed to feel equal. They had social outings, study forums, visits to the opera, all to encourage participation, debate, the creative spirit.

It was eleven years since Jade had joined GSW, taken on as a junior draughtsman by Kyle's father. He liked the work she had done previously although most of it got no further than paper. In particular the design for a sports centre in Paris. It had never been built, the contract was awarded to someone else, but Edmund Waverley had been impressed by the way she managed to combine styles. There was an eccentric side to him, she was to realise in time, and she appealed to that. 'You see what lies ahead, and you are not afraid to take risks,' he told her. She detected some condescension in his smile, but she let it go and took his words as a backhanded compliment, an implication that her eye was more ambitious than her hand was able. She wasn't quite sure what to make of Waverley, but it was that ambiguity that made her take the job. Because it left room for growth, because it said that someone else not only thought she had the qualifications, but actually liked her work. We all live in hope that someone, some day, will understand what we are trying to do.

'Awful mess.' Kyle leaned back in his chair, examining her as she sat down. 'Let's hope it just blows over.'

'I suppose so,' said Jade.

'Still, must have been a shock, dead man lying there and everything.'

'It was sad.'

'Oh dear, you do sound gloomy.'

Only it wasn't just sad, it was a tragic accident that should not have happened, that might be her fault. Her eyes passed over the London skyline and the river. A long dark barge was sliding through the water below.

'Any kind of trouble down there?'

'What kind of trouble were you expecting?'

'Nothing,' he shrugged. 'You know how things are. Police were there? Everything went according to the book, I hope. He wasn't anyone important, I gather.'

'Important?' Jade repeated, thinking it a strange word to use. 'The site manager seemed to think he had been sleeping there.'

'Aha, breach of regulations.' Kyle tapped his pen on the table

29

blotter. They both looked up as the door opened. No knock.

'Phone out of order?' asked Regan, as she walked in wearing that smug look that made you want to throw a chair at her. No one ever used her first name – she seemed to prefer it that way, and it suited her. She didn't look like a Philippa. She was just under six feet tall, her brown hair cropped close to her tight skull. A high achiever. Smart and aggressive. She had instinctively identified Jade, almost from her first day at work, as her main rival, the only real obstacle lying between herself and Kyle, the pinnacle of the company.

'I was underground.'

'Oh yes.' Regan nodded. 'I forgot.' Regan drove to work every morning in a Porsche cabriolet. She had acquired a mid-Atlantic sneer during a stint in the States somewhere. It was hard to tell who or what Regan really was. A mutant replica whose emotional range was limited to feeding her voracious ambition. Her own mother probably wouldn't recognise her voice, but the old dear had probably been abandoned to destitution years ago.

Jade turned towards Kyle. 'I'm not clear why we need this meeting.'

'Regan's idea,' conceded Kyle. 'We need a strategy on this.'

'You're expecting trouble?' asked Jade.

'He was a nobody,' said Regan. 'I know that sounds callous, but it's a fact.'

Jade wondered what in Regan's view she herself qualified as. She pulled out a chair and slumped down into it. 'Forgive me if I'm completely off the mark here, but doesn't that mean it matters even less?'

'He was an illegal immigrant. He was being employed by a construction company working on our project,' added Regan. She looked at Kyle, who squirmed, and finally got to his feet and paced over to the window.

'Look,' said Jade, 'aren't we making too much out of this? A tragedy, yes, but could we try to keep things in proportion?'

'Regan is concerned about what this might do to our profile. Who the man was is really of no interest. What matters is that there is a link between us and him.'

'It's a commonplace link. Everyone has some dealings

nowadays with people who are not legally in this country. They wash your windscreens at traffic lights. They stack the shelves at late-night supermarkets. They drive you home in minicabs.' Jade looked from one to the other. 'It's the state of the world.'

'I know someone at *The Times* who says there is a lot of interest in this story,' said Regan. 'Asylum seekers linked to the pharmaceutical industry can add up to a nice little scandal. Colombian drug cartels, that sort of thing.'

Jade couldn't help laughing. 'Drug cartels? Something you know a lot about? Since when did you suddenly develop a conscience?'

Regan addressed herself to Kyle. 'There's nothing personal about this. I am only thinking about the name of the firm.'

'Right,' said Jade, looking at Kyle. 'I still don't see how this can touch us. The building contractors, yes, but not us. As for the idea there could be a link to illicit trade in drugs, it's not even tenuous, it's ludicrous.'

Kyle seemed uncomfortable with the way the meeting was going. He stirred himself from the window and returned to the table. 'I need some coffee.' He lifted the telephone and waited. 'I think we should proceed with caution and not rule out any angle for the time being. I want to talk to everyone on the floor. If there are journalists about we have to be on our guard.'

'Against what?' asked Jade incredulously.

'That's just it. I don't know.' Kyle put the phone down without saying a word.

'I was thinking it might be an idea for me to go over there and take a look,' said Regan. 'It won't hurt to have a second witness on our side.'

'That might be prudent,' agreed Kyle. 'Keep us on top of developments.'

'And I have a contact at Snow Hill police station, not far from there. He might be able to tell me what their take on this is,' added Regan as she left the room. 'I'll get on to it straight away.'

A snort of derision escaped Jade. 'When she says "a contact", I suppose she means intimate? Probably had to buy her way out of a speeding fine.'

'Don't be nasty,' said Kyle. 'She is trying hard. I know she can seem a little earnest, but she means well, and you have to admit she comes up with some good ideas.'

'You mean the drug cartels and all that?'

There had been a time in the early days, when Kyle still had his father around to play the ogre, when he and Jade had been friends of a sort. In those days Kyle would stumble about in a haze, the designated office manager whom no one took seriously. He seemed to have concluded early on that he was never going to be able to match his father, in talent or dedication. Occasionally he would overdo it and then vanish for a few months to dry out. He seemed hell-bent on self-destruction. In Jade he saw something of an ally, an alternative to that public school world he was raised in. She drove him home a few times when he was too drunk to make it himself. She would haul him out of the way before he made a fool of himself at a reception. She sat and listened to him talk about how much he admired his father and how it hurt him to know how he could never fulfil his hopes for him. It was never more than platonic – she felt compassion for him, but nothing more. And she had a strong suspicion that he was more interested in men, although he could not bring himself to admit this. When Edmund Waverley died people were supportive, although no one seriously believed Kyle was capable of taking over the company. Everyone was expecting a fall. In the beginning he called in a lot of favours in his father's name, but to most people's surprise, including Jade, he was, for the first time in his life, genuinely determined to make it succeed. What he lacked in vision and scope he made up for with sheer effort. He needed Jade then. He needed people to help him. The old insecurities did not vanish completely. He made some bad decisions. He would lose confidence, feel threatened. He fired a number of people, and in doing so lost a good deal of experience and contacts. Then, in an inspired moment, he instigated a process of transformation, making sweeping changes to the structure and running of the company, hiring management consultancies, and finally renovating the studio completely. Giles, Stock & Waverley became GSW – a fancy logo, a trademark, and a public company. New faces, new ambitions, new priorities. Gone was the image of the small, old-fashioned firm. Nowadays Jade was one of the last remaining mementos of the past. One of the few who remembered what he was once like. There were times, particularly in the beginning under Edmund Waverley, when she wondered if they saw her as some kind of trophy, a colourful addition to the company profile. Kyle once jokingly suggested putting her name forward for a race achievement award. She laughed it off, but she still remembered it. And now there was the whole business with Regan, who was suddenly everywhere. Was it possible that Kyle, ever conscious of appearances, felt that this would be an opportune moment to ditch Jade. She had fast become the major creative force in the company, was generally liked, and this undermined his authority. She ought to have been made a full partner already. Everybody said so. She wasn't, and the harder she looked at her situation, the more convinced she was that this would now never happen.

'You've been around too long,' Verne once told her. 'You know all the family secrets.'

It might have been the effect of the accident, but it seemed to her as though everything had suddenly been knocked out of shape. She felt off balance. All she wanted was for the PharmaKorp building to be finished. But now, even that appeared to be too much to ask for. Suddenly, she longed more than anything to be away from here, away from all of this.

She got to her feet and walked over to the window. From the dome of St Paul's to the Lloyd's building, the ghosts of other architects, past and present, haunted the skyline; Christopher Wren, Richard Rogers, Norman Foster, Richard Seifert. Male architects draw the world, the women just fill in the shading. She was a woman and she was black, well, brown. What could she actually hope to achieve?

'Tell me what this is really about?'

'How do you mean?' asked Kyle.

'Regan. All of this about media interest and the company profile. Regan has about as much compassion in her as most human beings have in their left heel. She couldn't care less.'

'That is unfair,' he protested. 'Regan is genuinely concerned about this company. OK, I admit, she gets carried away sometimes.'

'So tell me I'm imagining all this.'

Kyle shrugged. 'You seem to be jumping a dozen fences at once. Firstly, you were responsible for the design, and it is a wonderful structure. Everyone says so. It won us the tender. Let's not forget that. Then there are the engineers and the constructors. Nobody went into this thing blind, not even the poor guy who was killed. He knew what he was getting into. Accidents happen. Look, it's been a shock for you. Why not take a few days off? Take a holiday. Go away.'

'Don't patronise me, Kyle.'

'I wasn't trying to.'

'I know this building,' she said. 'I put everything I have into it. The specifications were all one hundred per cent on the spot. You know that. If there was an accident it wasn't due to a failure on our part.'

'I know,' he nodded. 'We all know.'

'Then why do you need Regan to do your dirty work for you?'

'What do you mean?' Kyle frowned. Sometimes you talked to him and he didn't seem to be there; all you saw was a blank spot of grey.

If you are so desperate to get rid of me, she wanted to say, why don't you just come out with it? But she didn't say that. She gathered up her things.

'Look, you're the best we have,' Kyle said, walking her to the door. 'But we all need to take a break. That's all I'm saying. Just take some time for yourself.' He flashed her a broad smile. 'This thing will blow over. Believe me. And if you ever need to talk to me, just remember, I'll always be here.'

Rachel

The last time I saw England was when I attended my mother's funeral. My brother Matthew said I looked myself. I'm not sure what he meant by that, but at least he had the grace to pick me up from the airport. His poorly disguised impatience reminded me how much he really resented me for having stayed away for so long, especially now, in this difficult time. He could never understand my decision to leave Britain, certainly not at the beginning. To my brother I had abandoned my own family for the sake of a group of foreigners in a primitive and distant country. His witless jibes, banal attempts at humour about croco-diles and drums only put a satirical gloss on his contempt. He never took an interest, never once expressed curiosity. I didn't expect it from him. I had abdicated my responsibility towards Mother by moving so far away.

'She was asking for you,' he announced when we embraced, two middle-aged people reaching over expanding girths to cling briefly to one another amidst the glass and steel, the tumult of busy people and their luggage scraping furiously past one another in a clumsy dance of human emotions and machinery. His tone was cold enough to let me know how bitter he felt. He has always felt resentment, but never been capable of expressing it openly. From the occasional snippets about the Sudan that appear in the British newspapers I imagine it would be difficult for him to imagine how anyone could be happy under such squalid, not to say outright dangerous conditions. But I had not complained in thirty-odd years, had not come running home in tears – so he must have known I wasn't going to now.

Most of the time she was so far gone that she would have had difficulty distinguishing me from any one of the nurses who took care of her. With all the medication they pumped into her, and with her weak lungs, I imagine she was in a more or less comatose state. She barely recognised Matthew most of the time, kept asking him why he left silver when she had asked for gold-top milk. The nurse I spoke to later said they were all like that. 'Most of them wouldn't recognise themselves if you held a mirror up to them,' she explained prosaically.

You are no doubt curious to know how I learned of your existence. Well, actually, I found your letter tucked into an old family Bible. Something of a surprise, I can tell you, coming across that. It is a lovely volume that has been in the family for donkey's years. It contains the names of everyone on my mother's side, going back to 1822. The instant my fingertips brushed along the spine, rediscovering the beautifully tooled calfskin covers, I was carried back to a time when that book was the symbol of all that was good in the world. I saw myself in the St Joseph Convent school choir again, dressed in my grey and white pleated skirt and mauve blazer. Rehearsals on a Saturday afternoon. I much preferred the rehearsals to the concerts when I invariably became flustered and could not find the required note.

My father, our father, was not a religious man. We discussed the matter many times. As I recall, he viewed the church as a conspiracy of fools invented to close our eyes to the world. He was a strange figure, never really at ease, not even with the English language. I remember his hands, big hands, always busy, fiddling with his tools, pushing back his hat. I would stop by his workshop in the afternoons for a chat when I came home from school. We would talk about everything. Read it by all means, he would say, just don't believe everything in it. Just remember, he said, people tell stories for a reason.

My mother was the exact opposite, in this as in so many things. She was the one who had given me that Bible. Later, in a gesture of rebellion, I returned it to her. I converted to Islam, you see, officially at least, when I married. I suspected this was one of her ploys to tempt me back to the fold, never having really accepted Amin.

'It will never work,' she told me, quietly furious about what I had done. 'Marriage between people of different races, different backgrounds. How can you think that you know him?' She was talking of her own experience, of course.

It took me ten days of hard work to clear out the top-floor flat where she had remained a virtual prisoner the last years of her life. Each item, each object took on a weight of its own, as though reluctant to give up its usefulness to a person now gone.

I lay in my mother's old bed at night surrounded by boxes and bags ready to be taken down to Oxfam. The sheer emotional effort demanded was overwhelming. The energy needed to dispose of her personal effects: the bundles of girdles and old knickers, frayed at the edges, bands of elastic looping from them; leather handbags that she hadn't used in years; shoes with holes worn in the soles; dresses that had ceased to fit her twenty years ago; armfuls of mothballed coats; five dusty hatboxes; a set of curling tongs, circa 1959, which would no doubt have blown the fuses if you tried to use them, or set your hair on fire; two dozen bars of French soap which had been turned into powder by some kind of burrowing mite; a muffler made of fox fur, glassy eyes and bushy tail still attached – of course no one would take such a thing nowadays and Lydia (she used to read to my mother and visited her in the hospice more often than even Matthew) tearfully agreed to keep it; bottles of eyewash; tins of talcum powder; a collection of odd buttons; socks which needed darning, and the silver-backed hairbrush that Edith had inherited in turn from her mother and which I had always despised the sight of, with its worn-out bristles, and the memory of the nightly ritual of having my hair brushed, but nevertheless stuffed furtively into one of my suitcases at the last minute, overcome with sentiment.

As I surveyed that heap – as drab as any jumble sale – I was on the verge of despairing. There comes a point when you are clearing up after the death of a loved one when it all seems too much. Each object, no matter how ragged and worn, is painful to discard. It felt too soon to be doing it all again. I found myself clinging hopelessly to old scraps of paper, address books, trying to decipher scribbled notes, reading letters from friends of hers whom I had forgotten. The pile of objects grew, until I realised how foolish I was being and decided to make myself go back through a second time, and this time, I promised myself, I would be ruthless.

That was when I came across the Bible. I felt myself sinking down into the old armchair in the middle of the room and turning it over in my hands. Why did I open it up? Was I seeking consolation? Was I expecting to find some final message from her, a reprieve after all the years of estrangement? Perhaps. In any case, that is not what I found. What slipped from the pages into my lap was a creased and worn letter from a young woman of about fourteen years old. A curious letter. I took it from the envelope and unfolded it carefully. At first I thought I might have written it myself, despite the unfamiliarity of the handwriting. Who can recognise their own handwriting after half a century?

Why did she keep it? I wonder. Most women, I suspect, would have torn it to shreds the instant they had read it, tossed it straight into the fire. But she decided to keep it. She never showed it to anyone, but she kept it, nevertheless.

I imagine you must have written in secret. Your mother would have been opposed to the idea. The fanciful schemes of a teenage girl! You must have got hold of the address by piecing together the little bits of information you had and doing a bit of detective work, I shouldn't wonder.

I think that my father tried to tell me about you, years ago now, when I went to him in hospital. He was much changed. I barely recognised him. There was a bruised look about his features. His face seemed to have caved in and his skin had a bluish tint as though it had been beaten in some way. He could not speak a word. Along with the power of speech he had lost the use of his left arm, which had to be fixed with a sling to prevent it hanging loosely by his side. I used to sit there with him. He would hold on to my hand tightly with his good arm, as though he wanted me to pull him back into the world of the living. But I couldn't, nobody could. Sometimes I cried, but most of the time we just sat there and waited. He wanted to tell me something. I know he did. He lay there, gazing up at me with that look of fear which comes from knowing complete and utter despair. We become children again when we face death. All the worldly wisdom, the erudite sophistication, the learning we have acquired, all that has kept us afloat throughout life is suddenly rendered worthless, and we are left facing the brutal fact of the dark void with a kind of terrified wonder, as if we have never really understood life until that moment.

After my mother's funeral a few people came back to the old house for the last time. It is the house we grew up in as children. Built by my father after the war. He had a hand in designing it himself of course. He did not believe there was anything he could not do. Matthew had managed to persuade his own offspring to come along, both of them too overly concerned with themselves to convey any real conviction of sorrow. They are spoiled in the way of young people who have never managed to grow out of being pampered children. Poor Lydia had made enough sandwiches to feed a small tribe, and passed through the crowd holding out trays of them, along with the drinks, managing not to spill anything and to carry on weeping all the while. Matthew disliked Lydia because he could not understand anyone who offered their help free of charge. Elbowing her way into a private event, was how he put it, until I pointed out that without her we would have had to hire someone, although admittedly the tear-sodden sandwiches I could have done without.

I found myself in conversation with a tedious chap who kept beaming like a schoolboy who has just won something dull in the egg-and-spoon race.

'How long has the place been in the family, then?' he asked. Tim, or Timmy – Penny's husband. Penny is Matthew's daughter, my graceless niece. I had gathered from my brother that Tim earned an obscene amount of money doing whatever it was he did in the City. Swindling non-industrial nations out of their natural resources, probably. He must have possessed that special kind of intelligence which puts a person at a great advantage in one particular field while remaining to all intents and purposes as dumb as a doorknob in every other sense.

A man in a wheelchair, who seemed vaguely familiar, suddenly thrust himself into the midst of this conversation. I think the arm of his chair actually struck Matthew in the knee. A sinewy sort of figure with wild white hair and beard, and the most amazing blue eyes. 'Ernst?' he demanded harshly, causing a moment of confusion. There was a gangling, listless kind of young woman with him, rather poorly dressed for a funeral I thought, who I assumed must have been some kind of home help. She managed to manoeuvre the chair to one side. She was not flustered at all. On the contrary, she seemed to be more concerned with straightening her clothes and pushing her hair out of her face.

'This is Mr Schmidt,' she explained, making it sound almost like an apology.

'Of course.' I turned to my brother. 'Don't you remember Mr Schmidt, Matthew?'

'Mr Schmidt?' he repeated. But you could see it coming back to him. Like a long weighty shadow passing across his face. 'Yes, of course. How are you keeping?'

'Fine. Just fine.' Waldo Schmidt's face was a lined and shrunken copy of the vivid, disturbing figure I recalled. A friend of my father's. His closest friend perhaps. He was rather a mystery, and quite scary as I recalled. I don't think I ever knew what he actually did, although I had the impression that he had inherited a lot of money. 'Please, my hearing is excellent, thank you. Eyes, too. Fixed, with lasers. I can see like a hawk.' Schmidt was quivering with emotion. His hand shook in the air.

'You are a remarkable man, Mr Schmidt,' said Matthew.

The old man drew his elbows in. 'No,' he said soberly. 'Ernst was a remarkable man.' He looked down at his knees for a moment before looking up at us again. 'I am just an ordinary man who has lived a remarkably long time.'

Matthew had never liked Schmidt. Even when we were children. I think it was the fact that Schmidt was one of the only Germans who came to the house. I recall there was always something odd about Schmidt. His irreverence, his disdain for the norms of conventional life. It was a form of defiance and Matthew perceived him as a threat. It is true there was something wilfully aggravating about his manner. He liked annoying people, and plainly still did. If his staying alive was what irked them most, then he would do that for longer than anyone imagined he could. It was quite a performance. The man could barely stand up, his vital organs had either packed in already or their decay was held in check by heavy doses of pharmaceuticals. One heavy gust of wind and he would be scattered like an armful of twigs, and yet here he was, playing the old scallywag, cheerfully contemplating the miracle of his longevity.

'Have you met my children, Mr Schmidt?' Matthew asked, looking for a way out, beckoning to Vince and Penny. They came and hovered, reluctantly. Vince talked in a loud slow voice, eyes already drooping from the lager, and Penny fawned over the old man as though he were a cuddly toy.

'I was in love with your grandmother,' Schmidt winked at her while stroking her hand. 'Everyone was in those days.' He looked over at Matthew. 'So elegant and beautiful, Edith was.'

'Ah yes,' nodded Matthew. 'Always concerned about looking her best.'

'And you knew Grandpa, did you, Mr Schmidt?' Penny was mouthing her words loudly, and Schmidt, in turn, obligingly nodded his head in a doddery fashion. And all the time he was watching Matthew. I don't know about his eyes, but his mind was certainly sharp as a razor.

'It's funny,' he said at length. 'Your father was such a curious man.'

'Yes,' replied Matthew, straightening his back, 'I suppose he was something of an eccentric, in his own way.'

This amused Schmidt, who began to wheeze like a rusty accordion, wagging a finger in the air. 'No, I meant Ernst was curious, about things, everything. He had a true sense of wonder about the world, always wanted to know what made it tick.' Schmidt was turning his hands over and over, washing them in some invisible stream. 'I'm sorry if I startled you just now,' he mumbled. 'Weak moment of nostalgia. It is simply that I was struck by the fact of your resemblance to him.'

Everyone was looking at Matthew. 'My father?'

Waldo Schmidt nodded. 'I nearly had a heart attack when I saw you. I thought I was looking at a ghost.'

Seeing Waldo Schmidt again after all those years made me think about how little I really knew about my father. What I remember are the early years, when I was at school, when we were small. I was in my twenties when he died. I had always thought there would be time for us to talk as grown-ups, and now there never would be. It was soon after that that I decided to get married, to go away.

I didn't sleep that night, after my mother's funeral. I lay in the dark and I cried and cried, thinking how sad it was that I knew so little about my father. When they are gone, all we have left are odd bits and pieces, barely remembered fragments, mementos. We try in vain to construct a complete whole. But they stay like that, revenant histories, never concluded, the fruit of that nebulous, unresolved desire to make sense of it all.

Waldo Schmidt is the only person alive who might have more details, but heaven knows if he is willing to share them.

II

The Submarine Dreamer

'The drowning man is not troubled by rain.'
Persian proverb

5

What was it that led Ernst Frager to leave home in the spring of 1957, to put down his tools and walk out without saying a word? It was past midnight when Edith, roused from bed by the sound of the radio he had left on, came down to find the workshop deserted and her husband gone. The beginning of a long season of wandering.

By then he was hundreds of miles away, winding his way through the hills of North Wales to settle in the rocky bay of Tremadoc, where the landlord of the Marchioness told him the tale of 'Shelley's ghost'. The poet once claimed to have suffered some kind of assassination attempt, possibly an act of revenge. Shots fired in the night, windows smashed, and a narrow escape for Shelley himself. No witnesses to confirm the details, however, and soon people were saying he was going out of his mind, that he was having hallucinations, seeing spooks. Ernst took heart from the anecdote, as though it had been lying in wait for him. He saw it as a reward, a sign along the road, a vindication of his departure from home, restoring his faith in the world's capacity to renew itself, to instil wonder and surprise.

He found a cluttered bookshop in Bangor the next morning where he purchased a local guide and book of poetry by Percy Bysshe Shelley. He read *Queen Mab* in a small café over a pot of tea, learning how Shelley, believing the poem would never find success, had ordered only 250 copies to be printed. It put him in mind of his own inventions, many of which were doomed from the start, having little chance of finding a market. But that is not why we work, Ernst nodded to himself. Neither poets nor inventors work backwards from widespread expectations. No, you had to go the other way. It was about taking risks, following your instincts.

He walked along beaches and sat for long hours in his car (a 1955 2.4 litre Jaguar MK1) staring at the sea. He drove across the bridge to Anglesey and marvelled at curious shapes in the rugged landscape. The guidebook explained that what he was looking at was a rare example of mélange geology: a variety of rock fragments were swept together and embedded in a different bedrock. The bleached oval forms protruded from the landscape like petrified whales. He found a cramped but comfortable room in a bed-and-breakfast at Holyhead. The air was cold as he walked the windy clifftop paths, bringing tears to his eyes. In places it buffeted him so hard that he had to pause before daring to take the next step.

He coasted along the northern edge of the peninsula, seeing sunlight brushing across waves and old memories bobbing to the surface.

'Only give me a place to stand and I shall move the whole world.' Shelley borrowed Archimedes' aphorism to preface his poem. Shelley had dreamed of a refuge from the world, an ideal community, a utopia. Each canto of *Queen Mab* was aimed at denouncing a particular target: economic exploitation; warfare; tyranny; the monarchy; religion. Ernst found it to be less poetry than political manifesto. He read avidly about free love, the abolition of marriage; the very essence of love is liberty. He read the poem over and over, trying to decipher what it meant to him at this juncture of his life.

In a succession of unfamiliar dining rooms, each with its own cast of porcelain puppies and shepherd boys leaning against crooks on mantelpieces, idle conversation filled the silences measured by the tick of a carriage clock.

'It is very popular with holiday makers,' smiled the landlady, licking her lips as she ladled chicken broth into his bowl. He watched the wrinkles on her hand fold and unfold. His room smelt of burnt lard that rose up through the boards from the kitchen below. 'Were you in the services then, during the war?'

'The navy,' he replied, dipping his spoon beneath the filmy yellow surface to avoid explaining which side he had been on, or indeed which war he was talking of.

The sea had taught Ernst to love machines, instilled in him the knowledge that one's fate could depend on the reduced tensile strength of a rusty spring lever, or the spark created by friction between a flywheel and a badly fitted armature. That night forty years ago, trapped at the bottom of the Irish Sea while trying to slip through a minefield, the U39 whirred but would not budge, pinned down by jammed blades and a fast current. Willy, the man who had trained Ernst to watch bubbles floating through a pipe, was the one who performed the necessary miracle. Ernst did the odd jobs, winding up the extendable masts when they were running on the surface, fetching cocoa for the captain. He was small and agile and useful for clambering down into the galley, up through the narrow gaps between pistons and pipes. He lied when he ran away from Uncle Rudi's fishing smack and signed up for Kaiser Wilhem's navy. He told them he was almost seventeen years old and that he had sailed in fishing boats all his life. He was fourteen, but tall for his age and the cross-eyed recruiting officer didn't seem to care one way or another. He asked Ernst if he could swim. 'Like a fish,' he replied, with no hesitation, standing to attention and puffing his chest out. They swam in the Baltic, dressed in heavy leather boilersuits. They drilled on the parade ground for two weeks, learned to fire a variety of weapons, then they passed him on to Willy. Willy was short and stout with almost no neck to speak of. He had large round eyes and pale eyebrows which gave him the look of a rather inquisitive seal. As he led the way through the pistons and cylinders of the engine room he paused to indicate a picture of a girl draped in cowrie shells, strings of beads, bird feathers, bangles and nothing else. Mata Hari. 'I've heard it said,' Willy mused in a dreamy voice, 'that she never wore drawers, not ever, even in winter.'

'Must have been a little cold at times,' responded Ernst, missing the point.

'I like that. Sense of humour,' said the chief engineer, beads of sweat popping from his brow. 'They say she could suck the paint off a periscope.' Ernst laughed, though unsure quite what the significance of this skill might be.

You needed humour when you were trapped on the sea bottom. The drop keels were cast-iron counterweights that could be released from the outside of the hull in an emergency. The key had fallen from its hook and was trapped beneath the catwalk.

Ernst slipped through the oily floor plates and wriggled forwards to find it. Every one of the twenty-seven men held their breath, including Captain Usher, as Willy pumped out the ballast tanks by hand, one by one. Nothing. Finally, the keel trembled ever so slightly. Very slowly the vessel began to swing round in the current. The weight in the forward tank kept her anchored. Willy cranked the jammed hydroplane as far as she would go and working one against the other managed to lift the bow into the current. As they began to rise, Ernst begged God to let him see the sky once more.

And here he was, driving along the coast past Colwyn Bay, the wind blowing through the open window. He stood motionless on the beach for hours transfixed by the rhythmic turn of the waves, the frothy gouts breaking from the brown curl to sweep in around his feet. He lay in the dunes, his dark blond hair now the colour of dirty snow, watching the gulls snap their wings in the air above him like kites. He stared at the fading sun. He sat alone in saloon bars and tea houses, strolled up narrow streets and along rainswept promenades. He appeared to have no specific destination in mind.

In November 1918 the German fleet mutinied and the country descended into chaos. The war over, Germany was now at war with itself. The Kaiser went into exile. Ernst swore he would never go back to sea and went ashore to find that life was no longer what it had been. In Hamburg people spoke of the fear of civil war. His mother's life had changed, too, and there no longer appeared to be room left in it for him. She had a new suitor, a butcher who came to visit clutching armfuls of paper packages that leaked blood on the carpet. Horse meat.

The next three years he moved from one place to another, finding himself in the tumult of poverty and desperation that had seized a country in revolt. He wandered from one job to another, from one town to the next. In 1923, Ernst was sweeping up locks of fallen hair in a Berlin barber's shop when he heard on the radio about the failed putsch in Bavaria and that man Hitler going to prison. He delivered coal. He sold newspapers. For a while he trained as a tram driver's apprentice, but then the trams were stopped and the workers laid off. One day he saw a notice for machine operators. By the time he got there the last job had gone. And that was how he met Augustus Popinal.

'What shall we do with you, then?' Popinal asked, tilting his head to one side, tapping one foot while he studied the young man who stood before him. Ernst had never set eyes on such a strange person. He watched the small man closely. Popinal was no larger than a child of ten, and wore very formal and rather outdated attire. The monocle screwed into his right eye, the long-tailed coat, the grey homburg with a band of bright green silk around it, and spats. 'Times are hard, you know.' He spoke in a low, intense murmur. He was never at a loss for words and he never, ever repeated himself. There appeared to be no question in Popinal's mind that there would indeed be *something* for Ernst to do. He led him on a tour of his factory – a long shed on a narrow street on the outskirts of Berlin. 'The politicians can squabble, but it is people like you and I who keep the world ticking along.' The factory floor was crowded with row upon row of noisy machines punching out metal keys and levers with what seemed like an alarming expense of noise and energy.

'Herr Popinal, excuse me, but might I ask . . .'

'Typewriters, my boy, typewriters. The thing of the future.' The beaming little man spun around. 'Never apologise for asking a question.' The glass walls of the office and administration area were perched on a platform overlooking the factory. From up there Popinal could view the entire production line. In the beginning that was where Ernst would sleep, on a leather sofa in the waiting room, surrounded by Popinal's private collection of typewriting machines, some museum pieces already: 'Frister and Rossmann. And this one is a Stoewer Elite. Note the wooden base, very nice work. This one is a Creelman Blickensderfer No. 5 made in 1897. And this marvel is a Sphinx. Look at it! Over here . . .' And on it went. Popinal paused to see what effect all of this was having and was rewarded by the look of wonder in Ernst's eyes, which made a change from the usual dull incomprehension. Popinal spun on his heels to continue his guided tour: 'The first commercially produced machine was made by a Danish pastor, a dour fellow named Malling Hansen, would you believe? Proper production only began in America, of course.' His hand rested on the next machine. 'Note the legs, the flat pedal? It resembles a sewing machine, no? You depress it with your foot and the carriage revolves. Sholes and Glidden were the two men who devised it.' Popinal tapped the air like a conjuror producing a rabbit. 'Glidden was an apprentice in the sewing machine department.'

'Remington,' read Ernst aloud, his hand drawn magnetically to the name plaque, the smooth metallic poles, the elegant ivory keys.

'Yes, a name made famous by their rifles. A curious alliance between the manufacture of death and of great ideas, wouldn't you say?'

At the end of the tour Popinal rapped the tip of his stick against the floor decisively. 'I can't pay you much,' he said. 'But I can promise that what you will learn here will serve you for the rest of your life.' He seized Ernst by the shoulders. 'You are besotted, that much is clear. Very well then, I must offer you a job. I need an assistant. Can you do accurate technical drawings? If you have half a brain I can teach you. Let me see your hands. Can you take legible notes? Very well, then it is settled. You can sleep in here. The sofa I can vouch for and in the winter you will be as warm as fresh bread.' Popinal lifted his cane and gently tapped Ernst under the chin with the silver dolphin on the pommel. 'You can close that now.'

Popinal was a miracle, like nothing or no one Ernst had ever met in his life. He was an 'inventor'. Typewriters were simply a means to an end. On his cluttered office shelves he had plans for everything, from helicopters to egg-timers and alarm clocks that never needed winding. He had a rotating machine for peeling potatoes, and another version of the same mechanism for walking the dog, another for polishing silver. Whenever he became frustrated with his typewriters he would turn aside and begin sketching some new aspect of his vision. There was an instant rapport between the two of them. Popinal taught him about metallurgy and the importance of detail. 'It can always be improved. Never believe any different.' There were rumours that Augustus Popinal had once made a living as a travelling illusionist, that he had once had a terrible accident, that he was born a rich Russian aristocrat who had become involved with the Anarchists and had lost his fortune. What mattered to Ernst was that he showed him that life could be lived in ways other than the conventional. He taught Ernst to think, not to be afraid of suggesting ideas or modifications. Popinal was always enthusiastic, overlooking quite serious flaws in some of Ernst's early innovations, including a brass carriage as cumbersome as an artillery shell, and a persistent failure which could cause the return mechanism to slice through the thickest paper like a guillotine, or break your wrist.

Popinal, the eternal optimist, thought Hitler a passing annoyance, like a fruitfly that would be gone before you knew it. He was not the kind of person to look upon things in a bleak light. 'A beer-hall entertainer,' he explained. 'The man has no education. He can barely write his own name. He will not last.' Popinal may have been a forward-looking visionary in terms of writing machines, but as far as politics was concerned, he was quite hopeless. He was not alone in this. People lived in fear of the Bolsheviks, the Jews, the National Socialists, the bourgeoisie. The city was divided between extremes. The Weimar Republic went up in flames, just like those that lapped up the books that were thrown on bonfires, or nailed to pillories as in the Middle Ages. Ignorance declared bliss. Knowledge a tyranny. 'Students banning books? Whatever next!' said Popinal, as they watched a demonstration pass the factory door, tearing books to shreds in their hands. 'We celebrate stupidity. What an age we live in!'

More immediately there was also a rush to nationalise Jewish businesses. 'But I am only half Jewish, and even that is a very distant half,' Popinal fretted. 'It cannot apply to me.' It did. Orders were cancelled. Existing customers refused to pay what they owed, feeling utterly justified in doing so. One day a delegation arrived to commandeer the factory. The beady-eyed man with the clipboard explained that the property was being confiscated for military purposes. And so, sooner than either of them had thought, the day arrived when Ernst and Popinal stood in almost exactly the same spot where they had first met, nine years earlier, only this time the factory was dark and deserted. The workers had been laid off, the machinery sold. Popinal brushed hastily at a speck of rust that had settled on his lapel and it blurred into a yellow stain. 'This country has gone to the dogs,' he fretted. 'I never thought I should hear myself say that. When everyone else was doom and gloom, Popinal stood firm.' He let out a long sigh. 'Ah, but now . . .' He looked about him and pushed back his hat.

The day finally arrived when it was all over. Ernst set down his suitcase, the sound echoing through the cavernous hall of what had been the happiest home he had known. 'What will you do now?' he asked, unable to bear looking around the empty shed.

The energetic little man paused momentarily to consider. His hands turned the silver dolphin on the pommel of his walking cane. 'America,' he declared firmly. 'Yes, America. That is the future.' He put a hand on Ernst's shoulder. 'There is no room in this old world for dreamers like us. Why not join me?'

'In America?'

'Of course, my boy. Together, we shall create an empire of ingenious machines. I have been contemplating a movie camera that will be an absolute revelation. I have contacts in California. Why not?' Why not, indeed. The two men strolled together towards the wide entrance, now a blinding field of late autumn sunlight. 'Come to California,' Popinal called over his shoulder 'and we shall find an actress to marry you!' Ernst watched the little man walking away, moving with those firm little taps of his cane diminishing slowly against the cobbled road and he wondered if it might not all work out that way. But inside him, something told him that fate had other plans in store for him. He was right.

For a time he went back to walking the streets in search of work. He was eventually hired for a subsidiary of Krupp & Co., but found the work dull and routine. In his spare time he worked on his own prototype for a typewriter. In 1936 they asked him to go to London to visit the trade fair.

It seemed so long ago and yet hard to believe twenty-one years had passed since then. It all came back as he gazed out over the Merseyside skyline. It was late and he needed to find a bed, something to eat, a drink. The loneliness of Liverpool tugged at his sleeve. The consolation of iron and steel. An echo, too, of his lost childhood in Hamburg. But for the moment he was caught in the tangled path which had led him here to this. Black masts. The long necks of quayside cranes; antique gods raised against the fading twilight. The starved plume of a dirty funnel sketching an interrogation mark in the sky. The warehouse hulks like hollow tombs. The dying sigh of engines shutting down. The rising pitch of a steel cable running through a winch. There are times in life when you know instinctively that you are, by coincidence or fate, in the right place at the right moment. Ozymandias, he murmured to himself. A traveller from an ancient land. Look on my works, ye Mighty, and despair!

6

The startled pigeons snap into the air. She is running, clutching her mother's hand, the boom of the loudhailer somewhere high above – words drawn into a long echoing drone that drifts through the iron rafters above her head like an invisible balloon, bobbing between plumes of diesel exhaust. Skipping along the mauve flanks of the smoky London train as it shudders to a halt. The click of sliding compartment doors and the sharply ruled light falling down narrow aisles. Being lifted off her feet and twirled through the air, suddenly as light as a bird, by the strange, unfamiliar-smelling man who sets his hat on her head and clutches her hand in his. Porters tip their caps back and lean elbows on trolleys to watch the three of them walking up towards the street: a curious cock-eyed kind of family.

Jade emerged from a jerky, uncomfortable reel of sleep to find herself being shaken awake by an eager Maya. The upturned belly of an iron whale that was Lime Street Station sliding into view beneath the greasy clouds as the newspaper slipped from her lap to the floor. The sight of her daughter walking through the gloom ahead of her a memory of the little girl that was once herself, impatiently waiting for her father to arrive from London, as far away as the moon.

A harbour is a punctuation, marking the end of one story and the beginning of another. This was where her story began. The curl of the bay like an open palm fielding the unlimited abstraction of the sea. The past seemed to be pushing her back here. The letters from Rachel making Jade realise that she had unfinished business in this town. What was it that brought Ernst Frager here in the first place? Which story did he come here to end and which to begin?

Outside the station, the sun was tilting, poised to dip behind trees and buildings. In its wake it left a cold chill in the air. There, in the waning closure of day she was trapped for a moment like a moth in a ray of light; a slow-burning sodium flare sinking towards the earth. *Entre chien et loup*, the French say; twilight, a moment of transformation, of infinite possibility. The air filled with mystery and longing, as though she might just as well be able to reach back and touch the past. She was convinced that she was on the cusp of change, that everything in her life was about to collapse around her; work, her mother, these were the vital signs. She knew she was helpless to stop it. The only question was what would come next.

Later on in the kitchen Maya watched cartoons on the television set by the refrigerator, while shelling peas for lunch. Miranda would never dream of buying frozen peas in a bag. 'No character!' she said. She still insisted that Ben drive her to the market, refused to go to one of those big fancy places with lights and music and trolleys where she sent Ben for the essentials. The room reverberated to the whinny of screeching brakes, the sound of someone being hammered steadily and firmly into the ground. Thunk! Thunk! Thunk! Increasingly, Jade saw how her mother and her daughter were closer in character and temperament than she was to either of them. The genetic helix having skipped a beat, tripped over a generation.

'Tell her about the attic, Ben,' said Miranda. 'He's found all kinds of things of yours.'

'You mean the letters?' asked Jade.

'What letters?' Miranda frowned. 'Don't know about any letters.' She turned her attention back to Maya who was popping peas into her mouth.

Since his retirement Ben had been coming up with one project after another. What he enjoyed most of all was spending time at the hobby centre examining the new tools that were available. Now he was set on building a den. Why he needed it wasn't clear. There was plenty of space. Perhaps it was part of the ongoing need to claim the house as his territory.

'Anyway,' he said, as he removed his reading glasses. 'I've cleared all your old junk into the garage. Last chance for you if there is anything you want to keep.'

'He's itching to make a bonfire,' smiled Miranda, dreamily.

'He loves setting things alight and watching them burn.'

'I do not,' protested Ben. 'Just got to be done. That's all.'

Jade left them all to it, walked through to the front room with a glass of wine in her hand. She heard their voices behind her, engaging easily in conversation in her absence. She stood by the window and looked out into the street. How she used to hate that feeling of everything being the same, never changing. The same dull gleam, the calm acceptance of order repelled her.

The avenue was bisected by a grassy verge separating two lanes of traffic. Wide enough to kick a football around on. Long enough to hide in, if you lay down. And it was lying there, one swelteringly hot Saturday afternoon in August, she had first spied Ben walking into their lives. Slim impeccable Ben, dark as a peppercorn and shiny as a newly washed Hillman Imp – of which he was a proud owner. Ben was a very earnest and upstanding fellow. Benjamin K. Orville. The K. was for Kristensen, a nod to a line of ancestry that could be traced back through the tiny hoop of Danish Antillian rule on the island of St Thomas. Ben wore bow ties to work every day. He had an extensive collection: polka dots and humbug stripes, paisley green, butterscotch, navy chevrons, large and small, thick and thin. Ben also had a beard that was neat and very trim and contained two perfectly parallel streaks of grey, the only concessions to time upon an otherwise smooth and unblemished visage. He had loomed over their horizon with the solemnity of a bank of sullen cloud in a clear blue sky. Carrying his teacher's briefcase in one hand and a bunch of battered and rapidly wilting roses in the other, he came marching down Brodie Avenue with the conviction of a man who knows he could walk as far as Timbuktu without breaking his stride, if he set his heart on doing so.

Jade watched in horror as he stopped in front of *her* gate, saw him pause there to straighten his tie and tug at the lapels of his jacket while juggling his various burdens from hand to hand. He fumbled clumsily to release the latch before proceeding up the path towards the front door, aimed like a torpedo at the gently bobbing harmony that she and her mother had built together over nearly a decade alone.

'Don't look now, girl, but I think Orville the Oik has just come a-courtin'.'

They were hiding in the newly mown grass, smoking a spliff, she and Dave Lee, an accomplice in her teenage rebellion, and the most rocksteady dude in Merseyside according to Biff, who once said that if Dave Lee had been any more laid-back he would have been supine, which pleased Dave Lee greatly because he thought it meant something like sublime. Dave Lee had dropped out of school at fourteen and recently acquired a job as a municipal gardener. He wore pale-green overalls and drove a big yellow motorised lawnmower with flecks of wet grass stuck to the blades. His presence was always accompanied by a distinct and noticeable blend of aromatic herbs, of which only some were legal. All these elements combined to envelop him in constant haze, a heady kind of halo.

But this time there was no doubt that he was right: Benjamin K. Orville had indeed come a-courting, with the same stiff determination with which he approached teaching at the school around the corner in Booker Avenue. No matter how obstinate his pupils were they would leave his class with their lives improved. A similar resolve could be discerned in the wilting flowers, the box of Milk Tray, and a few select lines from the poetry of John Keats committed to memory and battened firmly down beneath the French beret which he wore in those days, although nobody was sure whether this was inspired by some artistic inclination, an admiration for the Black Panthers, or to cover the widening bald spot on his crown.

'It will never last,' sighed Jade, slumping back onto the cool grass and letting out a long stream of ganja smoke into the air. 'He's not Mum's type.'

'Love is a many-splendoured thing,' sighed Dave Lee, theatrically. 'Love is a drug. Love is all you need. Love on the rocks. Love hurts.'

'Please, spare me the details.'

'Love is a whirlwind. Love is a ticking clock.'

'You're making these up, aren't you?'

Perhaps he was, but there was no way of avoiding the facts. Love had come to stay. The courtship took root, anchoring itself like a stubborn barnacle on the edge of the singular continent of mother and daughter's solitude. It wasn't that Ben was unpleasant. He didn't stick his hand up her skirt, or fondly pat her behind, he didn't drink himself into a drooling stupor every night. He didn't shout. He didn't hit her mother. But he moved in to fill a space that had been left vacant, unoccupied. A void of latent possibility forever swallowed up. Their world, hers and her mother's, forged out of the absence of Ernst, who was never coming back.

To Jade, Ben's arrival also marked the end of a period of idle fantasy. She realised that, even at the tender age of fifteen, she had believed that her destiny lay elsewhere. Where was that idea from if not from her father, the fact that he had come from somewhere else, somewhere far away, about which she knew almost nothing? It wasn't just that he was white. She realised now that she had spent her entire life with a mystery she had built around him. He had become that malleable part of herself that never fitted in, the secret she carried in her skin; that which would always remain an abstract, unqualified and yet essential part of who she was.

Ben's arrival made her realise that she had a choice: she could either stay and resign herself to the thought that dreams are not meant to come true, or she could make herself free. By the time the wedding day was set eighteen months later, the end of her school days was in sight and she was assured a place at the London School of Architecture, which was about as far away as she could imagine.

Ben declared his upright values right from the start. He would not tolerate any mention of his wife's previous 'dalliances': 'I am as open-minded as the next Joe Bloggs, hear, but that man took advantage of you. He abused your trust and your charitable nature. He exploited you as surely as any white man ever enslaved an African soul. He left you with a blighted child who will never belong anywhere. I am happy to pick up the pieces left in the wake of that man, but by God I will not keep his bed warm for him.'

Others, too, encouraged this line of thought. Aunt Lillie, who had never disguised her animosity towards Ernst, abandoned any attempt at diplomacy when he died: 'You may not see it this way, but you're better off without him. I'm telling you. You my own sister, but you had no business getting involved with no white men and certainly no Germans.' Lillie approved of Ben. Ben went to church on Sunday. Ben was a teacher. Ben was black. Here was the reconciliation that all had individually dreamed of and there was Jade, stuck in the middle, not sure if she was fish or fowl, black or white. Ben was going to wash away the past and something of her would go with it.

But Miranda was not quite ready to throw her past life over the side just yet. She was having none of it. 'You can think what you like, but I'm telling you here and now that you'd better damn well put your pride away, Benjamin K. Orville, or you're going to be sleeping somewhere else, wedding or no wedding.'

Thus love was also a mystery, for if Ben truly loved Miranda then surely it was fully and unconditionally. Whatever had gone before was a part of what she was. It took Ben a while to realise that the two women had no need of rescue. For a time, in the beginning, Jade harboured a secret, malicious hope that this splinter would wear itself into a rift. They didn't need Ben. Hadn't they managed just fine on their own until he showed up?

'I need him,' Miranda explained patiently to her daughter. 'I can't go through life on my own. I need someone. You can't understand at your age, but when you are older you will.'

'Where did you go to, child?'
Jade turned to find her mother standing there. The light from the window made her look younger, took away the lines that had dug themselves into the corners of her face.

'Nowhere,' said Jade. 'I was just here.'

'Why are you hiding from us?' Miranda stepped closer to the window. 'I had an auntie like that. You must take after her. I must get these drapes changed, they need a good washing. Ben said you were having some kind of trouble at work?'

'It's nothing. I just think it may be a good time for a change.'

'You've made a good life for yourself and the girl,' said Miranda, turning to sweep a hand over the top of Ben's armchair, straightening the cover that hid the worn corners of the fabric. 'She says her teacher is bullying her.'

'Whose teacher?'

'Maya's, who else? A Miss Julie. She didn't tell you?' With a grunt Miranda turned and left the room as abruptly as she came.

The following morning Jade found herself surveying the collection of cardboard boxes, plastic bags, ancient suitcases with burst zips and snapped locks piled together against the far end of the garage. Like time left in a corner to rot, impregnated with the smell of damp. She picked out the once familiar shape of a canvas kitbag purchased at an army surplus store, so long ago she could not see herself as the person who had bought it. The kitbag looked slumped and paunchy, like a sagging aunt. It was like rediscovering a portion of her life she had finished with, a part of herself she no longer remembered. Objects that had fallen through a rip in the fabric of time. The first time she left Etienne she had come up here from London. She loaded everything she had into an old Ford Escort van borrowed from a painter friend (whose generosity was prompted by guilt; Jade knew she had had an affair with Etienne) and drove up with a four-year-old Maya who screamed for the entire length of the journey – eight solid hours. Some of those things had remained here ever since.

The weight of that time now came back to settle on her shoulders like a sack of wet sand. With a heavy sigh she sat down on a box and began to sift idly through the chaos. Dismayed at the thought of having to deal with so much of her past, she groaned her way through old cardigans and melted candles, cracked vases, a painting of a flamenco dancer in a red dress with a rose in her hair she had picked up at a fleamarket in Paris. She set aside a handful of old notebooks, which she had assumed lost for ever, and then found herself delving back into her childhood as she picked up a porcelain frog won at a funfair when she was seven. There were cocoa tins filled with assorted glass beads; a shoebox full of old gloves and socks; bundles of coloured string. Who on earth would store away stuff like this? She was horrified and fascinated at the same time, tossing things aside as fast as she could, muttering, 'Burn, baby, burn!'

She came across the photograph tucked away inside an old copy of *Wide Sargasso Sea*. She had thought the book lost. Jean

Rhys had once been a favourite of hers. She found herself turning the pages, which were yellowed and smelled of mould. Familiar phrases, scenes came back to her. Her fingers brushed the same corners she had once creased and bent back the way she used to mark her passage through a text. She was surprised that she could have forgotten this book.

Sargasso was the name given by Portuguese navigators in the sixteenth century to a patch of dead ocean which they encountered when sailing from Europe to the West Indies. In those latitudes the wind often dropped, leaving the ships stranded in a sea that was covered with a carpet of floating seagrass. They would drift for weeks at a time, jettisoning their livery of horses overboard to preserve their stocks of fresh water. A kind of madness descending while they were trapped in motion, unable to move. The memory of that haunting novel had stayed with her all these years. Finding the book again was like meeting her younger self across the span of years. More powerful even than the photograph tucked inside the cover. An apparition of herself aged sixteen. 'Summer 1979' was scrawled across the back of the photograph in her own teenage writing, the rounded, even letters showing that innocent, looping script; the penmanship told her almost more about the number of years that had passed than the photograph itself did.

Was it ambiguity that drew her to Jean Rhys, the fact that the author seemed to be neither of this world nor of that? Was it because as a child Jade had never really been sure if she was black or white. She knew less about what she was than what she was not. It wasn't about the colour of your skin so much as about the way you thought. She asked her mother about it, but all she got out of Miranda was that she was herself, and that was all that ever mattered. And most of the time it was all right except sometimes, like the time she heard Lou Reed singing 'Walk on the Wild Side'. And she had loved that song, until one day when they got to the part where they do the humming: 'And the colored girls go: Dup de dup de dup, dedupdup dup de dup'. And as the chorus fades into the background and the saxaphone comes in, it hit her. How many times had she heard that song before. Only now it struck her. What was a coloured girl doing in that song? What was she supposed to make of that? Would Lou Reed objectify her that way? Hi, Lou. Hi, this is the coloured girl I told you about.

In the following years Jade would watch riots in the streets and see injustice. People running away, policemen charging on horses, stones being thrown, cars set alight. She seemed to adopt parts of one identity or the other as it suited her. She listened to reggae bands and, yes, two-tone music, Ska, which was becoming popular. She was regularly to be found hanging around the Clarksville Social Club & Bingo Hall with people who had names like Biff and Bren, Ardman and Dave Lee, all smoking spliffs the size of cucumbers. She wore a faded green combat jacket and had her hair plaited in long rat tails which she tucked up into a knitted cap. A tea-cosy, her mother called it. It was layered in red, yellow and green. Green for the ganja we smoke, red for the blood of Africa that was spilled and yellow for the gold that was stolen from us. There was one boy they dubbed Manolito after a character in the television series, *High Chaparral*. His real name was Reginald Shale. He liked the poetry of Langston Hughes and had a sparse covering of wispy hairs on his chin that he was praying would turn into a beatnik beard some day. He also harboured high hopes regarding Jade since he believed he was in love with her, would confess this at toe-curling embarrassing moments as they all sat in a fish bar called Uncle Barley's High Tide & Fried Eats. Reggie had a way with words: he used too many long phrases which he did not quite understand and usually ended up tying himself in knots. He launched into interminable lectures about exploitation and workers' rights and people would get itchy feet. Biff and Bren would hunch their shoulders and saunter off to play pool at the Rackers Club, or go and see a kung-fu film at the Odeon.

She had not thought of those people or that time for years. She folded a creased corner gently back and took one final look at the girl in the picture. Hands in pockets, eyes and nose watery and red; she always seemed to have a cold in those days. Hair hanging down from her hat. The corner of a Bob Marley badge visible. How thin she was! The green canvas army jacket that she had worn night and day for years until it fell to pieces. Who took the photograph? What had happened to all those people? Reggie had a late-night chat show on local radio. She could hardly recognise his face from the pictures she saw in the window of Radio Merseyside one day. He had shaved off all his hair and grown a large beard. He was a well-known community figure, ran anti-crime, anti-drug, anti-violence campaigns, AIDS awareness, he appeared at charity events, opened shopping malls. And Dave Lee had given up the gardening. He rose up one day without warning, as though he had been dozing under a pile of autumn leaves all that time, shook himself down and promptly departed for the Caribbean where he went into the offshore banking business. He was now said to own a casino and several hotels in the Bahamas.

Maya appeared in the doorway behind her and surveyed the mess. 'It's like Rip Van Winkle's wardrobe,' she said. 'Where did all of this come from?'

'Here, look.' Jade held up a rabbit's foot. 'It used to be yours.'

'That's disgusting.' Maya screwed up her face.

'You don't remember. You were too small. You used to like it.'

Something in her voice made the girl put her hand on her mother's shoulder. 'I can't remember everything, Mummy.'

'No, of course you can't. Why didn't you tell me you were having trouble with your English teacher?'

'I tried,' said Maya. 'You just weren't interested.'

Where did that resentment in her daughter's voice come from? Jade wondered. Was it all going to be conflict and reprimand from now on? For a moment she was unable to think of what to say. The one ally she had always counted on was turning against her.

'Your father bought it for you in a market in Paris.'

Maya looked at her mother for a moment and then took the rabbit's foot and turned it over slowly in her hands. 'It's a dead animal's foot. Don't you think that's a crime?' Without waiting for an answer, she marched out of the garage, dropping the amputated limb into her mother's lap.

Jade turned her attention back to the task at hand, suddenly eager to finish with the whole thing. She sorted quickly through the remaining plastic bags and then took one last look around, for anything else to add fuel to Ben's bonfire, when she noticed an old carpet thrown over a collection of boxes in the corner. The edge of a wooden trunk was sticking out.

Pulling up the side of the carpet, Jade was hoping that the things underneath were not hers. Her skin itched and she wanted to take a bath. Aside from the trunk there was a woven basket that looked as though it would come apart if you tried to move it, and a cardboard box bound up with string. And there was one other object, tucked in at the back — a stiff black leather case, square, with a handle on top and metal clip fastenings that were rusted. It was heavy when she tried to lift it. She turned it around and with some difficulty managed to force the locks open. The top lifted and a side flap folded down. Inside was a handful of large black discs inserted within sleeves of waxed brown paper. Sliding one of these out onto the palm of her hand a ray of light strafed the shiny grooved surface. Old 78s. On the label she read the title: 'I thought I heard Buddy Bolden Say' — Sidney Bechet, His Master's Voice, 1940. The familiar little logo of the dog looking into the phonograph horn. She slid it carefully back into place and picked out another. A red label this time: Charlie Parker. Other records were by Duke Ellington, The Hot Sevens, Benny Goodman. Jade slid the fastenings back into place. Maya and her mother were calling her to come in for lunch. As she turned to leave, she hesitated a moment and then pushed the record case over to the door with her foot, ready to take with her.

Rachel

When I first arrived, this country was a rural paradise. We lived among fields that were waist-high with wavy cotton, and trees heavy with all manner of sweet fruits that I had never seen before, let alone tasted: limes, guavas, mangoes. And the sun shone all day, every day. Life was so natural, so simple, unimpeded by the industry and smog of the world I had known in London. I thought it was a dream. I would lie awake at night and listen to the chirping cicadas, the *thurrrp* of the frogs, and feel afraid that someone was going to pinch me and make it all go away.

I have never once questioned my right to be here. I married out of love. I was head over heels, and the more people tried to deflect me from my course the more determined I was to follow my heart. When we first moved here we lived in a house with Amin's relatives. Not one of them made me feel anything less than welcome. I was one of *them*; a woman, a wife, a sister. They took it upon themselves to educate me in the proper skills a wife needed and which I had not been trained in. His mother showed me how to cook the kind of food he had eaten as a child; impatient though she was at times, she was always considerate. The younger girls would spend hours trying on all my dresses and insisting that I try theirs. We spent long afternoons lazing about as they painted intricate henna patterns on the palms of my hands and the soles of my feet. They drenched me in perfume and showed me how to dance the way a bride would, turning in small steps, eyes closed and head tilted upwards. I am too old to blush, but I can assure you that the effect on my husband when I finally performed for him in private was quite sufficient evidence of the potency of such rituals.

In those early years there was not a moment's peace, people would barely leave you alone long enough to write a letter. It was considered unnatural to seek solitude, a sign of ill manners and not at all good for your health or well-being. I shall always be grateful to them. I was a foreigner. I imagined my father when he came to live in England. And I believe that finally I understood something of what Amin had felt when he was at university in England, being viewed as a curious animal, as though you had suddenly grown spots overnight, or an enormously long neck.

When the boys were small the days seemed full to bursting point. Little creatures take up so much space, and I recall those days as exhausting and wonderful. I had a job. I worked as a typist at the university. There was an air of great endeavour and optimism. Oh, I'm not saying there weren't problems, but the country was united in its determination to overcome the burdens of the past and find a way for itself in the newly independent world. Everything was alive, and vital to the diversity which makes this country unique. They were trying to turn that vast assembly of different peoples, herded together in colonial times, into a nation.

Where did it all go? All that goodwill, all that hope? All that political intrigue which used to keep Amin and his friends chattering away long into the early hours? I have no idea. I keep my opinions to myself nowadays. The whole political game is a minefield of personal grievances, debts and favours. It seemed silly at times, ludicrous, petty, but this was no game. People died. They put them up against the wall and shot them. They hung them by the neck until they were dead. They threw them in prison and left them to rot. This was no game.

Where we had hope we now have colossal debt. Honesty has been overtaken by corruption. Instead of dignity we now have cruelty. Slavery has made a comeback. We had religion, now we have hypocrisy. We had socialism, women's rights, now we have dogmatism and torture, ignorance where we had education. We have famine where we used to have irrigation schemes, and genocide where once there was hope of equality. I don't say these things out loud, of course. For one thing there are people around these days who would just as soon

66

see you swinging from the gallows for uttering such blasphemous thoughts. They claim to have enlisted Allah into their ranks. As we career senselessly into the third millennium, we are ruled by the anxieties and fears of fourteen centuries ago. Time not only stands still, it can also be made to walk backwards.

Even dear Amin, whom I hope you will eventually meet, has turned towards Mecca for comfort. Turned back to the old ways, as if all the time in between was nothing but a temporary amusement. When I first met him he was so full of fire, wanting to change the world, this country, this vast drum of a continent. Time is against us. It wears down our will. Our minds, once soft and pliable, bear the toll of the scars which the years laid down in passing. We settle back into the old ways. Oh, I have nothing against Islam, as such. It's no worse than anything else, I suppose. I think of the old men quietly passing the beads through their hands, counting off the ninety-nine names of Allah. It is comforting, I can see that. Amin has found his place among his elders. And if it feels like a betrayal of our love, that is only because I am not able to follow him.

It has not been easy for either of us. I think it is in moments of crisis or despair that our true nature reveals itself. After we lost Sayf, we went our separate ways. I see now that marrying an Englishwoman must have been more of a conflict for Amin than I realised. Going against the traditions. We used to be enemies, after all. The British marched in here and claimed it as theirs. Something like that does not fade away overnight. But if there was resentment, I rarely felt it. Now I am beginning to understand how difficult it was for him.

When we first met in London: all those years ago, he was dressed in a nice suit and tie. He always dressed well. He was handsome and charming amid all the greyness of the world I had grown up in: London after the war was a dreary place. Don't believe everything they tell you about cheerfulness and resolve. When all the speeches are said and the flags come down, you are left with a heap of rubble to clear up. Amin and his friends, all students preparing to go home and modernise their country, were so optimistic. They were young, of course, which helps. It felt as though we were on the edge of a great moment of change in the world. That after that terrible war things had to get better.

There were other wars to come, and turning dreams into reality is not as easy as it seems. Amin began to realise that there were too many obstacles, too little time. He devoted himself to work, to earning a living for his family. He had a wife and two children as well as countless relatives who all depended on him. I don't blame him for doing that. We went through some hard times together. But gradually you realise that your values have changed. It was Sayf, I think, who made Amin ask himself some hard questions about what he had done with his life. And some of those answers had to do with me.

Perhaps it was always there, that conservative streak, underneath the nice smile and the easygoing manner. Now I think that perhaps it was just a lull, a temporary breech in the wall that allowed us to find one another. Gradually that hole was filled in. But it was seeing his son embracing the religion he had shrugged off which made him think. And when that son was taken from him, well, I suppose it's not so astonishing that he saw it as a sign.

Oh, I have nothing against his choice, as such, though it does get a little wearing when he tries to convince me of the omniscience of his sacred book. We communicate so little these days that I feel obliged to listen. He tells me how you can find mention of latter-day inventions such as television and space satellites hidden within its pages, recorded far ahead of their time. I listen with all the resignation of the poor fool who married the dashing knight on the white charger only to discover in him some undeclared passion for trainspotting, say, or smutty pictures.

In the eyes of the world everything was against us; race was against us, nationality was against us. My family was against us. 'Your children will never be at home anywhere,' Matthew warned me. 'They will never belong.' My father only met Amin once. Those were strange years, he was away nearly all the time, and my parents hardly ever spoke to one another. Matthew and I had our own lives. It was when my father died that I decided to accept Amin's proposal, to marry him and leave England, maybe for ever.

We thought the world was changing, that we could change it, that there would be room in this new world for people like us, people who did not quite fit into the picture. We thought the world was growing wider, more inclusive. And now it seems it was actually drifting in the other direction.

7

They were in the conference room on the top floor. The view over the river was clouded by a troubled sky. Rain spat steadily at the glass. Kyle had caught a cold on a recent trip to New York. He was walking around the office with his overcoat on, pausing only to tug another handful of tissues from the box on his desk. He seemed to be evading her gaze.

'I'd like to know what's going on, Kyle,' she said.

Kyle held up a hand for a reprieve, then buried his face in a tissue and blew heftily before crossing the room to close the door, groaning.

'Oh God, I feel awful.'

'Don't play games with me, Kyle. Mason Chalmers has been meeting with Regan. Why wasn't I in on that?'

'OK . . . well, what happened is . . . As you know Mason Chalmers has a very tough schedule and I thought that, well, since you were still upset about the accident . . . It made sense to bring Regan in.'

'Regan knows nothing about that project, Kyle. That's my design you are discussing.'

'Not quite.' Kyle reached for another handful of Kleenex, as he sneezed.

'What do you mean?'

'The feeling is that Mason Chalmers wants to work with us, just that he is not too happy with the basic design.'

'I don't follow. He wants it changed?' asked Jade. 'What makes him think he can just order a particular design?'

'He has decided he wants a more classical touch, less innovative.'

'Suddenly everyone's an architect? And Regan is Albert Speer? What is she going to do, build him a Roman palazzo?'

Kyle sat down heavily behind the desk and picked at the buttons on the sleeve of his coat. He hadn't shaved. His eyes were red. 'Look, you don't need to make more out of this than necessary. We've always had a policy of pitch in and share the load. This makes sense, and you know it.' He paused to allow her to come in, and when she said nothing he went back to the window. 'I told you that I thought you should take some time off until things clear up. Well, I mean it.' He swung round to face her. 'You should give yourself time to think.'

'What do I need to think about?'

'I don't know. Everything.' He returned to his desk and sat down. 'Look, I have the impression you have been uncomfortable here for some time . . .'

'Kyle, what is this all about? The accident? I thought we were agreed that it was not our fault.'

'That's still our position.'

'Is it? Then why do I have the feeling I'm being made to carry this alone? You know what they used to do in the Middle Ages, when there was a plague or something? They used to find someone and throw them over the city walls as a sacrifice, a scapegoat they used to call it.'

'You're being over-sensitive. No one said you were on your own. We're with you all the way. That is a GSW project, says so on all the specifications, site hoardings, everywhere.'

'So what's the problem?'

Kyle pushed aside the box of tissues. 'There seems to be some discrepancy on the specification changes.'

'Steve OK'd any changes that were made.' All technical changes to the specifications were approved by the head of the project, in this case Jade, and the firm's engineer.

'Steve wasn't here for the changes directly related to the front forecourt suspended structure.' Kyle now met Jade's gaze evenly, no evasion. 'I checked the dates. He was on holiday in Tuscany with his wife.'

'Then who?'

'Brigit, the German girl, took over.'

Jade remembered her. Brigit was from Vienna, had been attached to the firm on a temporary basis for three months.

71

Spent most of her time clubbing, and bedding every available male in sight. 'Austrian, she was Austrian.'

'Well, whatever,' said Kyle. 'We are trying to locate Brigit. There seems to be a good chance that she is in Hong Kong right now.' He drew a circle on the desk with his hand. 'Look, the way it breaks down is that I think it would be better for all of us if you took a back seat on this one. Questions are going to be asked, and we can handle that a lot easier if you aren't around. It's as simple as that.'

'My design is what got us that deal. You can't cut me out at this stage.'

'Nobody is being cut out. We can't risk any of this jeopardising the Mason Chalmers contract.' He gave a loud sniff. 'Look, it's for your own good. Take some time off and you'll see that.'

'I can't believe you're doing this,' she said, her voice trembling with anger.

'Look, please. Don't make this hard for me. We both know that we have seen you in better shape, right? All I am saying is . . .'

He didn't finish whatever he was about to say. She was already on her feet heading for the door.

She took the rest of the day off, spent an hour or so in a wine bar feeding her self-pity with cold sweet Chardonnay, feeling her fury seething inside her. It felt like her time with GSW was coming to an end sooner than she thought. Where do I go from here? she wondered. She needed a cigarette and fumbled in her bag for the packet she sometimes carried for emergencies. Her hand found the little bundle of Rachel's letters. At first she had regarded the letters as another unwanted burden. A half-sister she knew nothing about, had not thought about since her teenage years: why was she writing to her now? What did she want? But now, her head thumping to the beat of surging alcohol and bitterness, Jade perceived, in the despair underlying the distracted, sometimes confused voice in the letters, an echo of her own state of mind.

Rachel seemed to be asking her to respond in some way.

But how? She glanced over the last lines of the letter she had just finished reading:

'Waldo Schmidt is the only person alive who might have more details, but heaven knows if he is willing to share them.'

This time, she noticed a little asterisk over the name Schmidt; at the foot of the page a number had been written. She reached into her bag for her phone and pressed the digits.

The house, when she arrived an hour or so later, was not what Jade what had been expecting. She had pictured a modest prefab bungalow at the remote end of a suburban estate, walls thin enough to punch a hole through. This was altogether more elegant. Convinced that she had the wrong number, wrong street, wrong Waldo Schmidt, Jade checked the address twice before deciding to push open the gate and walk up the drive.

Set well back from the road, the house was hidden behind a hedge and high iron railings running along the spine of a low wall. It appeared to float mysteriously in a lake of grey pebbles. The shadows of the pine trees on either side added to the effect. For a long time, Jade just stood there trying to make sense of the curiously hybrid structure. There was an element of Gothic revivalism in the mock ramparts and buttresses. But then this vanished into some rather impressive Japanese-type gabling under the roof. Looked like rather a lot of space for one old man.

Jade felt the weight under her arm of the enormous and very obtrusive box of assorted chocolates she had purchased as a last-minute offering. Searching high and low for what she wanted under the lecherous gaze of the gormless lunk behind the counter who licked his lips as he ran his eyes over her. All of this she endured for an overpriced and probably out-of-date box of confectionery with a nauseating picture of white kittens on the front. She considered chucking the thing over the fence, or burying it in the shrubs. Instead she marched towards the house of a man she knew nothing about, wasn't even sure what she wanted from him. By the time she reached the front door it all seemed like a bad idea. Ditch the chocolates and make a run for it. She was on the point of doing just that when the front door swung inwards and a diminutive girl with a face the colour of flour appeared. She frowned at Jade.

'Hello . . . I was looking for, ah . . . Mr Schmidt?'

The girl's expression gave no hint that she understood what Jade was saying. Jade thrust the box forwards. 'I brought these for him.'

The girl regarded the box for a moment but made no attempt to take it. Jade found herself inside a dark and cavernous hall. The girl indicated her coat.

'No,' Jade replied. 'It's all right. I'm not going to stay long.'

'You make telephone?' the girl enquired over her shoulder. Jade nodded.

'I make telephone.'

The heels of the girl's boots tapped out a brisk rhythm on varnished wood the colour of dark treacle. 'Upstairs,' she pointed. A doorway closed and Jade was left alone.

The interior of the house was, if anything, even more impressive than the exterior. A broad wooden staircase climbed up to meet a circular stained-glass window of unusual intricacy, over three metres in diameter, Jade estimated, with red roses, vines and green leaves. Here and there, strange creatures, half-animal half-human, were concealed in the greenery. Where it met the window the staircase divided into two halves; one leading right onto a hallway on the first floor while the second swept back on itself using a fairly unconventional system of hoists and suspension joists to spiral over the entrance hall to reach the upper floor.

Through the panes of coloured glass Jade caught a glimpse of a wide circumference of garden, neatly planed lawn, dotted with flower beds, long green canes of bamboo, and threaded by a path that led to an elongated pond covered by a wooden pergola or trellis. Craning her neck to peer upwards into the gloom which arched above the stairwell, she noted how the central section of the roof had been raised in the manner of a pagoda to let the light in. Very nice indeed.

'Makes your blood stir, eh?'

The voice floated down out of the dark air above her. She felt a touch of annoyance at having been observed secretly. Waldo Schmidt was shrouded in the shadows at the head of the staircase above her. She caught a glimpse of a face through the banister railings, low down. Seated.

'I take it you mean the house?'

'I mean the girl, Thérèse.' He wheeled back out of sight and it took Jade a while to work out that she was expected to follow. At the top of the staircase she found herself in the middle of an enormous square room. The windows had been widened in an oriental style with a series of shutters that tilted to control how much light came in. The man in the wheelchair spun round to face her. 'Not her real name. She says she's French, but I think she's Hungarian. She had a promising career in film before I met her. You would not believe the things she got up to. I pay her to talk to me in French. I find it stimulating. If I am surrounded by English all day my brain turns to jelly.'

It sounded like an elaborate alibi for an old man's lechery, but she did not want to start off on a bad foot. She took a moment to look around the room, examining the walls, the stout wooden columns that had been left exposed.

'This is quite an unusual house you have here. When was it built?'

'A long time ago,' he said, picking at the arm of his chair. 'Before you were born. Do you like it?'

'It has its charm.'

She moved about the room, which was mostly one wide-open space that took up practically all of the uppermost floor. It was divided into two halves, one light, the other dark. There was what looked like a hospital bed against the wall facing the window that looked out over the rear garden. The front, or light, half had the cluttered air of an artist's studio. A sofa heaped with what looked appeared to be rolls of canvas and bits of wood. The chaos spread across a low work bench and several shelves. Lengths of wire, pliers, a hammer, adhesive tape, tins of solvent, tubes of paint. Jars sprouted brushes like headless flowers. There were spatulas, knives, nails, cutters, rags that had been dragged through every colour in the spectrum. Close to the window, behind Waldo Schmidt, there was a collection of rolled-up canvases stacked all along the wall. He sat there, watching her take stock. His face, thin and shrunken, was a mask of impassiveness. The eyes were a cool, pale blue. He still had that perverse little smile playing on his face.

75

'The rest of the house I leave to her and her friends. Anything up to a dozen at a time. I envy them their youth. I'd love to know what they get up to. I thought about installing a surveillance system.'

Schmidt was clearly trying to needle her and so she smiled, turning her attention to the large crucifix by the door. It was about five feet tall and made of teak.

'From the Philippines,' he explained. 'A sixteenth-century relic to remind me of when I used to enjoy travelling, and what lies ahead of me, I suppose. Nowadays I am more concerned with what is on the inside.'

'You mean spiritual matters?'

'No.' Schmidt tapped a finger to his chest. 'I mean my deteriorating health.' But he clearly didn't like the subject and straightened up. 'The girl said you wanted to see me about the house. You're a property developer?'

'Not exactly,' said Jade. The girl, whatever her name, had not been hired for her English, she had told her that she was an architect.

There was almost no furniture in the room. No carpets, no paintings on the walls. It was as though everything had been cleared away. The paints and canvases seemed to have been overlooked, perhaps for sentimental reasons. It didn't look as though they were still in use.

'Then what?' Schmidt asked, the silver spines of his eyebrows rising. 'I don't understand.'

'I'm not sure where to start. I believe you knew my father.'

'Your father?' snorted Schmidt. He started to say something else, but stopped and instead fell silent.

Jade looked around for something to sit on. The bed was too intimate, and clearing the old sofa would have taken an afternoon.

'I take it you don't have a lot of guests.'

'Out of the habit, I'm afraid.'

Close to the glass, she peered down into the garden. It was like standing on the edge of a verdant mysterious valley. Huge shadowy trees – cedar, pine, mossy-looking spruce, azaleas. There were clumps of long-stemmed rushes that gently swayed, lilacs, juniper saplings, milk-white lilies, even a rock garden in one corner, inhabited by giant feldspar nodules and pink quartz.

'My little corner of paradise.' The quick blue eyes darted. 'You are wondering how I can afford all this?'

She turned back to face him, shaking her head. 'Actually, no, I wasn't.'

Waldo Schmidt grunted his approval. 'Fairly convincing liar. Well, I'll tell you for nothing. I sold a painting,'

'A painting?'

'Not a very big painting, either.' Schmidt's long thin hair hung down over his temples, the strands gleamed with the jaundiced texture of raw sinews on a skinned chicken. He didn't bother to stroke them out of the way. 'A Monet. Rather nice, I thought. That was in 1954.'

'Monets don't come cheap to begin with.'

'Oh, I had plenty of others. Monet, Manet, an early Modigliano or two. I specialised in the Masters. Very ambitious in those days. As a rule it's best to stay away from the big names, too many experts around.' He was watching her carefully for her reaction.

'Forgeries? That's what you do, paint forgeries?'

Schmidt emitted a low growl of laughter. 'Lost masterpieces, that was my speciality. You know how many old paintings have gone missing, never seen for centuries?'

'Perhaps you shouldn't be telling me this.'

Waldo Schmidt shook his head. He didn't care.

'It must get a little lonely here. Do you really need all this space?'

'Spoken like a true property developer,' cackled Schmidt. 'I don't get lonely. Besides, I have Nathalie.'

'Thérèse, I thought her name was. And I'm an architect, not a property developer.'

'It's not her real name anyway, whatever it is.' Schmidt was peering intently at her. 'Would you mind?' he gestured towards the bed.

Jade remained where she was. Was all of this some sort of test? Forged paintings. And now this? And where was the home help when you needed them? Where was Nathalie, or Thérèse, or whatever her name was? Waldo Schmidt wheeled himself over to the bed and waited, watching her observantly. There seemed to be little option. Taking a deep breath Jade stepped forwards. One bony hand reached for her as she leaned over him, hooking her arms around his back to take his weight. He smelled faintly of sweat and talcum powder mixed with the antiseptic odour of plastic sheeting and medication. She felt the faint pulse of his breath going through him. He weighed hardly anything. They made the manoeuvre without difficulty, and he slumped back onto the bed, breathless, his hair falling in lank nictotine-yellow strands over his face. He remained like that for what seemed like a long time, her hand trapped beneath his weight. He opened his eyes and looked up into hers, a dirty smile on his face. 'I keep praying for an erection,' he wheezed.

'I see,' said Jade, pulling away.

'I doubt whether you do.' More breathless gasps which might have been laughter or distress. Schmidt leaned himself back into the pillows, pointing towards his feet. Jade lifted them up from the floor, saying:

'They have pills for that kind of thing nowadays.'

'Those are the ones the doctor won't give me. He says the excitement would kill me.'

'Perhaps he has a point.' Jade was growing tired of this fencing. They seemed to have struck out in the wrong direction and it looked increasingly difficult to get back to the kind of conversation she had envisaged. For a time neither of them said anything. Schmidt lay on his back looking at the ceiling.

'I sold everything that I didn't need,' he said, after a time. 'They can have me cleared out of here in under half an hour when I go.'

'Mr Schmidt . . .'

'Waldo, please.' The eyelids were drooping, the chest rose and fell unevenly with his laboured breathing. He bared his teeth in what might have been a smile. The teeth seemed huge compared with the shrunken size of his skull. The flesh hung down over the sharp angles of his face. 'I'd like it if you called me Waldo, like your father used to do.'

Those two words, 'your father', were somehow compensation enough; everything else diminished into the soft distance.

'Waldo, then,' she said softly.

'Good.' He closed his eyes and waved a hand dismissively.

'You'll have to move that box. Take it with you. I don't eat the stuff and she only likes dark chocolate and those kittens are absolutely vile.'

Jade stared malevolently at the box she had propped up on the end of the bed.

'How did you find me?' he asked quietly.

'Rachel has been writing to me for some time,' explained Jade. 'Since her mother died. I was only given the letters recently.'

'So what do you want from me?'

'How well did you actually know my father, Mr Schmidt?'

'Mr Schmidt again. Now she is getting serious.' He was silent for a moment. 'I knew him as well as anyone, I suppose. He was the best friend I had. What do you want to know?'

'Well, to begin with, what was he doing in Liverpool in 1957? How did he meet my mother?'

8

When her father died, her mother said it was Miranda who had put him in his grave; 'What with all your carrying on, and singing in a nightclub and barely sixteen and all, like you Ella bloody Fitzgerald!'

But she didn't care. She was going to be a singer. None of their hopes and scrubbing floors was ever going to get them anywhere in this world. She knew that. All the years she had watched her father working in the post office, how he sat quietly by, watching as young boys still wet behind their ears came in through one door and went right past him out the other side, up to the manager's office, to head office, to senior positions, and he never once said a word. Not a whisper. Yes sir, no sir, three bags full sir. His reward would come, he claimed. He spent his whole damn life waiting for them to give him his due. One day, he would say, one day they gonna realise their mistake. That day never came. It doesn't work like that. Who knows if it ever did. All the savings in the world can't buy you your dream house if the neighbours don't want no black people on that street. You have to fight for your dreams.

And this was where Miranda's dreams had led her: down the narrow staircase of a small insalubrious basement where the sailors used to go. In those days the Blue Nile was not so much a club as a form of bewitchment, a kind of spell. More than just a run-down dump on a neglected side street, it was a confluence of dreams.

The music was a cacophony of places and styles from every corner of the planet. Most of the time it was just plain old Dixieland waterfront jazz. Out-of-tune four-piece combos of machine fitters and stevedores, off-duty tug pilots who could manage a passable imitation of New Orleans syncopation. Those were the regulars. On other nights there was a steady stream of musicians passing through, bringing with them mournful songs from other ports. One night it might be Portuguese fado, the next night it would be a tango trio from Buenos Aires, or a bouzouki troupe from Piraeus; an Icelandic ragtime pianist; a nineteen-piece orchestra complete with tuba, all the way from Turku; Brazilian crooners nobody could understand until they started moving their hips; once even a trio of mournful zither players from the Black Sea. Who these musicians were and how they got here, where they went to, what ever became of them was part of the great untold mystery of the world, of the sea, of harbour life and finally of the Blue Nile. They came and they went, drawn to the club by recommendation, by rumour, by accident. All styles were valid.

The proprietor was a big man, an ex-merchant sailor named Ismail Bilal who had dreamed of a jazz club like they had in New York, though he knew next to nothing about jazz. As far as he could tell it was a sinuous, flexible kind of abstract thing, hard to wrestle to the ground. 'You sure this jazz you playing?' 'Sure, man, sure. Jazz merengue.' 'Never heard of him. Play a little more so I can get the feel. We don't just let any damn fool play this place, you know.' A profusion of musical innovations blew in through the door before blowing off, down the street, across the sea, some of them never to be seen or heard of again. Django Reinhardt meets Trini Lopez. Cajun crosses Texas honkytonk. Jamaican ska cut up by a soaring Ornette Coleman aspirant playing a kettle like a muted trumpet. Bilal may not have been able to explain what it was but he understood that it came from the same place all music came from, if it was good. His weakness for variety led him at times to hire people simply on the basis of what they looked like. If there was something intriguing about their appearance, or if they came up with a witty remark, a sympathetic gesture, he lowered his guard, said, oh, all right, then. But I am warning you, the clientele we get in this establishment is top notch. Which was also part of his wishful thinking. Oh, they did pull in their share of devotees, but the majority of the punters were undistinguished drunks. They liked to hear something that was not too jarring, a little wayward, perhaps, but with sway, with feeling. At least in the early days, before times got hard, the music changed and the club, as Miranda put it, just went downright sleazy.

During the daytime the interior of the Blue Nile club was a dreary sight to behold. The chipped counter, the ripped panelling. All in all it appeared a far cry from the glamour of 52nd Street, but to Ismail Bilal it was more than he could have dared hope for. His Nubian childhood was a muddy river that flowed beside date palms and the crumbled ancient ruins of a civilisation nobody remembered anything about: somebody else's kings and queens, glory, ostrich hunts and elephants roaring in the dusk. The past was a conundrum whose keys lay scattered in the Roman mosaics hidden in the sand, in the broken miniature pyramids once said to have been filled with gold. The future, as far as he was concerned, lay in the slow creak of the shadoof that lifted water into the fields, the bellow of an ass in the distance, a lifetime tending date palms. So he ran away across the Bayuda desert and took to the sea. He never looked back. The Blue Nile club wasn't New York, but he could live with that. The music was the magic that dispelled cobwebs, chipped glasses, burn marks in the linoleum. The lighting was low and the mirrors were smoked – in here everyone looked good. Once the music began to flow you could be anything or anyone you wanted to be.

Ernst Frager himself had no real idea what he was doing in there. He knew nothing of Liverpool. Well, next to nothing. He had read once that when Herman Melville stepped ashore in 1839 he saw before him the Eighth Wonder of the world, comparable in his eyes to the Great Wall of China and the Pyramids of Egypt. Then, at the height of the industrial revolution, there were sixty kilometres of quayside bustling with activity. Melville was entranced. He felt a compulsive fascination and at the same time a deep repulsion for the place. He witnessed how wealth and industry rubbed up against abject human misery and squalor. The town writhed in a bubbling of foreign babble; the heated patois of Germans, Dutchmen, Icelanders and Danes, Chinese, Swedes, Spaniards, and of course the Irish, all falling over one another to be heard. One in two sailors was a foreigner. At night the public houses and taverns rattled and shook to the guttural sound of people negotiating the gulf of their alienation. Singing, dancing, fighting and fucking being the most common forms of contact available. This is where the ships came in, bringing the goods to fill the warehouses, line the pockets of the merchants up on the hill and put bread on the tables of the ferrymen, stevedores, taverners and all the rest of them.

Shaking himself out of his cocoon, Ernst found himself dancing clumsily with a black girl less than half his age, her soft body moving lightly under his hands, realising that he knew this music. He recalled Christmas in Berlin in 1945, rather drunk, listening to a Dixieland band over in the American base. He watched a man get to his feet, put the clarinet to his lips and play Sidney Bechet's 'I thought I heard Buddy Bolden Say': 'Ashes to ashes and dust to dust; if the women don't get you, the liquor must.' And he remembered the black sergeant in the Rangers platoon with Lieutenant Burdon's men. The tiny village in the Bavarian alps. And long ago, the sound of a piano tinkling at the bottom of the Irish Sea . . . His head swirled him through the dark, and the girl kept him from stumbling.

There was nothing too unusual about this mixed couple. The Blue Nile was a place where people hung their normal lives in the cloakroom for a few hours of affordable glamour, complete with lacklustre upholstery and cracks in the plaster. This is what Ismail Bilal provided. An enchanted cave. A magic carpet. He was the genie, the djinn, the big chocolate giant winking in the oil lamp. People settled down beneath the fluorescent constellations painted on the black ceiling and let themselves go. The moon was a gyrating mirrored ball twinkling over the buzz of conversation and the bubbling swell of laughter, half-notes and quavers, until everyone was neatly syncopated, and usually quite inebriated into the bargain. This, Ernst thought, is the friction which keeps us clinging to the whirling surface of the blue planet in the lonely black void. A measure of our incompleteness, our humanity.

With a long drum roll Ismail Bilal stepped onto the stage as master of cermonies; 'Good evening, ladies and gentlemen. How are you are all doing? Nice to see some familiar faces. All right, love? Nice little dress you've got there. Did he give you a discount? No? Shame. He ought to, you know – he sold the other half to someone else.' A clash of cymbals punctuates the punchline, extracting a thin trickle of laughter. Someone at the back squealed uncontrollably. 'Couple of new faces, I see. No, it's not the vice squad. We had them in on Tuesday. '

The mad silver orb bounced rays of light off the walls, cutting through the fug of smoke and laughter. Nobody seemed to mind his lame humour. It was a trademark, part of the atmosphere. Miranda belonged to the penumbra, the pale edges of shadow along the gauze of glamour, the constellation of illusion. She was the hat check girl who sat in the tiny booth inside the door, pulling tickets from a roll. Some nights they let her sing a couple of numbers. In fishnet stockings and a costume underwired with something like a coat hanger that dug into her sides. She was afraid to laugh for fear of puncturing a lung. She didn't have to dance with the customers. As Bilal said, 'No woman gonna *prostitate* herself fee my club.' The Arabic within him straining to get out, drumming at his skin, sending his sentences stuttering out of shape. She danced with people who made her laugh, or the ones who wore their loneliness like fog.

That first week on Merseyside, driving across from North Wales, Ernst found himself a room in a boarding house behind the Adelphi Hotel. Famous, his landlady proudly proclaimed, for the fact that Roy Rogers once rode through the lobby on his horse, the equally – if not more – famous Trigger.

'Why would anyone take a horse into a hotel?' Miranda asked, slipping onto a bar stool beside him. 'Just think of the mess it would make.' When he laughed she took a closer look at him: 'What made you come into this place?'

'I don't really know,' he said, looking around. 'The music, the jazz.'

She nodded her head. 'It's nice sometimes.'

Ernst watched her for a long time across the room. How she moved with a grace that seemed a feral combination of beauty and tenderness. The hooped dress that made her legs look like the stipules of a bell magnolia. He bought a packet of cork-tipped cigarettes from her. She lifted her face and smiled.

It felt like the first sign of compassion he had experienced in a long, long time.

'The first time I heard jazz I was underwater.'

'Underwater?' she raised her pencilled eyebrows.

'It's a long story. It was a record by Scott Joplin. That was a long time ago. But I never forgot it. The music was like a spell. I can't explain it.'

'That's why we need music, to tell us the things we can't explain.'

'During the war, somehow, the only thing that made sense was the music. When I hear Bud Powell it is as though he is playing my life on his piano.'

'That's sweet. You make it sound like God was talking to you.'

He smiled. 'That's a nice way of putting it.' It was a little scary to hear himself talk. But maybe it was the loneliness of the past week or the fact that she was still a complete stranger, which implied that whatever passed between them would theoretically never have to be spoken of again. A conversation without consequences, and yet he meant every word he said. He was not lying to her, or putting her on, he was trying to tell a truth. He was trying to explain to himself what he was doing in this gloomy club full of Africans and West Indians far away from his wife and children, his job, his life, everything he knew and had worked to establish. He had never been unfaithful in twenty years of marriage.

In silence, they walked through the streets, with no recollection later of where they went or what they talked about. Her tired feet, released from their high heels, found a new lease of life in simple pumps which tapped a gentle thrumming sound against the tarmac, leathery and muted, like the valves of a sleeping heart.

'Don't you have a wife or something to get home to?'

She pushed a key into a lock, turned a corner in the stairs, lifted a latch, pulled back the covers. She let his white hands explore her face, her soft flanks. She pushed her fingers through the spiky ends of his greying hair, like fine metal filaments springing back against the light of her touch. A blind couple scrabbling for a match, they burrowed deep inside one another, away from the world, away from dismay and disapproval. He remembered later how, when she took his hand and led him out onto the chequered floor, she whispered, this is how we dance, this is our love. It's black. It's white. It goes round in circles.

9

How many days did he spend hiding up there that first time? In the afternoons he lay down in his rented room waiting for her to join him. Closing his eyes, he found himself floating out into the dark sea of his memory. The images coming in waves: a curious eye gazing skyward through a watery lens. Graceful, somnambulant creatures floating out there in the blue depths. Bulbous relics of a forgotten world. Gliding barnacled and effortless through the void, carving invisible striations across ocean currents, rising and sinking on spiral eddies and drift tides, following ancient unwritten cycles, communicating over vast distances in impenetrable languages.

Ernst Frager read about such creatures as a child. First in the Bible, and later, tracing lines with a wavy finger across the pages of a book. Pictures of men in small boats, poised in the bow, harpoon aloft. Captain Ahab tumbling from the back of the great White Whale. 'There she blows, there she blows!' He saw in those pictures the horror men were capable of, hunting the whales like vast floating mines of golden oil, hoisting them on chains, slicing long white strips from their noble flanks with hooked blades. Milky blubber bared against indigo skin. Wine-dark blood spilling into the frothy sea. The mystery of it all seized the boy by his imagination. As a child he lived as far away from the sea as it was possible to get, in a vast black forest of tall trees, beneath which he ran, through the leafy green light, dreaming of submarine worlds, lush oceanic foliage, the sway of sea grasses.

In the autumn of 1914, Ernst's elder brother, Hugo, returned from the Western Front looking thinner than a rake, ribs protruding through his skin and with the pallor of a dead trout, his spine cleaved apart by a piece of shrapnel the size of a thumbnail surgically inserted by a six-inch Vickers field gun at a distance of fourteen miles. He should have died instantly, but he didn't. He survived and was sent home with a discharge notice. The army had no further use for him. He was dragged clumsily through the door of the house on a stretcher carried by two medical orderlies. One of them was a boy no older than Ernst who carried a cigarette tucked nonchalantly behind his right ear. Wherever they tried to lay him down, Hugo screamed as though a hot knife had been plunged into him. Finally, they shot him full of morphine and stretched him out on the table in the front room, mumbling insanely, conversing with demons only he could see. He was supposed to be dead, the orderly told Ernst confidently as the two boys stood outside the house and listened to the screams of Hugo and his mother, the medical orderly who smelled of herring, trying to calm her down while drinking all her schnapps. Ernst watched the boy pluck the cigarette from behind his ear and expertly lick both ends before lighting it. He took a couple of long, leisurely puffs before handing it to Ernst. Nothing more the doctors could do for him, he said, it cost time and money to look after such a patient. Ernst inhaled, broke into fits of violent coughing and then vomited all over his shoes.

Hugo lasted almost a week, screaming day and night, obscenities that Ernst had never heard spoken inside a house before, by anyone. He would lapse into terrible silence and Ernst would tiptoe through the darkened parlour to look down into the cloudy blue pools of those eyes staring fixedly upwards, and wonder what it was his brother was seeing. Finally, his mother tied a rag across the boy's mouth to spare them all from going insane, then she sat down beside him sobbing and held his hand.

Ernst woke up one morning to inexplicable stillness. In the gloomy front room Hugo lay stretched out motionless, his eyes closed, at peace at last. Next to him Ernst's mother was rocking silently back and forth on her knees, a pillow clutched to her chest. She seemed unaware of her younger son's presence. Looking up, her eyes met his. What passed between them could not be spoken in words, either that day or on any other. It was understood, and never mentioned, ever.

Soon after that they moved to Hamburg. His mother told him that that was where his father lived, but if it was he certainly kept himself out of their way. They lived in a small two-room place above a curio shop full of relics brought in by sailors: shark jaws, shrunken Jivaro Indian heads, Kachina dolls, ivory elephants. His mother went out in the evenings and stayed away, often until the light came through the window when he opened his eyes at the sound of the key. Sometimes she was not alone. It was a strange new life in a strange town. The cold sea rushed in to crush itself in a hard smack against the iron girders of the harbour. How Ernst wished he could escape from that house, and his mother's fathomless sadness, which only got deeper and more inconsolable the more she tried to drown it in drink and the company of men. She finally decided to send Ernst away to work for his uncle Rudi, who fished the waters off the Friesian coast. She said she had already lost one son and couldn't bear to think that the army might one day come to take him away from her. He wanted to believe her.

And there Ernst would have remained, working with Uncle Rudi, sending money home every week to his mother, waiting for the war to end. Except that one day the stories he read as a child climbed out of the sea to claim him: God sent up a great fish to swallow Ernst Frager.

In the Bible, he had read, the Lord commanded Jonah the son of Amittai to go to Nineveh and fight the wicked sore of disbelief which festered there. Jonah decided he wasn't ready for this, so he ran away. He headed for Joppa where he boarded a ship bound for Tarshish. Once at sea, however, the ship encountered a tempest and the terrified crew put the blame on the stranger in their midst, and threw him overboard. And that was when the great fish swallowed him down. It kept him in its belly for three days and nights to teach him a lesson. When he rose up again he swore never to defy God again, and who can blame him?

It was a balmy week in late April. The warm sunlight flashing on the sea made the crew of the boat drowsy, inclining them to close their eyes and lie back against the wheelhouse, trawling up stories one after the other to while away their day until it was time to haul in the nets. The sea was dead calm and there was no wind, nothing but the gentle creak of the mast flexing above them and the flatulent putter of the motor. Then, unaccountably, they felt the stern begin to swivel like the needle on a compass. One by one they stopped talking, instinctively sensing that something was amiss. It was unnerving, as though a malevolent spirit had seized hold of their ship. Someone gave a cry of alarm, another began to curse repeatedly, shouting wildly at the sea, daring the spirit to reveal itself. But the only answer was for the deck to tilt itself more severely. The men fell silent as the keel began to swing further, until, incredibly, the fishing smack began moving backwards. Water poured over the stern in lashing gulps. Thinking quickly, Uncle Rudi threw himself down and began cutting through the taut lines that fed out to the nets, calling to the others to do the same. Ernst was drenched, retching from mouthfuls of salt water. He fumbled to hold on to the rope, the knife jumping in his hand as he tried to saw through the manila. Then, just as suddenly as it had begun, it stopped. The boat came to rest, bobbing up and down violently. The men began to curse their luck, furiously and fiercely. Uncle Rudi hauled in his torn nets. Then came an explosion of water to the starboard side and a huge snout emerged from the sea less than two boat lengths away. The water was frothing wildly and there was a rush of air escaping. Ernst got to his feet to see the dark tapered nose rising gracefully into the air, glistening majestically for a moment before plunging back into a vale of spray.

'It's a whale!' he shouted, jumping up and down with excitement until the sound of laughter around him made him pause and look again. A figure could be made out now, riding on the back of the beast. A man waving from the conning tower. The crew cheered and waved back. The U-boat was turned towards the coast and making good speed, water breaking over the dark prow in glistening sheets, the hull gleaming smoothly in the bright light.

'Where are they heading for?' asked Ernst, mouth agape. The men around him were bent over with laughter. They slapped him on the shoulder. Funny kid, they said. A whale. They howled some more. Uncle Rudi cursed everything in sight, fishing nets, the navy and the Kaiser.

'The Jade Basin,' someone said, pointing into the distance, 'Wilhelmshaven. Safest harbour in the world. Closed on all sides, narrow entrance, nothing gets in or out of her without them wanting it to.' Ernst stood rooted to the spot. He was in the grip of a vivid, breathless sense of exhilaration. As though past, present and future had just collided and the vessel he had just seen had sailed out of his imagination. His whale. Its lungs were rubber flanges and its fins driven by diesel fuel and electrical current – like the *Nautilus*, Jules Verne's fantastical ship. Now he knew how to conquer the vast unfathomable blue – it was done by machines.

10

Unlike a whale, a submarine has two skins: an inner hull of nickel steel, and an outer sheath of tinplate. This was the second thing he learned in basic training at Kiel.

It was in the early months of 1918. They had been towed out of Wilhelmshaven into the North Sea to be jettisoned off the north-west coast of Scotland, from where they had made their own way down into the Irish Sea. Their mission was to pick up a high-ranking German officer who was being held prisoner in a camp somewhere north of the River Mersey. They had no clue to the identity of this mystery passenger and the crew speculated endlessly as to who he might be. Kaiser Wilhelm's favourite cabin boy was the most popular candidate. All they really knew was that he was due to make his escape on one of two consecutive moonless nights at the end of the month. Whoever he was, he was important enough to risk crew and vessel in such a dangerous exercise.

It was Captain Usher who had decided to sail headfirst into an area clearly marked on the charts as being heavily mined. The worst hazard a submarine could encounter, mines accounted for one third of all losses, and that included all those U-boats sunk through ramming, torpedo, destroyer sweeps, depth charges, gunfire and other various causes. Mines were the worst. When you were submerged, you had no eyes. To sail with the periscope up was to risk discovery. Mines were dropped overboard with an anchor. Where they floated depended on how well they had calculated the depth of the water.

'The only way forward,' Usher announced, dropping his pencil on the chart table to point straight as an arrow towards the shoreline marked LIVERPOOL, 'is dead ahead.' The men crowding around the folding table in the control room glanced around at one another. The captain had something up his sleeve, no doubt about it. He was the wiliest fellow any of them had ever met. As a breed, sailors are superstitious enough, but the most superstitious of all are U-boat men. A strange lot by any measure, as one might expect from men who entrusted their lives to an iron coffin. They were to be the most highly decorated service of any of the armed forces in both world wars simply because they had the worst chances of survival.

There was a bit of a legend around the persona of Captain Usher. His father was rumoured to have been a whaler lost in the icy waters west of the Nuussuaq Peninsula off the jagged western coast of Greenland. Since a whale had caused the death of his father, the sea owed him a life, or so the story went. Until he and that whale met to settle their differences, Usher would be safe from any danger.

Old wives' tales, superstitious hocus-pocus, but to these men the sea was a dark myth into which they willingly slipped time and again. There was a shark's fin tied up in the conning tower. There were Madonnas and phials of holy water hanging in the engine room, anything that might help. There was no U13 in the fleet; it had been renumbered. Usher was their lucky talisman. They would follow him anywhere, even headfirst into a British minefield. He was ensured a charmed life, and so, by extension, was anyone who sailed with him.

'Very few whales would actually attack a man,' Ernst pointed out with youthful scepticism when first fed this yarn during a spirited night on the town. 'Perhaps his father drowned.' His new comrades shook their heads in despair at this poor naïve little country boy. As if drowning were a simple matter. A maudlin train of music seeped from the casinos and bars along the waterfront of Wilhelmshaven, rolling out across the foggy bay of the Jade Basin. An organ ground out a wheezy ballad somewhere behind them. Ernst Frager's head was already spinning as they filled his glass to the brim yet again.

'When the whale dives she makes the most unearthly sound. If you ever hear it you will never forget it. It sits right here,' said the speaker, punching a fist into his ribs. 'It is a special scream. It is the sound a drowning man makes as he goes down for the last time. No one can hear it but the dead.'

Ernst Frager might have been tipsy, but he wasn't drunk enough to avoid observing (to himself) that he had never imagined sailors to be such a sentimental bunch of old women. But he was astute enough to realise, glancing at that cast of blurred and bloated heads which bobbed about him in the smoky red light, that perhaps there was more to it than simply the wonders of modern machinery. They stank of stale beer, cabbage and pickled herring, but perhaps something profound happened to your spirit when you left behind light and air to plunge into the depths.

'It's a bluff,' Usher announced, with an impetuous grunt. The men looked at their captain. They nudged one another and winked. Sure, the captain was right. A bluff. Usher sketched lines in the air with a deft hand; 'The shelf is too deep and the current moves too fast,' he indicated. The British mines, poorly designed to begin with, were unreliable at best, he went on. Out here they would be a floating hazard to their own vessels. 'We go straight through the middle without waking a soul.'

So they entered the minefield like a dolphin diving blindly into the circle of a net, confident that it will find its way out again. The cautious men held their breath and crossed their fingers, touched a hand to a St Christopher's medal hanging around their neck and prayed. They travelled due east for two hours before turning their nose into the current and sinking down to a shelf on the seabed to wait out nightfall. They had a pocket dinghy lashed to the deck ready to launch the moment they sighted the signal from their passenger ashore.

It was a long wait. Down there it was eerily silent and still. Even in rough seas little movement could be felt when you went beyond seventy feet, only a gentle lulling motion. After the evening meal Captain Usher appeared in the hatchway to the seaman's mess carrying a gramophone machine under one arm. They all gathered round to watch as he set it on the table and then placed a heavy lacquered disc onto the turntable. At first it seemed indecipherable, the scratchy shriek of a needle, but gradually the lines on their faces turned to smiles. The oppressive atmosphere lifted by the sheer verve of the music. How could you do that to a piano? Soon they were bobbing their heads and tapping their feet in time and asking the captain to play it again. Which is exactly what he did. The 'Maple Leaf Rag' by Scott Joplin went round and round on the bottom of the Irish Sea. The first jazz record Ernst ever heard, well, ragtime to be precise.

At three a.m. the men were roused from their uneasy slumber. It was time. They made ready to rise to periscope depth. The crew silently took up their posts. Ernst Frager was at the ballast tubes in the control room, his eye on the bubbles. The helmsman spun the handwheels of the hydroplanes. The bow began to lift and they slid off the shelf into deep water.

'Nice and slow, please,' came the captain's voice, reassuring in the half dark. A minute passed and then another. There was silence in the control room, just the hum of the electric motors and the occasional murmur from the captain. 'Level out the bow and down fifteen degrees on the stern.' Diesel oil, sweat and the wax of leather suits combined into a distinctive smell which stayed with Ernst Frager for the rest of his life. The scent was the closest he could come to defining raw fear.

They were still eight fathoms down, when there came a tapping, scraping kind of sound. The men looked at one another. The noise grew more intense, like the tiny hands of hundreds of children scratching on the hull.

'Stop rising,' ordered the captain. The men moved quickly. The compression pumps to the regulating tank fell silent. The bubbles slowed and then stopped moving. The engines were disengaged. For a time their momentum continued to carry them upwards. The scratching dragged out like nails being drawn down a blackboard. The depth gauge read five fathoms. No one moved. Nobody even breathed. The captain's voice came out of the gloom again. 'Flood the aft tanks,' he whispered, 'very gently.'

The bow was tangled in a cluster of mines; the scratching sound was made by the suspension chains dragging against the hull as they tightened their grip, bringing the mines closer and closer. The captain's plan was to try and extract the ship by letting her fall out of the tangle the same way she had come in. It was an unorthodox manoeuvre. Ernst watched the bubbles start again, flowing out of the aft tank. Too swiftly, the deck began to tilt. The current was pushing down on the stern,

forcing them into a much steeper angle than they had antici-
pated. In moments it was clear something was wrong. The tanks
were flooding unevenly and they were beginning to descend
in a steep, uncontrolled dive. There was a burning smell coming
from the engine room. The batteries were overflowing. The
sting of chlorine gas hit Ernst, making him choke; his eyes hurt
so badly that he could barely see. He was hanging on to an
overhead pipe, trying to hold himself upright, his eyes unable
to get a fix on the observation tube windows. They were gaining
speed. Around him things were crashing about. He heard a man
fall, saw one of the pilots tumble across the deck. Something
or someone hit him hard in the legs causing him to fall, his
weight hanging on his wrist. The men on the hydroplanes were
struggling to turn the big iron wheels against the weight of
water. They were calling for assistance, but no one could reach
them. Something hard crashed into his leg. Someone nearby
begin to swear, over and over again, rhythmically like an incantation. The lights waned, dimmed, blinked once and then went
out. They continued to sink, onwards into darkness.

Rachel

The electricity went off yesterday evening and still has not returned, nearly twenty hours later! So you see, you should be grateful for the little things in life. I am writing this to you by candlelight. It is early evening and the mosquitoes have not quite woken up yet. Everything is so very peaceful and still when the lights are off, one almost wishes it would stay that way.

Now that the rainy season is officially over we shall have the ceilings repainted and Amin wants to do the outside as well – they use tar paper here, which is effective most of the year, when it never rains at all. The problem is that the roof is flat and tends to warp into hollows and craters where the water collects. So when the heavens really let loose, the water simply wears its way through. The paint falls away in great big flat flakes. This year's rains have been alarming, the worst I can remember. Altogether though, the damage has not been too bad – my lovely blue carpet and some handwoven rugs being the worst casualties. Our worries are puny, of course, compared to those poor people whose homes were totally destroyed in the floods. The worst affected were those already living a rather precarious existence, perched on the outskirts in shacks made of cardboard, the same rounded shape as the huts they used to build traditionally. The government paid no attention to them before, except to send out the bulldozers once in a while to raze the whole thing to the ground. Most depressing of all is the fact that all 350 planeloads of international aid – tents, blankets, food, etc. – did not reach those who suffered most; I know of university lecturers who got sacks of flour, and the blankets you can find for sale in town, clearly stamped as donations – I have been offered a couple myself. They say that a lot of the tents went to the army. People who lost their houses have received nothing. Everyone has to pay for their own repairs themselves... But the government received millions of dollars in actual cash – where is it all? Bah!

On the night it started, I was stranded in town. The car flooded three times. Inconsiderate people in large Land Cruisers (we are inundated by aid organisations who sweep imperiously through our midst) swept past splashing huge waves over the poor thing. The windscreen wipers wouldn't work (probably packed up in fright – never having seen so much water in their life!). Two hundred and ten centimetres fell that night. Poor Amin was on his knees praying for my safe return when I finally got back, after six hours! (Normally it takes fifteen minutes.) People began comparing it to the great floods of 1946. That was when, rumour has it, those living by the river found stranded crocodiles wandering about in their front gardens! Sounds like a tall story, and one I must remember to tell my brother, Matthew. He is genuinely shocked that there are actually people who live in places like this. I think he believes they only exist in those documentary films about the natural world which he snores his way through on Sunday afternoons.

Ah! A chorus of sighs from the neighbouring houses tells me the power is back. It is like falling back into the present century with a jolt.

What I wanted to say when I began writing this is that sometimes, when you are blown off course, when your centre of gravity is gone and everything seems to be flying outwards, you reach in desperation for anything that might bring comfort. Amin's response to our loss was to turn away from me and go back to the old ways to which he had been born. I took that badly. It felt like a personal betrayal. As though he had decided that all of our life together, our marriage, meant nothing to him. I suppose I could have joined him. I considered the idea, but it wouldn't have been honest. I couldn't go through with it.

All of this is by way of explaining perhaps why I think of you as being very close, almost as if I were speaking to you each evening instead of writing. There is so much to tell, and yet it is often not clear, to oneself, I mean, what is significant and what is simply upsetting.

Oh, this won't do. My thoughts are leading me away from what I wanted to tell you. Let me start again. Right. I usually go to the market in town once a week. It is always so full of life. Hot and full of flies too, you would no doubt remark, but life is abundant in the brightly coloured hillocks of spices, and the shiny peppers and aubergines, freshly sprinkled with water, and that wet dusty smell of damp sacking they are spread on. Of course, prices have gone through the roof and inflation means that you now need an absolute brick of cash with you. A kilo of tomatoes would cost a policeman his monthly salary. How do people survive? A flock of little boys follow you, jostling one another for the job of carrying your basket. Some of them are so small I sometimes feel I ought to carry the damn thing for them. The tiny ones get pushed aside and trampled as they press forwards, waving their hands, sticking out their chests. 'Tarzan!' they shout, slapping their chests. They are dressed in assorted rags, some of which are recognisable, as I used to give out the boys' old clothes when they outgrew them. They sleep on a scrap of cardboard somewhere. To see them is to be reminded of how hard and stony human existence can be, how enduring the spirit.

There is a woman there who sells spices. Small in build, with two parallel scars on either cheek. She wears a large bracelet of old Bedouin silver which she told me belonged to her great-grandmother and which must have come from far across the desert. I used to tease her that I wanted to buy it, and she said it would bring bad luck to part with it. It is all she had left, she said, to remind her of where she came from. We have known one another, in a manner of speaking, for more than twenty years. We are roughly the same age, I believe, and I feel an affection for her which is quite out of proportion. We hardly know each other, after all. But still, when she is not there I enquire after her at the other stalls. If I fail to make an appearance one week she will ask why I did not come the next time. It is a tiny fragment of our lives that brings us into contact with one another, and yet it means an immense amount to me. I cannot tell what it means to her. But we have watched one another growing older, and I suppose that counts for something.

Some years ago she told me how she lost her son in the war. I mean the war here, the civil war, which is not civil at all, of course, no war ever is. 'He went to town one morning and he never came back,' she said. At that time they had taken to picking people off the street at random and sending them south. I was angry. I might even have mistaken her attitude for indifference. But it wasn't that. 'Sometimes they bring the body back,' she told me, 'usually they don't.' A delegation of army officers came to her house with the news. They told her to rejoice, her son was a martyr who had died in holy jihad and that he was in paradise now with seventy virgins as his reward.

It makes me laugh out loud when I hear those experts they get on the World Service sometimes. They seem to have this idea that they are still running the world from their little corner of England, Bush House, or whatever. They don't have a clue, and more to the point, they don't seem to care. Truth, like light, bends the further away you get. Today it is us, tomorrow it is Tibet, or Tasmania. We seem to have been consigned to a kind of unending postscript to world history. I am told the country is in danger of dissolving into mayhem and secession. The government has been busy arming civilians in the provinces, forming their own vicious little militias to carry out their dirty work, which is cheaper than having a proper army. It is an extension of the ancient conflicts by modern means. There are slave raids, people are burned alive in cattle cars, thousands fleeing into the nothingness of the desert. At the time, I thought, how sad for her to lose a son, how terribly sad, but she is tough, she will get over it, people like that always do.

It is a long time since I last saw her. At one stage I just couldn't bring myself to go. I didn't realise this until I was sitting in the car one morning about to drive to the market, just as I have always done. I couldn't do it. I simply couldn't. I switched off the engine and just sat there, which is where Amin found me when he came home that afternoon.

I need to take my time before I can tell you how I feel. How it feels to lose a child. Before I get to what I want to say, though, I should like you to know something of me, of the life I have lived here. This seems important to me. I feel as though I have gone through life with my eyes closed and suddenly, looking around me, I wonder where I am and how I got here.

Maybe I am encouraged by the fact that I am sitting alone in the darkness writing to someone I have never set eyes upon. If you find this correspondence a burden, please forgive me. Ever since I learned of your existence I have felt the way one might feel after driving for hours through the dark in the middle of nowhere, when suddenly there appears, dead ahead and far away in the distance, a tiny pinprick of light.

II

'You're sure you want to go through with this?'

Arthur Quail had a very sad-looking face. His eyebrows slanted steeply down at the edges making him seem lost and forlorn. Altogether, you might say he was a remarkably plain-looking man doing an unusual job. Mousy-haired, he wore wire-framed spectacles that enhanced the rounded rodent-like aspect of his features. He had a nervous tick that involved shutting both eyes tightly at the same time as though in pain. He sat behind his desk and tapped a pen on the top of the blotting pad as if trying to recall a rather tuneless piece of music he had once heard. On the coat stand beside his chair hung a selection of jackets. A leather one with elasticated cuffs, a blue mountain anorak with a hood, a long gabardine raincoat – all part of his repertoire of disguises, Jade surmised.

'I've thought about this a good deal. I want you to find out what you can.'

Quail nodded. 'Do you mind if I ask you a question? What exactly does this mean to you?'

'Is that relevant to the case?'

The detective sighed. 'You are asking me to find a dead man. A man with no fixed address, no history.' His eyes surveyed the notes he had been taking of their interview. 'Possible asylum seeker. No known family in this country. No education records.' He set down his pen. 'I would be starting from scratch, scraping in the dirt with a stick, if you like. So I need every little detail I can get hold of. Anything you can give me might be a help.'

The windows of the office were grimy with black soot. The noise of the traffic below in High Holborn sounded an unrelenting drone in the background, punctuated regularly by the louder grumble of a bus or lorry, which made the floor shake and the glass rattle in its frame, or the high-pitched whine of a motorcycle.

'I suppose I feel responsible.'

'For his death? But it was an accident. Do I understand correctly? So, even assuming there was a flaw in the design, for which I am not qualified to make a judgement, and not a material failure, there is still the matter of what this man . . . Thursday . . . was doing on the building site alone in the first place. You cannot possibly be held responsible for that.'

'I don't mean I am afraid of being held responsible, just that I feel a personal sense of . . . complicity.'

Arthur Quail lifted up his fountain pen and began tapping once again on the blotter. 'There is no reason to feel responsible.'

'No rational reason.' Jade nodded. 'I know.' She closed her eyes. The image of the dead man lying in the mud, anonymous and broken, came back to her.

'No rational reason,' repeated Quail, shifting uncomfortably in his chair.

'Is it so unusual to feel responsible for the consequences of your actions? I mean, so much of what we do causes suffering, doesn't it?' She realised she wasn't making a lot of sense, and fumbled for an example to illustrate her point: 'Pollution. The petrol we put in our cars, the food we eat. So much is done to allow us to live the way we do. The depletion of the seas by over-fishing, the extinction of tuna.'

'Tuna?' echoed Arthur Quail.

'The thing is that we go through life closing our minds to this. Supposing there is a limit. Supposing it matters to stop and take responsibility.'

'And this is what you are doing? By trying to find this man, you are trying to set things right?'

She didn't know why it was important to retrace Thursday's steps. She only knew that she needed to try.

'Do your clients always have to give you a reason?'

'Not at all,' said Quail, setting his pen down and locking his fingers together. 'But the reason why we insist on this interview before accepting a case is to get a real idea of what personal importance this investigation has to our client. This might have a bearing on our work, as you can imagine.'

'I want to know who he was.'

'It won't change things.'

'Maybe not, but . . . it seems to me there are moments in life. We don't plan them. We don't seek them out. But they come to us, and how we react at that moment determines who we are, what we are and how we go on. Does that make any sense?'

'Yes.' Arthur Quail nodded. 'Yes, I think it does.'

There didn't seem to be much more to say. After a moment he made as if to get to his feet, and she followed suit. As he led her to the door of his office the detective reached into his pocket and held out a business card for her to take.

'My partner,' he explained. 'Perhaps you should consider making an appointment.'

'But I thought you were taking the case?' asked Jade, confused.

'Oh, yes, of course.' Arthur Quail laughed as though he were sneezing. His eyes blinked tightly shut. 'I mean my partner, personal, not business. She does meditation, healing. You might like to consider giving her a call.'

Jade thanked him, and went on her way, wondering if she had made a terrible mistake. Outside, she stood in the busy street and watched the traffic go by, trying to remember what she was supposed to do next.

12

It was a sullen day, the air wringing with moisture. Not ideal weather for a stroll in the garden, but Waldo Schmidt insisted. 'I need to get outside,' he wheezed, his lungs sounding like sandpaper. 'I need the open space.'

Waldo Schmidt clearly liked an audience, despite the years of isolation – the man was virtually a recluse. She wheeled him into the tiny lift, big enough only for the wheelchair, and then descended the stairs, hearing his voice echoing through the gloom as he sank downward in the cage alongside her.

'This is the high point of my day. That and a regular bowel movement.'

They rolled down a dark ramp and out into the garden. Somewhere in the house, Eastern music was murmuring; drums like soft hands tapping on water. Outside the light was draining from the sky through the trees.

'I first came to London in 1937. A young man with huge ambitions. I wanted to paint. Things were difficult for us in Germany. Adolf Hitler, the ultimate example of the failed artist taking his frustrations out on the world. I think he despised himself, but he also hated anyone who had enjoyed more success than he, which effectively meant anyone who ever lifted a brush. It had little to do with whether they were Jewish or not. That same year, Hitler had staged an exhibition of Degenerate Art to show how bad it all was for the German soul. To the fascists classical art was everything. We wanted to break that hold. After the exhibition they burned all the paintings. You can't fight violence with culture. I can claim the distinction of having watched my work go up in flames alongside that of Marc Chagall. That was the end of that. Why Britain? I don't know. It was never meant to be anything more than a temporary shelter, and Britain has always been generous that way.' Schmidt's nose looked red and swollen in the cold air. But it was his choice. Jade stopped to help arrange the blanket around his shoulders as he went on. 'I had money, family money, but it was cut off when I came here. I was forced to fend for myself, for the first time in my life really. I was totally unknown, outside a select circle of degenerate specialists, that is, so I had to think how to earn a living. It took me a year of struggling in a draughty old warehouse off the Farringdon Road to realise that dying a cold and lonely death as an artist had little appeal. To keep warm I used to go and sit in the Royal Gallery and study the beautiful paintings. And it struck me one day that those artists had reached a pinnacle of a certain kind, and that all our efforts to create something of a similar nature were going to be in vain. A truly great painter is capable of looking beyond. Think of Turner's wonderful seascapes. I was cold and hungry and that is the time to be brutally honest with yourself. I was never going to achieve more than a brilliant mediocrity. So, I decided to perfect my skills by learning how the Old Masters did what they did. I became completely absorbed by matters such as different types of paint, canvas, all kinds of technical details. I began to experiment with structure and colour. I researched the history of paint manufacture and improvised methods of incorporating a variety of materials, some conventional, others not, such as soot, dust, ground bone, anything to achieve the required texture. In the beginning I specialised in Flemish fifteenth-century works. People were more trusting in those days, I suppose, But I had a fair amount of luck, I dare say. I visited several dealers, posing as an exiled Russian aristocrat. My accent helped, as did my shabby outfits, which had obviously once been cut by a good tailor. London was awash with refugees down on their luck, trying to make a new start, and there were ripe pickings for those who had an eye for such things. People were looking for safe investments. Currency could be devalued, art works retained their worth. Slowly, I began to sell.'

It was having embarked on his new career as a forger that Waldo Schmidt made the acquaintance of Ernst Frager at the London Trade Fair where he had gone looking for buyers.

Ernst had been in London for about a year then, having decided not to go back to Germany. Waldo and Ernst were opposites. Ernst, quiet, honest, diligent, loyal and Waldo, well: 'I was after the contacts he had and he wanted the ones I had. We all had to help one another. I introduced him to a wealthy industrialist who had already invested in a rather fine Goya of mine.'

Enter A. J. Preston, of Preston, Pike and Sons, Engineering Co. Ltd. Except there was no Pike, as he had passed on years ago, and there were no sons, either. They had been cut down, like Ernst's brother, on the bloody fields of northern France. Preston was an old-fashioned Northerner who had pulled himself up by his bootstraps. But like many self-made men he saw himself as a man of vision.

'Ideas are like works of art,' he would declare. 'They guide us into the great beyond. The Egyptians had the wheel. We have combustion.'

In Ernst, Preston found an attentive ear for his grandiose theories. Ernst not only agreed with Preston, he thought it was all perfectly feasible. He believed that in the not-so-distant future machines would cook for us, feed us, even replenish themselves. Plants would grow in greenhouses without any tending. Animals would be reared, fed, milked, and slaughtered according to strict scientific methods to measure and optimise their yield. One man could manage an entire herd. It sounded like one of Swift's satirical parables. Preston had no real idea of what he was dealing with, not really, but he thought Ernst did.

'Where did you say you were from?' demanded A. J. Preston, slightly deaf, pulling himself up to his full six foot three and one-half inches, hands like huge floundering trout seeking the deep pockets of his ermine-lined overcoat.

'Altersbach.'

'Where's that when it's at 'ome, then?'

Ernst could not have failed to notice the effect he was having on the enchanting creature at the big man's elbow. Edith seemed to enjoy watching him squirm. She toyed with the buttons on her ivory yellow gloves while Ernst looked Preston in the eye.

'It's a small unremarkable corner of Europe, very much off the beaten path.'

'Well at least you're not a Hun then!' surmised Arthur Preston with a loud laugh. The British Empire was still riding high on a tide of textiles, spinning and weaving, ladies' fashions, the stocks of haberdashery departments, and Preston's weak grasp of geography could perhaps be explained by the fact that the Schwartzwald was further removed to his mind than Burma, Bombay, or Durban, say, where he had his customers, associates and investments. Spinning and weaving machinery. He exported all over the world.

From behind the formidable shield of her father, Edith was studying Ernst closely. The sheltered flower. She had been brought up all her life by nannies and tutors. Her mother had withdrawn from maternal duties early on, due to an 'attack of the nerves'. A fleet of medical authorities were brought in, some from as far away as Switzerland, but none could prescribe anything but rest and isolation. Her nerves never really recovered and she later came to live with Ernst and Edith after they were married. An artistic temperament was blamed. To A. J. Preston this was worse than having been diagnosed with typhus or consumption. Preston took measures to restrain the malaise: he sealed his wife off in a remote wing of the family estate and ensured that she did not interfere in the education of their daughter. Arthur Preston worried about his daughter. He wanted her to emerge from beneath the stifling shadow of her hysterical mother and be allowed to blossom fully. He needn't have worried. In many ways, Edith took after her father. She liked the open air, and she liked to play dangerously. Her artistic temperament expressed itself benignly in watercolours and piano recitals.

To Edith, Ernest Frager seemed like an attractively dangerous sort of man to get involved with. She saw immediately how different he was from the suitors her father had been encouraging her to meet – lumpish landowners and morose ball-bearing manufacturers. There was something distinct about Ernst. His foreignness to begin with, and his hilarious accent, his intense seriousness balanced by a rather funny gleam in his eye. He was a challenge, she decided. She adored the *idea* of falling in love with him as much as actually being in love with the man himself.

'Ernst had managed to acquire the manners of a gentleman.

He looked rather quaint, with his cardboard briefcase and his trilby. He knew his subject and he had an infectious kind of naïve enthusiasm for things which, combined with his European accent, added up to a formula for mysterious wizardry. He showed the old man his ideas on paper and Preston offered him a contract there and then. Told all his friends that he had discovered a "flippin' genius".' Waldo Schmidt smiled, 'I saw him for what he was, a fraud, like me, playing for time, hoping one day to fulfil his dreams.'

Preston Patents (times being what they were Ernst could not possibly use his own name) began in the abandoned brick kiln, overgrown with weeds and wild gooseberry bushes, behind the Preston family home in Hendon. It remained a small-time venture with Ernst now on the shop floor, now on the telephone. One minute drumming up customers, the next at the drawing board doing what he enjoyed most, inventing new machines. Ideas sprouted from Ernst's imagination like tiny little shoots, springy wires spilling out onto the rough work bench. Waldo, whose work discipline was, to put it mildly, undisciplined, would drop by to keep Ernst company. He did useful things like opening beer bottles with a screwdriver while Ernst hammered out his prototypes. The entire length and breadth of the workshop was cluttered with strange objects. The benches were strewn with half-finished models that nobody could make head or tail of. It looked like the aftermath of a mechanical massacre with the scattered remains of dismantled motor engines. There were propellers and water pumps, railway signals and generators, gramophone players and radios, each of them mined for one unique part that could be useful in a way never imagined by its makers. The result was a tide of debris, tangles of wire and iron levers, buckets of springs and ball bearings and every manner of minutiae, all waiting for an idea to attach themselves to.

'It was a mess,' recalled Waldo. 'Right from the start. Nobody understood what he was up to, not even me. But he was furious with energy.'

Ernst would work on half a dozen ideas at the same time. He would make garden shears with extendable arms to reach high branches; a revolving clockwork stand for teapots to ensure perfectly steeped tea; a hollow walking cane with in-built compass and hip flask for gentlemen out observing a fox hunt; an ingenious magnetic hatstand where you simply threw your hat and it would stick to the wall. There were early break-throughs, such as the Folding Reader, which was like a music stand, only this one rested beside your plate on the dining table with the morning paper on it. Invaluable for holding up docu-ments while typing – *folds up instantly to tuck away in the filing cabinet or sideboard with the cutlery!* There were coatstands with retractable arms; typewriters with interchangeable keys to allow you to use different lettering; a shoe-polishing device to carry in your suitcase; a card-shuffling box for bridge players; a trav-elling washbasin and shaving case with a spring-loaded mirror that flipped over.

'He was a sort of genius, I suppose. He was able to work out the entire mechanism for a new device in his head, before even putting pen to paper. He once explained how he could see it all happening, each little cog turning. I never knew whether to believe him,' sighed Schmidt.

What Ernst came up with was a series of gadgets; useless devices that cluttered up the back pages of the *Illustrated News*. No great breakthroughs in science. These 'ingenious devices', brilliant though they were, and successful, some of them, were nevertheless of their time. Their appeal faded quickly as tech-nology overtook them. So many of Ernst's inventions were forgettable, dispensable curiosities that you might easily decide you could live without. But that was precisely the point of them; they were luxury items, displaying for all the world the level of decadent comfort you had achieved. Mechanical items to ease the physical tasks of the modern age. The mainstay of the firm, its staple product, its bread and butter, turned out to be one of its simplest and earliest innovations: a rubber roller for cleaning the typeface on a typewriter. With a smooth, varnished wooden handle and a spool and bobbin device coated with sticky rubber:

A simple device to renew your typewriter in a matter of minutes! Ensure crisply typed letters on every document. No more illegible blurs! Make every word count! One quick roll over each morning and the special adhesive rubber picks out all the excess ink, dirt and paper lodged in the keys. Saves on wear and tear. Guarantees fewer complaints! Don't let your image be marred by smudged letters. Order now!

Maintenance became an extinct element, like the dodo, or the trilobite. Ernst's beloved Stamp Appliance – *Just depress the handle and it affixes a stamp onto an envelope, saves hours of sticky fiddling!* – was replaced by an electronic franking machine. But finally, the nail in the coffin was shaped like a ball, a spherical type-writer head that whirled around itself like a tiny mad planet, replacing the sedate assembly of static iron keys that rose behind the platen like an amphitheatre waiting in reverent anticipa-tion. The word sings electric. Electronic circuits replacing the ingenuous mechanical devices Ernst was so good at devising. He was looking the future in the face. No more repairs: you didn't roll a golf ball clean. You replaced it.

Waldo Schmidt chuckled to himself as they trundled along the little path that curved out across the green lawn. 'Ernst was always dreaming of the one ingenious device that would make his fortune, but his ambition was flawed by impatience. He would cast something aside and set off in another direction as the ideas came to him. He did not have the patience to finish one thing before starting another. The adding machine, for example, was a beauty, but it took him decades. He took the principle of the Chinese abacus: divisions of units, threes and fives, turning on poles along which sleeves slid back and forth. It was faster and lighter than any adding machine anyone had seen before.' He jabbed a hand in the direction of the pergola. They took a left fork past a fine little cherry tree. Jade noted potentilla and berberis.

What Ernst didn't know was that Preston was on the verge of bankruptcy. When the old man died it all went into receiver-ship. The family property was sold, leaving just enough for the house in Hendon. Edith never really recovered from the shock, said Waldo.

Perhaps in America it might have grown into an enormous financial concern, but in Britain it stayed small. A handful of workers slipping bobbins onto reels. Sealing boxes of twelve dozen units of typewriter cleaners. The market was small and people were cautious. Ernst delivered orders himself when the driver called in sick or the customer was in no mood to wait. He had one late success, an automated billiard game; a handsome miniature table carved out of oak with spring-loaded wooden figures and smooth Welsh slate under the green baize.

They had reached the elongated pond. Schmidt was an avid collector of Japanese koi carp. He had dozens of the things, he explained. The common orange and white variety, then the *showa*, which had black bands called *sumi*. Some were pure alabaster, and one was a dull silver colour; a platinum *ogon*. Each fish cost several thousand pounds. The entire pool was rigged with a complex electronic system with infra-red sensors to deter burglars.

'People will stoop to anything nowadays to make a few shillings.'

The pool itself was a beauty. It had an extremely sensitive filtration system. The ecology of the environment being all important. The shade from the wooden trellis kept the light out and stopped the growth of algae. Schmidt opened a bag he had been carrying and started tossing little pellets or worms or something into the water using a tiny catapult. The fish jostled around one another at the surface. Mouths opening and closing like strange flowers in the water.

'He went back to Germany after the war, to act as an interpreter for Military Intelligence. That was at the end of 1945. I was against the idea. No good would come of it, I said. You think the British went into the war for moral reasons? They had no choice, I told him. And now you want to go and help them against the Soviets? I suppose it was all that business of being interned during the war. He wanted to prove something and there was nothing I or anyone else could do.'

'So what happened while he was over there?'

Waldo Schmidt squinted at the pool. Jade could smell the moisture in the trees and the strong fragrance of pine. The bony figure remained motionless for a time before raising the catapult to flick another handful of pellets into the water. Smooth tangerine flashes darted through the mineral blue water. Waldo

Schmidt fell silent and she had the sense that he was holding something back. When he spoke again his voice was changed. 'We lost contact for a time. When he came back things between us had changed. I was part of the old world and he wanted a new one.'

Jade was beginning to feel the cold. Schmidt looked withered, his nose running, the spokes of his wheelchair gleaming as tiny bubbles of fragile water condensed out of the air around them and the frail bands of spring light slowly drained. There was a shout from behind them. They both started guiltily and turned towards the house from where the French girl was now bearing down on them, running across the damp grass clutching a large blanket to her.

'Ah,' muttered Waldo Schmidt. 'Time to get back into my coffin, I think.'

13

One of the few distinct recollections Jade had of her father was an excursion to Ainsdale. She was about four years old. They drove the big Jaguar straight down onto the beach. The wind blew in punchy thrusts along the long, wide strip of sand. They sat in the car waiting for the downpour to pass, watching the rain hitting the sea, feeling the car gently rocking around them. Peppery clouds revolved over their heads, tumbling with effervescent energy. Then the sun broke through and they pushed open the doors, feeling the wind trying to rip them from their hands. A disaster of an outing, Miranda was laughing. They left her there, struggling to hammer the striped windbreak into the ground and prepare the picnic while they went exploring. The grass in the dunes slashed like tiny paper knives against Jade's ankles making her squeal and screw up her face. She ran down the steep incline into the arms of the strangely familiar man in the baggy trousers and the shapeless tweed jacket. His clothes were damp from the spray, and she smelled that curious combination of engine oil and sea water. The wind pulled back her curls and made her clap her hands in delight. She stared at how white his feet were as he danced up and down the beach, lifting her onto his shoulders, turning round and round, her arms flying outwards as the sky turned above her head.

In the distance, a point of reference, was his car, the worn-looking Jaguar, glinting dully on the otherwise deserted beach.

She laughed so much she couldn't catch her breath. They tumbled to the sand in a heap and stared at the sky.

'Where do you come from, Daddy?'

'What do you mean?' He frowned.

'You're so funny. I bet you come from the moon.'

'The moon? No.' He smiled and pulled her close. 'I'll tell

you a secret,' he whispered into her hair; 'I come from out there.' He pointed at the sea. She looked and saw only grey water, the scummy white froth of tumbling waves: the viscous geometry of impossibility.

It was the happiest memory Jade had of the three of them together, as a family. When she was going through her own divorce she often dreamed of that time on the beach – she didn't want her daughter to grow up longing for an absent father. It was what she had always promised herself she would never do, and yet it was happening. The dream seemed to come back to haunt her.

It was the offer of a job at Giles, Stock & Waverley that was to mark the beginning of her career and the end of her marriage. It was for Jade's sake they decided to move to London. For Etienne it was not a happy change. He missed his beloved Paris, his friends. He also missed his work, being able to travel, to sit bouncing in the back of a rundown bus for fifteen hours from Peshawar to Kabul. He had given all that up, he said, for her, and for their life together as a family, for Maya.

They had met at an exhibition of photography. Two pictures in a corner, one showed a toothless woman in Soweto smoking a pipe; the gaze from her eyes penetrating the wraiths of smoke around her head and infusing the image with an occult power. The other was a girl hanging gaily from the doorway of a tram in Lisbon, her gaze utterly lost in thought.

'Did you know her?' Jade asked. The first conversation they ever had.

'No,' said Etienne, 'but I have been looking for her ever since.'

For three months they lived a tangled, reckless kind of passion which they only realised soberly might actually be love when they found out she was pregnant. They got married, quietly and without fuss, for practical reasons, they agreed, chastened by what they were embarking on. They moved her suitcases and one trunk into Etienne's tiny flat behind the Bastille, and for a time lived the romantic life, of long summer evenings in cafés and friends who talked passionately of the ambitions they were sure they would one day realise. She had no room for dreams. She was twenty-six years old and she was about to become a mother. Nothing would come easily. She knew that. If she didn't work harder than anyone else she would get nowhere. She would wind up living with her mother again like all the other damn fools who had made the mistake of putting their hearts before their heads. Everything lay in the future: parenthood, buildings, photographs, greatness. She was realistic. They would do it all. They could do it. All they had to do was try. Life was a shining orb, burning fiercely with hope and possibility. She was happy. *They* were happy.

The memory of those early years remained strong, tempered by questions that were still unanswered, questions such as what went wrong and why. Then, she had been trying to finish her apprenticeship. Etienne was the one who earned the money, and his work took him away. There were long periods of loneliness for her to get used to. He went to Beirut, then to Angola, to Colombia, to Kabul. It scared her, but it seemed that wherever there was trouble in the world, he had to go. There would be time for them later, but he had to establish himself, to make his name first. There were hundreds of photographers out there, but only a few of them were willing to take the risks and that meant going out to find the edge. But she told herself that if he could do it then she could be strong. He went to Bosnia, talking from a noisy candlelit bar in Sarajevo. The steady rattle of percussion behind him. Broken rhythms. He said the firing was a long way off. Then there was a roar like the sea striking a pebbly beach and then silence, the line went dead. She cried for him that night. She held her baby to her breast and wept. For almost eight hours she could think of nothing but the fact that Etienne was gone. She could not think of who to call, or what to say. In the morning she rose up and looked out over the still blue rooftops and thought how much she hated this city, the passive sense of normality it had instilled in her. The world was burning, coming apart at the seams, and here was the smell of fresh bread and drunken laughter clattering home through the dawn streets. When he called her back at eleven that morning to let her know he was all right she told him that she loved him and begged him to come home. She believed it, when she spoke the words, but she knew she would never allow herself to become so dependent on another person ever again.

Even before their move to London he was beginning to go a little off the rails. She had thought a change of scene might help, and it was a good job. But Etienne never really found his footing in London. He went through a phase of conceptual photography, studio experiments, using light and shade. Trying to reach for art, trying too hard, revealing a void in his talent that he had never thought he would find. To Jade they all looked like portraits of unhappy people. They didn't sell well. A few exhibitions in small galleries, but nothing substantial. Etienne's ambition was gradually replaced by an odd collection of bohemian friends he had managed to dredge up – artists, painters, writers. London was full of them. They all claimed to be trying to get somewhere, but they seemed to spend most of their time drinking and smoking and complaining about how dingy and provincial England was; the primary qualification for joining the group seemed to Jade to be expatriotism: Italian poets, Lebanese painters, Greek installationists, Spanish filmmakers. While they dreamed of getting into the Saatchi collection, Jade was the one paying the bills. Etienne would forget to pick Maya up from nursery, the only absolutely essential duty in his day. She would arrive home and find everything in the same state of disarray as she had left it that morning. Etienne needed change, he said, variation. She had long since taken for granted that, as far as other women were concerned, he had been getting plenty of variety, but he was stifled creatively, he said. He needed to go. A part of him, she realised, had discovered that he was like everyone else, he had limitations. So now he needed to find his way back to where he knew who he was and what he wanted to do. There seemed no point in fighting it. Maya was almost six when it finally ended and she took it remarkably well. Their life together grew simpler. They knew they depended on one another. Three years into her independence and she was on the verge of being made a partner when Edmund Waverley had a fatal heart attack at his villa in Antibes and everything went on hold.

She missed the sense of purpose Etienne had given to her life. Just having him around, to argue, to debate, to agree, and finally, to love. Despite his absences, perhaps even because of them. The determination to keep things working. He went away. He came back. She was responsible for maintaining his sanity. In return, his movements to the dark points of the world punctuated her ordered life with meaning. It became exhausting to carry on, easier to slowly let go. But she missed the drive of those days, despite the pain and the fury.

Everything in her life seemed to have been leading her up to this point. The accident, the falling arc, the dead man, the letters from Rachel. All of it suggested that she had reached a point of no return. Rachel's letters provided a line of escape that led away from the chaos of the present into the labyrinth of her past. It was a tempting offer. A necessary one, too. But it would not be easy. It made Jade aware of how much she had cut herself off, from her mother, from anything to do with herself, in the process of making herself into what she was today. There was a pleading note, a vulnerability in Rachel's letters which set off a tremoring echo deep in Jade's memory, a buried mirror that she had cast away from herself long ago.

When she had first left home, she had tried to get so far away from her own life story she even lied about who she was and where she came from. It seemed absurd to think about now, and the fact was that she had not thought about that time for years, but it was true. Her determination had made her distant, cold, secretive. She had little time for people and few friends. If she decided people were of no use to her she pushed them away, cut them off. She lied in an effort to consolidate an image of herself as someone able to succeed, capable of crossing into a world she had not been born into. Quite simply she told people her parents had passed away, that she had been brought up in an orphanage, that she had been adopted as a child. The places she came from, the school she went to, all of it was erased, as though one fragment of that story might bring her crashing down to earth. It all seemed so far-fetched now. Had it all been necessary? At the time she had thought so. For a long period she refused to see Miranda. Everyone else went home, for Christmas, Easter, occasional weekends. Jade never did. 'You've got the same hair as me,' this from Melanie, a Birmingham sociology student, seeing in Jade's skin a pale shadow of sisterhood. 'It comes in a bottle,' she replied, not wishing to be tied down to ethnic specifics. She wanted freedom, an open road, and was concerned with any feature that might impede her progress. 'There are so few black architects in this country, you'll be wonderful': her tutor, Geoff Sheen, woolly-haired academic liberal who wore baggy jumpers and a Sergeant Pepper walrus moustache. He begged her to come away with him for a CND protest weekend. But she couldn't accept his terms. She wanted no limitations. She wanted, simply, to be the best, or at least die trying. 'I'm not going to be a black architect,' she retorted, 'just an architect.' Which only made him want her more. When she decided to move to France it was not so much for any high ideals, intellectual endeavour, or deconstructionism, nor was it really out of a love for French architecture – though she often declared this as a motive when asked. Probably the real reason she went was because it allowed her to cross yet another river and slip further into the trees of anonymity she craved to recreate herself. To add another layer of distance between herself and the person she used to be.

She found herself looking for precedents, role models, theories to explain her choices, discovering them partly in an affinity with Hannah Arendt and her ideas on exile and the human condition. In order to survive, the exile had to move on, had to transcend all those things they had been brought up to believe were a part of them: home, religious destiny – *Gemeinschaft*. She became an architect because she dreamed of transforming the world she came from, the world she was born in, which yet seemed to have no space for her. She went to Paris, she said, to try and understand that need to free herself, as Arendt put it, from the chains of memory.

Haussmann's Paris, the first truly modern city. Most of the time she just liked being there. It was Paris that showed her how the cities we seek exist only in our imagination. Like Venice as painted by Canaletto, who moved buildings and bridges around to suit the vision in his head. She needed the complexity of cities, that conspiracy of vanity and lies. A series of alibis, a mathematical progression that stretched back to zero, to infinity, to cavemen and handprints on the wall.

She found other examples of imaginary places. The early frescoes in the Museo Archeologico Nazionale di Napoli: softly faded colours, coral, cinnabar, avocado; a figure crossing a misty bridge reminiscent of Chinese Han dynasty ink paintings, all dissolved into a chalky white abstraction. These were not depictions of places that really existed, but invented views. Extensions, as she saw it, of a hunger to describe what the mind wished to inhabit: a landscape of dreams. The palaces of Roman emperors were lined with images of such imaginary places, which helped inspire the conquest of the world they were planning. The same with the Dutch sixteenth-century painters, whose imaginings offered wide open spaces for the empire to grow into. Lone figures lost in the dead emptiness of it all; palaces, turbans, peacocks, the fire-plumed birds that spoke of remote exoticism, distant marvels, and the wealth needed to seize them. To possess the world you had first to imagine it. Francisco Gutierrez depicted Moses being discovered floating in his basket with the bulrushes reduced to a trim moustache of green along the rectilinear kerb of a stone canal. Elegant ladies and gentlemen descending the steps towards the water at their ease. An imagining of Egypt in antiquity based on a model of Rome or Venice, complete with its palazzi and gondolas.

It was in Paris, she recalled, that she first saw Victor Hugo's tower in a storm, *Le Burg dans l'orage*: a dark edifice rising from a flat landscape. The tapered pile emerging from the obscurity of a sandstorm in the desert, in which the viewer was utterly lost. Impossible to know what else was hidden in there, what the complete structure might look like. She had always seen it as an optimistic picture, the construction emerging from the swirling clouds of sepia, beige and cinnamon. Order being made out of the confusion of the modern world. Now it seemed that vision had abandoned her. Ever since that brass arc had come falling down she had been lost, unable to tell where the earth left off and the sky began.

14

On Wednesday morning she called in sick. At twelve-thirty she took the tube to Green Park to meet Francis Arburgh. The solicitor had suggested a small place off Cork Street. At one o'clock sharp she walked through the door and instantly regretted agreeing to the venue. The dark veneer and the leaded windows weighed heavily on the room. Old England; a place you could visit, but where she would never belong. It wasn't so much a question of race, as of environment. This was not her territory. The only woman in sight was serving drinks. A row of men stood by the bar talking loudly, their voices booming with boorish affluence. They turned to watch her as she entered. She picked out Francis Arburgh right away. He was standing alone, dressed in a light grey suit, striped shirt, pale lemon tie. Unobtrusive, and clearly in his element. He was obviously a regular visitor, greeting the waiter with familiar ease as they were led to their table. Jade felt her confidence evaporating as she became that graceless Northern girl she once was, clumsy, lost for words.

'Sorry, what would you . . .?' Francis Arburgh and the waiter turned towards Jade. He had ordered the day's special without even looking at the menu.

'I'll have the same,' she smiled quickly, with no idea what it was. She was not feeling particularly hungry.

'So.' Arburgh broke a bread roll and began to butter it fastidiously. 'How are you getting along?'

'I'm not sure. It all seems very confusing. Difficult to think of the company you have worked for for nearly eleven years as your adversary, I suppose.'

'Sure it is. Of course.' He popped the piece of buttered bread into his mouth and began to chew with quick, efficient movements of the jaw. 'Tell me a bit about yourself, outside of work. Social life, that sort of thing.'

'What has that got to do with anything?' she asked.

'Everything has bearing.' He beamed, eyes bobbing back to knife and butter.

'I am a working mother. I have an adolescent daughter. Between her and the job, I don't really have much of a private life.'

'I understand.'

'Would you mind telling me where this is leading?'

'Leading? Ah, yes, of course. Well, how can I put this . . .'

A sinking feeling came over her. Francis Arburgh put down his butter knife.

'All right,' he said. 'I shall try to be candid. How would you feel about playing the race card?'

'Well, I wouldn't have picked you for a start. Is this some kind of joke?'

'No joke. No. I assure you.' Francis Arburgh lowered his voice and sniffed loudly. 'How about sex?'

'Sex?' The waiter came and went without her noticing. She looked down at what appeared to be shredded black pudding and Brussels sprouts covered in melted Stilton.

'Gender, I mean.' Francis Arburgh dug straight in, speaking while chewing quickly. 'Can't be easy, making a name for yourself in the architecture game – as a woman, I mean.'

'There are more women in the profession than you would think, but somehow they are not visible. It's a man's game in many ways, building things. Freud would say that it had something to do with men trying to escape the creative powers of their mothers. The fact is that the decision-makers are men in most cases. To me, it's just one more obstacle. Either you let your life be ruled by adversity or you take it in your stride. I don't believe in making excuses for myself.'

Francis Arburgh was listening attentively as she spoke. He nodded, whether in acknowledgement or approval was not clear. Jade pushed the tip of her fork around the plate hoping to find something she might be able to swallow and managed to spear a sprout.

'You could order something else, if you don't like that. They rather specialise in innovative approaches to traditional English fayre.' Arburgh smiled wanly. 'Makes a change from all that fettuccine, I find.'

She changed the subject. 'You seem to be pretty sure this will end in court.'

'That's what I am counting on.' Arburgh raised his eyebrows. 'I mean, I presume that you have sought out legal advice because you have surmised that Giles, Scott & Waverley are preparing to use this unfortunate accident to try and get rid of you.' He took another mouthful and took his time, waiting for her answer.

'It looks that way to me.'

'Good. Now from what I can gather of your work for them over the years you should be in a far higher earning bracket than you are now. That is why I think we should be able to make a pretty good case for discrimination. Sexual, largely, but maybe we can throw in a bit of racial prejudice for good measure.'

'Do you have much experience of this kind of claim?'

'Presumably you read the newspapers? People have a lot of grievances these days – no longer content to sit back and take it any longer . . . Hello, Bill.' Arburgh broke off to greet a passerby before turning back to her. 'When someone steps on you and you don't bite, you know what they do? They step on you again. Well, I am in the business of helping people bite back.'

He certainly made a convincing case, but Jade was uncomfortable with the idea of becoming a test case, or worse, a pet exhibit. What would it do to her career? She wanted to be an architect, no tags attached. Even if she won the case her name would be forever associated with the word discrimination. If she lost she would have to emigrate to a non-English-speaking country, like Greenland, say.

She folded her napkin, giving up all pretence of trying to eat. 'I wanted this meeting because I need to know what my options are. I mean, I have no real evidence that Kyle is planning to use this accident against me. But I need to have a defence prepared. I think that if any accusations came our way I might find myself on my own. He is not the only person who would like to see me gone from the firm.'

'Well, of course.' Arburgh nodded. 'And I understand that completely. You have emotional ties to the company. Loyalties.

You've watched it grow. It doesn't feel right. Only natural. But you have just made a good case for being prepared. OK, let me tell you how I appraise the situation. Do you mind?' Jade shook her head. 'Any case like this is less about guilt or innocence than about character.'

'Which means?'

He held his plate in the air. A waiter appeared to take it. He reached into his jacket for a leatherbound notebook. 'They look for personal flaws. A weakness they can exploit. I have been talking to a few people. Making enquires. Exploratory work. I have been in this business a long time and I know a lot of people. The best way of finding out what the other side know is to make enquiries of one's own.'

'You mean you've been making enquiries about me?'

'The operatives I use are very discreet, I can assure you.'

He was smiling that smile again, a blend of smug knowingness. At this point she felt she would dearly like to have hit him with something.

'And what did they tell you, these operatives of yours?'

'We are dealing with professionals, intelligent people like yourself. People who are good at hiding their weaknesses. If Giles, Stock & Waverley decided to hang you out to dry they would need something that would make you appear unreliable. We look for flaws, the little things, clues that tell us how someone behaves when they don't have their guard up, when they are under stress.'

'It sounds like one of those self-help manuals you find in supermarkets. How to improve your chances of winning. Yoga Without Pain. Zen the Easy Way.' Jade sat back and folded her arms. 'You're going to have to spell this out for me.'

Francis Arburgh dabbed at his lips with the white napkin. 'Very well. Let's say that your behaviour of late has been a little eccentric. For example, you engage a private investigator to research the life of the man who died in the accident. Hard to explain what good can come from something like that.'

'It's not a crime, is it?'

'Obsession can be an unhealthy thing, a sign of mental and emotional instability. There are other signs.'

'Such as?'

'Well, that's your third glass of wine in, what, half an hour?'
She was stung, as if someone had struck her.

Arburgh waited before going on. 'There's nothing unusual about people leaning on alcohol more than perhaps is advisable. Statistics show that women are particularly prone, professional women. You didn't drive here, I take it?'

Jade dug her nails into the palm of her hand. 'What is your point?'

'If they try to float the idea that you are, well, hitting the bottle, for want of a less offensive term, then I need a counterplay, something to shift the blame back to them. If it comes up we might have to use it to argue your case for mental abuse, maltreatment. I need to know how far I can go. Your professional judgement, of course, will be at stake. Ever tried any counselling, detoxification?'

'This is ridiculous,' snorted Jade. 'Look around you. I don't drink any more than your average healthy active adult.'

'You drink at home?'

'Sometimes.'

'Every day?'

'Maybe.'

'How many measures do you get through in a week? Just a rough guess.'

'I have no idea and I'm not counting.'

'I told you, I need your full cooperation otherwise I can't take your case.'

'I don't have a drink problem.'

'Of course not. Not you, nor the half a million estimated heavy drinkers in this country. You don't have to have a beer gut, or to fall over in the street to have a problem. It just has to affect your judgement. Any drunk-driving convictions?'

'Look, I have a daughter. You think I would risk her welfare or safety? I'm a responsible mother.'

'That isn't answering the question. The fact is that you were convicted of drunk-driving.'

'That was years ago.'

'Two and a half to be exact, still on the record.' The waiter turned up to enquire about dessert. Arburgh waved him away with a deft flick of his hand, didn't even look up.

'The specifications on the PharmaKorp project were changed after commencement. Nothing drastic. The carbon composite masts supporting the brass mezzanine walkway. The suppliers made a mistake. Two of them were a different diameter from what was in the original specifications. Slight difference and it shouldn't have affected their ability to do the job. I'm not saying that difference caused the accident because it probably didn't, but someone else could make that case. The site engineers asked for written confirmation of changes, as is normal in these cases. As is also common practice the changes were approved verbally, over the phone. No records. The legally binding documents were promised for the following day. They never arrived. No one else knew about it. You were alone in the office that evening. You had work to do so you stayed on. Had you been drinking that night?'

Jade met his gaze. 'I don't remember.'

He glanced down at his notebook. 'Are you in the habit of popping into an off-licence on Blackfriars Road named Prado Lindo for a bottle of wine when you work late?' When she said nothing, he went on: 'Would the staff there recognise you?' Jade pushed back her chair and got to her feet. Francis Arburgh gestured for her to sit down. 'Please. I think we need to finish this.' She hesitated, and then sat down. Arburgh signalled to the hovering waiter to bring the coffee. He resumed his argument, speaking steadily and with a frank intensity she had not seen so far. His eyes never deviated from her. 'A man died. That is the gravity of this situation. In the eyes of the court everything will be measured against that simple fact. The case, as you know, has been drawing some media attention. I'll be frank, nobody really cares about the plight of a nameless illegal migrant from an equally nameless war-torn hell that the majority of people in this country could not find on a map without help. What people care about are stories: stories that move you, that make your heart tick, bring a tear to your eye, or make you livid with outrage. If Kyle's legal team try to discredit you they will do it by painting a portrait of an ambitious and bitter woman, disappointed with life. Everybody can identify with that. She drinks a little more than is good for her, and one day she makes a mistake and a man dies because of it.'

Francis Arburgh tucked his notebook into his inside pocket. 'That is the gist of it.' A flat look settled on his face. 'All I can do is tell you how I see it. The rest is up to you.' As he got to his feet, he said, 'I suggest you think about this matter very carefully before proceeding. If you want to engage my services you will have to agree to every term I impose. If we do that I have every confidence we can win a substantial amount in compensation. The courts are generally favourable to single mothers these days.' The waiter came hurrying up with Arburgh's coat. He held out a hand in farewell, a parting smile on his face. 'Unfortunately I have to rush, appointment in court. Please don't wait too long to make a decision.'

She watched him go. Then she slumped back down in her chair and covered her eyes with one hand. She wished the whole mess would just go away and leave her alone. After a few moments the waiter returned.

'Can I get you anything else?'

'No, thank you. Just bring me the bill please.'

The waiter beamed confidently. 'Mr Arburgh has already made arrangements.'

She fixed her eyes on his. 'Just bring me the fucking bill,' she snapped.

Rachel

I suppose that the beginning of it all was the day my son came home and announced that he had joined the army. I wasn't quite sure what he meant. Had he been conscripted? No, he said. They would have let him wait until his studies were finished, but he was impatient. He wanted to help, he said, to fight the ignorance that filled the world. He felt it was his duty to go to the south.

Did I tell you about the war? Well, this is an endless kind of war. A fruitless struggle that neither side can win; everyone loses. It is a vicious sawing back and forth, wearing away the land, the people. A war of attrition. The front line moves back and forth according to the time of year. When the rains come the army pulls back. They bomb the camps while waiting for the roads to dry out and then they launch a new offensive. It seems hopeless but the government describes it enthusiastically as jihad, a holy war against the unbelievers, which makes it sound nice and simple.

As far as the world at large is concerned it is a peripheral, distant, insignificant kind of war. The value of human life diminishes with each passing mile between front line and newsdesk. We are off the beaten track, a backwater of the world, and thus we are left to the savagery such obscurity deserves. But this is a lie. One day I was struck by the simple thought that wars cost money. Millions and millions of dollars. Money that could be well spent somewhere else. And where is it all coming from? You cannot wage war for so many years without outside support, without arms. So the world must know this is going on. Why does it remain silent?

This is a war fought by children. Some of them are simply picked up off the streets where they have been living rough.

They may have run away. Some, it is said, were sold by their mothers to keep their younger siblings alive. They live and work like slaves until they can no longer stand it, and then they run away, and wind up in the only place they can turn to, the streets. They arm them, they provide them with a kind of home, with food and a place to sleep. War feeds on its own hunger like a fever, drawing from humanity the replenishment it needs to sustain itself. People have begun to believe their own fantasies. This is a war that is bringing the light of religion to the world and thereby good. Children make good soldiers. The younger they are the better. A twelve-year-old knows no fear. It is all still a game to him. They have no understanding of the meaning of death. They think they are immortal, like all children everywhere. They move quickly. They run in where a grown man might hesitate. Sometimes they die like that too, I imagine – swiftly, on their feet, holes punched abruptly through their frail bodies between one breath and the next. The unlucky ones take longer. It is only when they are dead, when they are lying there inert, that they come to resemble little children again, sleeping peacefully.

My son was not a child when he joined up. He was twenty-two years old. A responsible adult. He knew what he was doing, proud of it in fact. I remember clearly the moment when he told me. I was standing at the back of the house, outside the kitchen, telling Musa, who is our cook, how to prepare the fish for lunch that day. It was a Friday. Amin was visiting his mother and would be late for lunch. Our two boys would both be there, Sayf back from the university, and his older brother, Mekki, who is trained as a construction engineer but has been unable to find vocational work and so has gone into business, importing electric fans, blenders and such items. It is somewhat less glorious than the career he had envisaged, but he is pragmatic and resigned to do the best he can under the circumstances. It was to be a big get-together, as the two boys were rarely home at the same time. I was concerned about the Nile perch I had bought because Musa had in the past committed atrocious things to some excellent fish. I wanted to make sure that he was not left alone with the thing for too long, in case he started getting ideas.

I have to say that we had been concerned about Sayf for some time. You always read that children go through phases. 'He's going through a phase.' How often I have used that expression myself, defending the quirky moods of my children. But I too was beginning to be worried. He was growing out of our hands, out of our reach. At that time he was attending Medani University, which is a couple of hours away by road. Amin's family comes from there. A small town in a pleasant corner of the country, on the rim of the huge Gezira delta of cotton plantations, although Amin mutters darkly of these having also gone to pot.

The changes began during Sayf's first year. He was staying at the student hostel on the campus and I believe this was something of an eye-opener for him. Away from the comforts and shelter of home, perhaps he felt vulnerable. He was living with strangers for the first time. He started to come home every weekend, which was not so bad, although we began to wonder, as we knew that not all the students could afford this. It wasn't that we minded having him back, just that we had the feeling that he was coming less to visit us than to avoid something else. I suspected that he had found himself among people whose lives had not been as easy as his, that he was discovering the world in a new way. I thought this might not be a bad thing. I sometimes feared we were too soft on him, let him get away with too much, placed too much responsibility on the shoulders of his elder brother. I was the younger child, and I had suffered as a result my mother's favouritism towards Matthew, so perhaps I was compensating. I was glad to see Sayf growing out of it. I could see it would not be easy, and we accepted it when he became uncommunicative. He was moody when he came home and would lock himself away in his room and sleep all day.

'One of his phases,' I said to Amin. Although I admit, I had expected him to be over these kinds of humour swings by this stage. He also stopped seeing his old friends. I began to consider the idea of drugs. Then, just as suddenly as they had started, the moods ended. He seemed to settle down, and now it was all we could do to get him to come home once a month.

'What about all the horror stories?' we asked. He used to

delight in feeding us nauseating titbits about how awful the hostel food was, how filthy the facilities were. It is good for him, his father would say, make a man of him and all that. Suddenly no more complaints, nothing of the sort. It was not so bad, he would say. If the others can live with it, then so can I. Your son has become a stoic, I told Amin, who immediately launched into one of his fond soliloquies about the virtues of his family, which as you may have grasped by now, are seemingly endless. Oh, we are all very tough in my family, hardened by the years and the hardships and so on and so forth ad nauseam – there are times when I feel like strangling him.

I've joined the army, Sayf said as he came in that afternoon, with Musa complaining that I had bought a fish with too many bones in it and I, my hands covered in flour, explaining that they don't come any other way than with bones in them, and that if he was careful enough to check he would find that all Nile perch have exactly the same number of bones in them, no more and no less, and all decided by the very same merciful and compassionate Lord who had provided him with a job in such a generous home. He shut up after that. I asked Sayf to repeat what he had just said, which he did: 'I've joined the army.' It took a long time to sink in. Needless to say the fish was forgotten and when Amin arrived home he found the house in uproar and no lunch ready, which did not put him in the best of moods to begin with.

'What on earth for?' was his first reaction. Why would anyone *want* to join the army? For once, I had no ready answer, I was as stumped as he was. We tried to reason with Sayf. What about his studies?

'Wait until you are finished, then see if they call you.'

The army was full of bullies and brutes, I argued, and people who had no choice: 'You have a choice. You are privileged. You have an education, a chance to make something of yourself.'

'We can take care of this,' Amin reasoned. We were not poor, he was not without influence.

'That's always your answer!' shouted Sayf furiously. 'Buy your way out! The wealthy are not interested in doing what is right. You know why? Because they have already bought their way into paradise. But the poor, the poor have no choice but to pray that one day they might be allowed in. Prayer is all they have.'

I was dumbstruck by his words, his outrage. He had become a revolutionary. My little boy. He believed that he was going to make the world a better place by killing people who did not share his beliefs. Oh, Amin carried on, trying to reason with him, of course. But not me. I could see it was a lost battle. I don't know how it happened, but Sayf truly believed that he was right. He had all the answers. There was nothing we could do.

It had happened gradually. We later learned, through his brother Mekki, that Sayf and his new friends had been coming to the capital regularly to demonstrate, to express solidarity with their brothers abroad. Lorries full of cheering students, waving banners and branches torn from trees along the way. They would march in defence of the Palestinians, in defiance of imperialism. All of it in strict adherence to government policy. You can't demonstrate against the regime. So they chanted, set fire to flags in the street and threw stones at the American embassy.

I was confused. I felt a surge of pride at seeing the passion my son felt about injustice, but couldn't understand how it could be so misplaced. I didn't see the logic of his complaint. The war was wrong. Surely he realised that the government was engaged in a steady campaign of the persistent erasure of one ethnic group after another. They were forcing them from their homelands – which just happen to be swimming in huge deposits of crude oil. In the west and south of the country local militias, mounted on horseback and pick-ups, armed by the government, would set fire to cattle cars filled with fleeing refugees and burn them alive. There are reports of murder, mass rape. They had helicopter gunships purchased from dodgy Russian entrepreneurs and piloted by Ukranians who had learned their trade in the mountains of Afghanistan. You say it is to spread Islam, I argued, but religion is not the issue, it never was. Oil is the issue. I made no impression at all.

We were too soft on him, Amin said, not enough discipline. He is confused. He grew up in an age of optimism, when the house was full of artists, painters, people who could think for themselves, creative people who did not want limits. My son grew up craving the opposite of what we had offered him. He wanted those bearded men with their archaic laws and their parochial views. I could hardly believe it.

'We gave you choices, the freedom to make up your own mind. Now you want to impose your will on others because they are different from you.'

'Sometimes choice is not what we need. I am proud of who I am, where I come from, what I believe in. Why should I be ashamed of my beliefs?'

We thought the world would change, that our children would grow up to embrace difference, not reject it. Sayf found the remedy for his confusion in the mosque. I suddenly felt very old. I was reminded of my brother, all his recriminations, and blame. And so God wins the day and the rest of us shall no doubt rot seven times over in hell. We cling to the world as if it might fling us outward at any moment, into the great nothingness beyond. We find comfort where we can. I sometimes wonder whether in an earthquake, say, or a shipwreck, the most unsettling thing might not be the slow realisation of what is happening to you, knowing that it is too late to do anything about it.

III

The Drift Latitudes

'It's not down in any map; true places never are.'
Herman Melville, *Moby Dick*

15

The jazz is the stuff that stops the universe from whirling apart, is what pushes the stars into pretty shapes in the sky. It makes all the notes hang together, hooks them in and sets them jangling in harmony. Without the jazz those disparate sounds would drop out of the air like so many dead birds. You can't analyse it. If you take it apart, there is no logic to it, no real beginning and no end, just a number of dots on a sheet of music. And this is one of them: the sound of a foghorn rising over a distant skyline.

That was the way Ismail Bilal would tell it, many years later. Of how fate, or jazz, delivered him to Liverpool in the winter of 1955 to begin a new life. Salt water and tears. The merchant ship, the *Fata Morgana*, was on her last legs and would be locked in the Merseyside shipyard for months as one problem fell away to reveal another and the owners ran out of funds to pay for repairs or wages. She arrived carrying bales of long-staple cotton grown between the Blue and White Niles in the fertile silt of the Gezira, along with dusty copper ore, barrels of gum arabic, half a ton of coral from Durban, sugar from Barbados, a spotted lynx from Boston zoo, and one very tall Nubian who had always known deep down inside that the sea was not for him.

Ismail Bilal's deviation from the plotted course had begun three short weeks earlier beneath the Manhattan skyline. The *Fata Morgana* docked in New York after a long, roundabout voyage that first led south from the Red Sea, around the Cape of Good Hope, then up to Port of Spain, Panama City, Vera Cruz and finally north to New York via Miami. As he stepped off the gangway onto the frozen quay in Brooklyn Harbour he found himself enveloped in a mysterious living cloud. The large white flakes brushed gently against his face, making him smile.

The sky pressed down and the air was crisp and silent. Of the seven crew members who stood on the dockside around him, only one had ever seen snow before: a Portuguese Communist named Hector Balboa who had fled Mozambique after becoming implicated in some kind of unrest involving a gold mine; the details were sketchy. He claimed to have seen everything the world had to offer, at least once. He threw his head back and laughed at their astonishment. 'Hey! You're not in the jungle any more.' Most of the time the rest of the crew, who hailed from places like Massawa, Dakar, Durban, and Gdansk, never understood what he was saying, whether he spoke in English, French, Portuguese, or Arabic, but he was a lively sort to have around.

The looming shadow of the great iron ship, big and silent as a dark hill, rose behind them to meet the night sky, luminous with snowflakes trapped in the arc lights like falling stars as the sailors waved goodnight to the duty watch before turning to walk on, pausing to gyrate, slide or walk backwards for a stretch, just to see the patterns their footprints made in the thin carpet of white. Their onshore odyssey began in the low dives of the Jersey waterfront before edging its way up to Manhattan where Hector had promised to show them the sights.

'You can't look at the lights in Times Square without having a few drinks first. It's too much for any human being, especially people like you who just parked your camels in the desert like yesterday.' There were peals of laughter as they helped one another to their feet, slipping and falling on the icy ground. Cars hooted as they crossed the street with no regard for the traffic. Hector jumped up onto a lamp-post, leaning out in a camp imitation of Gene Kelly in *Singin' in the Rain*, a lookout in a crow's-nest. He pointed away down the street and wailed.

There was an endless supply of bars waiting to be discovered, it seemed, but a limited amount you could siphon into the human body. Three hours later five of them had backed off or passed out and were now deposited across the city in a variety of taxi-cabs, bus stations, doorways, run-down hostels and the arms of some rather dubious female company. That left Bilal and the increasingly frenetic Hector, eager to prove his claim that he knew *all* the great places in New York. Hector was also determined to be the last man standing. But Bilal was a hard man to drink under the table. He was the size of an electric generator, broad and tall. Twice the weight, approximately, of his guide, who had already begun to stumble and slur. As they staggered in circles, the snow began to fall more thickly. Heavy flakes floated down, splayed out like sea polyps sinking through viscous water. Suddenly they were caught in the stunning glare of a spotlight.

'*Cojinúa!*' Hector turned to Bilal who was busy vomiting on a lamp-post. 'You know where we are?'

Bilal had trouble getting the syllables past his tongue in the right order. 'Ne-yow Yerk? Unired Stays of Marica?' Everything seemed to be floating and he felt a tremendous urge to sit down and weep for some inexplicable reason.

'No no no. I mean, right here, right now.' Hector was turning, looking for evidence in the softly padded pavements; signs wrapped in puffy sleeves of white. A car slewed by them, horn yawning in a long-drawn-out moan. Hector threw his arms out: '52nd Street!'

Bilal tried to take in the significance of this fact. One number was pretty much the same as another and he was growing concerned that he could no longer feel his feet. The town was closing down with the thickening storm and the late hour. He was tired, and more than a little drunk. He wanted to go home. His head was spinning. He felt guilty. *Ya satir, ya rub,* he hiccuped. Allah forgive me for my weakness, I shall never let a drop of it pass my lips again. He wanted to go to bed. The image of his bunk, narrow and small for his frame, but soft and quiet, filled the sky, warm and beckoning. But the world had other plans; with dismay he watched Hector striding into the circle of light with great determination.

It had appeared out of nowhere: a hole in the great black, impermeable wall of the world. As he stood swaying in the icy wind, Ismail Bilal had no idea that going through that entrance would take him into the last phase of his life, would bring him a wife, a child and a source of income for the remainder of his days. Reminiscing, as he was often inclined to do in later years, he would tell anyone who asked that his life was divided into a before and after, and the line ran along that carpeted runway leading from his feet to the doorway of that club. The braided cordons, the uniformed doorman clapping his hands against the cold. That entrance, he said, was to him like the parting of the Red Sea was to Musa. Not that the sea parted for them right away. As the two mariners made for the door, the doorman, taking one look at the state of them, held up a gloved hand.

'Sorry, sir, only by special invitation.'

Hector was taken aback. This was a man who had fought his way across the high veld of Rhodesia with only a machete. He wasn't going to be turned away by a *bobo* dressed in a monkey-suit. The problem was clearly Bilal. He was not a large man, no, he was a *gigante*. Hector had seen him lift a wheel-house door off singlehandedly just to grease the hinges. He had fingers the size of Havana cigars, and not those little *puritos* either, real Cohibas. A man that size could do a lot of damage if he lost his rag. A couple of drinks too many and he could wreck the joint with one hand tied behind his back. The walls would come down so fast it would make Solomon's tour in the temple look like a Sunday school picnic.

Bilal just stood there feeling uncomfortable in his borrowed jacket, the sleeves drawing to a halt halfway down his forearms. The flash of the light bulbs around the doorway tapped out a steady beat across his eyeballs.

'Special invitation, huh?' Hector winked up at Ismail as he stepped forwards, holding his hand at a curious angle, wrist down, a five-dollar bill folded neatly between his fingers. 'How special does that read?' The doorman pulled a bored look and jerked his thumb in the direction of down the street. Beat it. Disappointed, Hector was about to let fly a tirade of lusophone abuse before turning his big friend loose on the jerk, when a man in a sharp tuxedo strolled by them and straight towards the front door of the club.

'Evening, Chester, having a spot of trouble?'

'No trouble at all, Mr Byas.'

'Mr Byas? Mr Don Byas?' The Portuguese mariner's jaw gaped. He reached around blindly to tug at Bilal's sleeve. 'Do you know who that is?' And of course Bilal did not know, had no clue, so he just stood there, as big and silent as a dimmed lighthouse. The side parting he had shaved through his tight curls in honour of coming ashore shone like a tramline in the hot lights. 'This is the man who made this street a legend, along with the immortal Dizzy, of course.' Hector slapped himself in slow motion, wiping one hand and then the other across his cheek, as though trying to wake himself up. 'The 52nd Street sound. What a day, what a day! Didn't I tell you that New York was the place where dreams fall over themselves on the side-walks just waiting to get at you?'

Chester had lowered his guard, and as for Don Byas, he was grinning like a chipmunk. 'Where're you boys from?'

'We're from Africa, same as you,' said Hector, straightening up. And while he didn't quite understand what his friend meant, Ismail Bilal nevertheless felt a surge of pride on hearing these words and he too drew himself up to his full height. Don Byas and Chester both took a step back, looking him up and down, not quite sure what to make of this Goliath. 'We jumped ship just to take in a little jazz. I promised my friend here that I would show him where it all began. He's a big fan of your music, Senhor Byas. Real big.'

'He's big all right.' Don Byas seemed amused. With a wave of his hand he turned to walk into the club calling over his shoulder: 'Night like this we'll be lucky if anyone else shows up. Let 'em in, Chester. Let 'em right on in.'

The curtain drew aside and Bilal had the sense that he was floating down a long corridor of velvet darkness, at the end of which was a glowing, tumbling diamond of turbulent light. A fluttering peacock fan of sound and colour, mauve, vermilion and turquoise, snapping golden discs of vibrating cymbals, trembling silver crescents snaked by drum snares, blue moons and clarinets, saxophones rising and falling, leaping like chromium fish from a river of satin and sequins. It was like entering a secret world, like nothing he had ever imagined.

'Jazz,' Bilal murmured to himself, grinning like a fool. 'This is jazz.'

Whatever it was, from that moment on he was in the grip of its spell, the enchanting mystery of it all, the champagne buckets and rustle of fine clothes, the velvet booths, the faces softly lit by table lamps, people walking in and out, fur coats and tuxedos. And they were all here to listen. To jazz.

His heart beat in his throat. Men like him playing. Africans, and this was their music. He had never thought to find such a thing here, in the richest country in the world. Light ricocheted off metal. Long fingers ran along piano keys with reckless abandon. If smoke had started to come up through the floorboards under his size-twelve feet and people had begun yelling 'fire!' Bilal still wouldn't have budged an inch. He would have stayed until the smoke was coming out of his ears. Charred to a cinder. There he was, and there he stayed, until the last note was played and the audience had pulled on their hats and coats and had all gone home and the waiter was shaking Hector awake and pushing them out of the door to begin the slow trudge back to the ship, and still it didn't feel real.

'I told you,' grumbled Hector, more than half asleep. 'There's nowhere like it in the world. Well, except maybe Manila. Have you ever been there? No? Well, the girls they have there, spectacular, let me tell you . . .'

But Bilal wasn't listening, didn't care about Manila, or girls for that matter. His ears still ringing, at that moment all he wanted was jazz. And that was how it came to be that his heart ran aground in Merseyside. He decided to jump ship. Stranded high and dry on the charms of an Irish girl named Marjoram Meads, he declared in that rumbling tenor voice of his that he was going to quit the sea and settle down.

'But how are we going to make ends meet?' asked Marge, gazing up at the Nubian colossus sitting beside her on a bench in Sefton Park, her tiny ivory hand all but lost in that huge palm of his. 'I'm going to open a club,' he beamed, as though the idea had just fallen out of the tree above his head like a ripe fruit. 'A jazz club.'

16

Jade had a recurring dream in which all of her work came undone: buildings dismantling themselves, walls fragmenting, rivets popping out, seams coming apart like zippers, windows tumbling from frames, concrete dissolving into soft gooey heaps, steel pylons clattering down like handfuls of spaghetti. The world flying slowly apart beneath her gaze. Time moving backwards.

'Growing older is really all about coming to terms with our mortality. The rational side of our brain tells us to accept what is happening to us. It's the irrational side which causes the problems. When life fails to deliver, it causes frustration, instability, which can lead to substance dependency, violence. The most powerful means of evading reality, however, are in the mind itself.'

The charismatic Dr Varsad's manner suggested some affinity with a modern-day guru. His style was chatty, informal and bordered on the mystical. He ought to be based in California, Jade thought, catering to pampered suntanned clients rather than occupying a dreary little room in an underfunded hospital dealing with her mother.

'How exactly do you know when someone is having a nervous breakdown?'

A firm shake of the head. 'Your mother is not having a nervous breakdown.'

'I wasn't thinking of my mother.'

The intelligent look deepened. Dr Varsad leaned back in his chair, fingertips rising into a steeple onto which he rested his bearded chin, and he contemplated her face carefully.

That was Monday morning's crisis meeting. Her mother's condition had worsened. No one seemed to know what was wrong with her. Was it depression, was it the onset of Alzheimer's? Tests were inconclusive. The effect of all this meant that Jade was back in her office by Tuesday, wondering what she was still doing there, feeling incapable of summoning the will to fight. She struggled to find the ability to lose herself in her work. A skill that had always served her well, allowing her to slip without a splash beneath the surface of her drawing board. To wrestle there with whatever tangle awaited, her mind cutting out all the unhelpful clutter of noise and distraction, husband, wailing baby, even back in the tiny flat in Paris. Unresolved problems involving angles and weights took over. Tensile strengths, shear coefficients would circle through her head until a stray thought insinuated itself and a resolution emerged between her eye and the paper. Nowadays she was all loose ends. Her concentration eluded her, left her hanging, pencil poised in the air, her thoughts wandering off, over the top of the white board and out into the city skyline beyond.

She looked up to find Regan standing self-consciously in the doorway, observing her. Lamely, she lifted her hand as if to knock. Jade got to her feet automatically as the other woman came in, ready to do battle.

'I thought maybe we should talk.'

Regan lingered, hesitant, reaching idly for the metal question mark lying on the desk. A micrometer: a type of gauge used for the accurate measurement of width, the precision tool of an engineer. Turn the ratchet and the bar closes the circular gap. It carried with it the image of a man with thinning silvery hair brushed back from his high forehead. The round face, the awkward smile. The jaundiced light of the standard lamp in the front room. The little girl twisting it round and round in her hands, making the ratchet whirr. An instrument used to measure infinitesimal increments, like the distance between father and daughter, say. She had pulled it out from inside his old leather briefcase. He laughed and tousled the child's hair, while she rotated the brushed-steel instrument. In her hands it became a magical key for making time speed up, or slow down.

Jade leaned forwards now and plucked the object from Regan's hands.

'What do you want to talk about?'

'I think there are some issues between us,' said Regan, pushing her hands through her hair. 'It would be better all round if we could work them out between us.' She said, adding an unconvincing smile as an afterthought.

Jade folded her arms. 'OK, where do you want to start?'

'Look, I understand you are upset about the Mason Chalmers project.'

'It was my project, for goodness' sakes. I worked on it. I came up with a design they liked. Then you started elbowing your way in.'

Regan sighed. 'That's not exactly how it happened.'

'Oh no? Then who was it who persuaded them the design was not good enough? The last time I saw Mason Chalmers' people, they liked it.'

'It's too complex, it needs simplifying.'

'Simplifying means cutting corners. People come to us for quality work. Good work takes time.'

'There's a difference between quality, and the excessive use of complex mechanics. I think the PharmaKorp fiasco made that point abundantly clear.'

Jade was beginning to see where Kyle and Regan overlapped in their thinking. They were both looking for quick and easy solutions. Homogenisation. Domestication. They gleaned the best elements they could pick up and rationalised, throwing them together in a swiftly administered package of blandness.

'I don't work like that,' said Jade.

Regan nodded. 'Sure. I think we all know that.' She smiled and moved around the room to examine the diagrams and sketches hung on the walls – projects that were finished and done with. 'Kyle says you've met with Francis Arburgh,' she said, and when Jade made no attempt to reply, she went on. 'He's the best there is.'

'He ought to be at the rates he charges,' Jade said. Then it dawned on her why Regan had been surprised to see her. 'You didn't expect to find me here, did you?'

'I understood that you were taking some time off.' Regan shrugged.

'So you came in here . . . for what? To try out the desk for size?'

Regan held up a hand. 'Look, let's drop the protocol for a moment. We both know that you got to where you are today because Kyle's father had a few liberal ideas about equal opportunities, right? You've been persistently holding back the progress of this company with your quirky designs and your inconsistent behaviour. No one knows where you are half the time, and when you are supposed to be taking time off, here you are skulking around the office.'

Jade had to smile. 'You really want me out of here badly, don't you?'

'Are you going to make a case against GSW?'

'Why would I do that?' asked Jade. 'On what grounds?'

'Racial discrimination,' suggested Regan. 'Attack being the best form of defence.'

'Do I need a defence?'

'Kyle seems to think that's what you are up to.'

'And you, what do you think?'

'In my view, you are a liability to the firm. The sooner GSW are shot of you the better. It's nothing personal. Look at it another way. Maybe you would be happier somewhere else.'

'Why are you telling me all this?' asked Jade, finally.

'I don't know,' confessed Regan. 'I really don't know why I am bothering.'

'I mean, you seem to have made up your minds already.'

'You're right,' said Regan abruptly. 'Maybe this was a mistake.' There was a moment's silence and then without another word she turned and walked out of the room.

Jade slumped back into her chair, exhausted from this sparring. The idea of work now firmly consigned to the realm of impossibility.

'Ashes to ashes and dust to dust,' she muttered. 'If the women don't get you, the liquor must.' But she didn't want a drink. For the first time in a long while Jade felt the need to remain clear-headed. She picked up her bag and coat and left the office with barely a word to anyone. She travelled across town without any particular destination in mind and found herself wandering around the West End, half-convinced that she was going to cheer herself up by going shopping. The mannequins gazed out of the windows looking imperious and impossibly thin. There was nothing she wanted. Finally, she wound up outside a record shop in Soho she had never seen before. A sad-looking figure was stretched out full-length on the pavement outside, bound up like a mummy in a heap of filthy blankets. Human? Man or woman? Sleeping on a strip of cardboard on the ground. The image recalled the sight of the man lying on the stretcher covered by a white sheet, being ferried across the muddy battle-field of a building site, one arm hanging down, fingers brushing the ground, reaching back to touch the earth.

A sheet of newspaper had blown up to rest against the lumpy brown cocoon. The sports pages. 'Transfer Hopes Dashed!' a headline blazed, as though someone had drawn a cartoon bubble over the sleeping figure, the words flushed from a dream.

She had been drawn to the shop window by a vast black and white photograph of Charlie Parker. His shirt wrinkled and the wings of his shirt collar askew – one up, one down, like an origami bird someone had sat on. He had his eyes fixed on a spot high up in the air somewhere over the chimney pots, the rooftops, the greasy London sky. A bead of sweat shone like mercury on his brow. What did he see when he was playing? 'Birdland', read the letters across the bottom of the picture. Jazz had always struck Jade as an affected, overrated kind of music replete with self-conscious displays of virtuoso technical mastery that only a tutored fan could appreciate. A brief fling with a boy in the Jazz Society at university had left her with memo-ries of an artificially forced atmosphere where everyone wore oversized suits and hand-me-down hats from Oxfam shops. All seeking to acquire a degree of eccentricity, essentially, to become black. She broke up with him when she began to suspect that she was simply some kind of trophy.

'What are you looking for?' demanded a voice. The man behind the desk, of indeterminate racial origin; some oriental in there, mostly white, a dash of afro. Late thirties, the ubiqui-tous stubble and pony tail. 'Funk, Trad, Modern, Dixie, Fusion?'

'Just, you know, the old stuff,' she shrugged, waving a vague hand to cover her ignorance, to indicate that she was speaking in broad terms, non-specific. She also felt a strange sense of inadequacy, as though this music was something she ought to have absorbed, through the pores of her skin.

'Stomp, jive, rag, Latin?' He lifted a bent roll-up that was smouldering on the edge of the counter and took a drag. 'Vinyl, compact, rare recordings, out-takes?' He droned on, as they used to say, like a broken record.

'I'll just, you know, have a look around.'

'Right.' The half-nod condemning her as a time-waster.

Her fingers clicked over the plastic cases. Red Rusty Ratchett Riverboat. Names fluttered through her head. Jarrett Kruper Little Miles. She was submerged within the free flow of history running by. Like she had just dipped a hand into a stream. It is the music of displacement, she thought. Music for people like you and me, the in-betweens.

She had always wondered if it didn't also have something to do with buildings. Adorno concluded that jazz was a degenerate kind of sport for black people with acoustics thrown in, a popular replacement for real culture in the age of reproduction. Marx would have argued the same thing probably, if he had been around. The great European philosophers never understood jazz. Freud, Jung, Adorno, none of them saw what it meant. Why? Because it breaks all logic, breaks down the idea of progress because it breaks up linear notions of time. Time stands still, it moves in circles, it takes unpredictable leaps. Jazz doesn't repeat the same phrase the same way every time, it improvises.

From the country roads of Huddie Leadbetter and John Lee Hooker the blues turned in towards the city, to find Kansas and Chicago. T-Bone Walker and Stormy Monday. The story of jazz was born in dingy basements and dubious establishments, neighbourhoods where children play in the streets and the baby in the next flat is always crying. People play music because there is nowhere else to go. So they put their loneliness and frustration together and blow it all out through a single note of harmony. A note that shimmies like polished brass and rises up into the air with all the grace and slender enchantment of a wisp of smoke, or a building that can only be imagined in the dreams of a city that no one has ever yet set eyes on. Amen and Goodbye Pork Pie Hat.

The great cities, like jazz, she thought, were composed of thousands of discordant notes that come together at times to create harmony. The jazz of cities is the syncopated distillation of unexpected elements which allows us to live together: none of it makes sense, except the sense we give it.

'You want all of these?' The man behind the counter nodded at the heap of discs she had just dumped in front of him.

'Why not?' she replied, in a hurry now to get back and start writing down her ideas. The music gave her a sense of purpose which carried her all the way home where she sat in her study and began pushing one disc after another into the player, impatient to hear each and every one of them. To know it all. The whole story.

She was listening to Nina Simone when it struck her why she felt comforted by this music, because she had always associated it with her mother. Miranda used to listen to jazz records when Jade was very small; and she used to sing along, too. When did her mother stop doing that? And why?

Jade's life at this moment seemed to be receding, a train flying away from her along a sequence of disjointed points on a line. That night, in her dream, a little girl was running past her along the pavement, four or five years old and racing with all the joy and pleasure of being able to do so, of feeling the wind in her curls, of making the ground move in a blur beneath her shiny red shoes. Completely absorbed in the shadow of her feet over the cracks between the paving stones. Alive and oblivious to the world, the slow unwinding coil of traffic alongside her. She did not look, paid no heed to her mother calling for her to slow down, to bloody well stop. Jade watched the little girl leap blindly out, across the boundary between pavement and running road. With a cry she stretched out a hand to catch hold. For an instant the little girl was suspended in mid-air. Confused, she let out a wail. She was already out there and could not understand why the course of her jump had been abruptly curtailed. When she looked up she saw a woman she had never seen before, but who might have been her own image glimpsed through the pool of time. Then the moment was past and they were pulled apart. Instinctively, Jade stepped back. Above the cruising metal snarl she heard the little girl sobbing, the mother's repeated tirade. She would undoubtedly have been knocked down. She watched them go, the little girl, being tugged along reluctantly, twisted round, looking over her shoulder.

Rachel

I gradually convinced myself that I harboured within me a source of malevolence. I slowly came to the terrible conclusion that this thing, whatever you might call it, this malignant spirit, was poisoning me from inside.

I didn't realise at once. For weeks I felt fatigued, tired all the time. I had no energy. I was despondent, lethargic. I had no desire to get up in the morning and face the day. Amin tried to encourage me at first. When that failed, he began to blame me, as though I had unwittingly cut into a vein of bile between us. Thirty-seven years of built-up disgust. That is the word. Disgust.

My health deteriorated. I contracted jaundice and this weakened me considerably. Weeks of daily injections and boiled chicken – the only thing I was allowed to eat. I can still summon up the smell just by closing my eyes. I was confined to bed where I lingered, sweating away for weeks. By the end of this time I was exhausted and beside myself with utter desperation. I wanted to die. I felt crippled, mentally and physically, unable to go on. I was distraught, convinced that I was dying. When tests showed this not to be the case I wondered if I was going out of my mind. By this time I was unable to sleep, eat or rest. I was driving myself and everyone around me to their wits' end. A gormless professor of psychiatry came to visit a couple of times, an old crony of Amin's from his card-playing days. He suggested rather bluntly that it was menopausal. Honestly! Finally, I began to see that nobody could help me, that no amount of counselling or sedatives was going to make me feel better. All their medicine and rot.

I turned in another direction and sought the advice of a woman I knew had some experience of these matters. She is what you might call a healer, I can't really think of any other way of explaining it. It was Suad, an old and dear friend ever since the early days, who told me about her. She immediately agreed to introduce me. Suad, I realised, knew quite a lot about it, having attended a number of these sessions herself over the years. As she was speaking I realised that I had heard her telling me all of this before. I found it encouraging that a possible remedy to my torment had been there all the time, right under my very nose. It was as though the pain was necessary to prepare me for this next move.

A *zar* is really a kind of celebration that women perform alone, no men allowed, which of course only adds to the air of mystery and makes it seem all the more illicit and intriguing. Where exactly it stems from I couldn't tell you. There is some Islam mixed in but its roots really stretch much further back in time. The most enduring rituals being those that manage to adapt themselves to changing currents. It goes far back, to the earth, the trees and the river.

The women gather in the house of one person or another, usually outside in the yard under the stars. For the most part it is just an informal get-together, what you might call a girls' night. The women just let themselves go, do all the things that convention prevents them from doing most of the time. They drink and smoke and play music and they sing, for hours and hours, all through the night. At the heart of this revelry, however, there is a purpose.

The one I attended was held in a small house in a poor quarter on the outskirts of the city, an area I did not know. I drove the car and Suad directed me. Just as we were approaching the collection of mud walls there was a power cut and everything was plunged into darkness. We were driving across a stretch of open land from the main road when the streetlights ahead of us suddenly went out. It was like a string of white pearls vanishing beneath a blanket – an illusionist's trick.

It was an unremarkable house, the outer walls were bare except for the whitewashed bricks that framed the entrance. A naked light bulb over the cracked wooden door illuminated a simple yard with a few rusty bedsteads. In the far corner a couple of goats were chewing *birseem* spread on the ground.

They looked up from their meal to see who we were before going on with their business. There were four or five rooms facing onto the dusty courtyard. As we entered we were met by a young girl who led us to a large room on the left. Inside we found ourselves in a salon lit by oil lamps. The floor was covered with uneven black and white tiles over which reed mats had been laid. The air was so hot in there and so thick with sweat, perfume and incense that entering was like passing through an invisible but palpable veil. Already there were about twenty women gathered, all seated around the sides talking among themselves, making themselves ready.

At the far end of the long room sat the Sheikha, the spiritual guide, the healer, although I hardly recognised her now. When Suad had taken me to her house the previous week I recalled having met a rather plain old woman wrapped in a shawl, bent over a bowl of aubergines she was slicing. That person bore little resemblance to the charismatic figure I was now looking at, her arms bare but for tattooed patterns and dozens of gold and silver bracelets, leather amulets, copper and ivory bands all the way up above the elbow. Her hair was hennaed a bright red colour and tied close to her head in braids. With the heel of her hand she was striking a *dellouka*, a big flat drum. At the Sheikha's side sat another three women, each of these also had a musical instrument. One of them paused from time to time to spray the air with an old glass atomiser marked Chanel, although I suspect the label had no bearing on the contents. People made way for us to sit on the floor as we entered.

'Greetings to the foreigner in our midst,' boomed the Sheikha, without looking in my direction, never once breaking the rhythm of her hand on the drum. Bowls of scent with petals of hibiscus and jasmine floating in them were passed around. Smoke coiled from oil of sandalwood and myrrh on hot coals in small clay braziers. The music was a soft pounding beat which seemed to reach into your heart and take hold of it, so that when the drum slowed, your heart went with it, and when it speeded up, you felt your head was about to burst a blood vessel.

The Sheikha was pouring with sweat – her face gleamed in

the glow of the oil lamps. Impulsively, one woman stood up to dance. Two others helped her, gently removing the diaphanous veil wrapped around her body to leave her standing there in a rather ordinary dress, hands hanging limply by her sides, head down, motionless. A remarkable change came over her. The music seemed to enter her body through her feet. First one and then the other began to lift and fall in slow succession causing her to vibrate like the string of an instrument. The women around me were clapping and wailing, making that ululating noise with their tongues. The woman was dancing faster now, with her heels, shuffling her feet forwards like a bird, one at a time. Rising and falling, her head tilted back and her eyelids closed and fluttering in a most sensual way. From where I sat I could see that her face was resplendent with utter serenity.

A *zar* spirit is a kind of djinn. When Allah made Adam it is said that he breathed life into clay. Instead of clay, djinns are made of fire and air, otherwise they are just like us. They move in the world all around us. Once you are possessed by a *zar* spirit you are never free. And while you cannot escape it, the spirit will be fed and satiated. That was the real purpose of these meetings, to draw these spirits out from within and allow them to be entertained, to enjoy themselves so that they might withdraw and leave the person they usually occupy in peace.

I was taken aside to speak to the Sheikha. She was resting outside in the cool air, a towel over her head like a champ fighter between rounds, sipping from a bowl. She said it was good we had come. She had thought about what we had told her and it was not so strange. Suad asked her if she could cure me. The Sheikha looked at me carefully and asked if I was ready. I nodded. I can't explain the feeling of warmth and trust I felt for this woman. I felt safe. She summoned an absolutely ancient old woman whose face was like a shrunken mask. She wore a plain white shift and supported herself on a cane stick. This woman was a kind of 'doctor', the Sheikha said, as though trying to explain things in my terms. The toothless old woman began to murmur a kind of litany in a language I could not understand. Not Arabic, but a *rutana* which is hardly used any more.

All she did was touch a hand to my back, but instantly I was nauseous with fear and a terrible anxiety, more acute than I had ever experienced. It was like the worst nightmare I had ever had. As though every bad dream and sleepless night were rolled into one. I was crippled with anxiety and could barely stand up. Suad looked worried. I clutched her shoulder, holding my stomach and groaning like a sick child.

Back inside the room I found all my inhibitions had gone. Before, seeing all those women there I had worried about being called upon to make an exhibition of myself but I no longer cared about that. I needed to be cured. I was in the grip of something worse than I had imagined. I had come there out of curiosity, not entirely sure, but now I was convinced. It was all suddenly very real. Not a game, not a charade, not a women's knees-up. The only way out was to go through with it.

I felt the women gathered around me as one. I was in the embrace of an enormous entity, warm, fleshy and protective, the way I once felt as a child. So there I was, a foreigner in a strange house in a strange part of town, unable to stop myself sobbing with emotion. Someone handed me a cigarette which I took, although I have smoked on no more than a dozen times in my entire life. I inhaled, realising then that it was not ordinary tobacco, but the local marijuana, *bangho*, which is rather different altogether. Then someone handed me a bowl containing *merissa*, a viscous home-made beer, very nutritious, but now highly illegal, of course. I did not hesitate. I lifted the bowl to my lips and drank deeply.

All of this time the music was drumming away. It never stopped, but ran up and down my spine in little circles. I felt their hands on me, their gentle hands, painted with henna petals and leaves, like I was floating through a field of waving flowers. I was moving in a spiral, my clumsy feet blindly managing to find their own way. Strangely, I did not feel any shame about displaying such personal emotion, or performing in such an undignified manner. The music rose higher and I, with my skirt rucked up to my thighs, my blouse undone, my eyes closed, felt myself swaying. I was filled with the intoxication of fear and God knows what else, but there I was. My entire being, my whole body felt alive in a way that it once had, in the early years, when Amin and I used to retire in the sweltering afternoons and spend hours delighting one another, our skins charged and swollen with love. I had forgotten what that was like, I had lost touch with my body. Now I was possessed by another desire, all the more disconcerting for being unfamiliar. I was drained and shivering with chills and exhaustion. The Sheikha reappeared. Even before my eyes could focus enough to pick her out I could sense her powerful aura. She stood before me and cupped my face in her hands. Two sets of cicatrices, thin furrows, were cut into the skin below her temples, at the edges of her deep, dark eyes. Each formed a three-legged shape, like the footprints of a bird. She turned away from me, and when I looked again she was holding two chickens upside down by their legs, one black and the other white. Someone took my hand and dipped it into a sticky bowl of henna paste held up to me. Then, taking my hand, she made me draw a line down the front of first one bird and then the other. They were very still, held firmly by the wings. From throat to hindquarters I drew my fingers. I could feel the trembling of their warmth beneath the plump surface of their breasts as I passed. I was being supported by two women, one on either side, to stop me falling down. I no longer heard the music. I no longer heard anything. The Sheikha went outside, followed by a small group of women, including the old 'doctor' in white.

I knew what they were going to do.

It had passed from me to one of the birds; the _zar_ spirit which was haunting me. It had chosen white or black, and now it was inside one of them, trapped, and they were going to set it free. They were going to set my son free. Man is made of clay just as djinn are made of fire and air. It was going back to the air. This djinn had entered me after my poor boy left this world, the Sheikha said, having found a hole in my spirit made by the grief. And now they were going to set him free and I could not stop them. I tried to. I wailed and kicked and screamed, trying to fight my way out of the room, to stop them, but they held me. They clutched me in their arms tightly and would not let me go. I didn't want them to set him free. I didn't want to lose him. I wanted him to stay with me, inside me. I called his name over and over, and then I suppose I must have fainted for a moment.

When I came to it was done. They pressed the bloody knife into my hand, told me that I was to keep it with me at all times to prevent the djinn from returning. They daubed chicken blood from a bowl into my armpits, on my forehead. They dipped a cloth into the bowl and wrung it until it was deep red and then they knotted it around my wrist. I think it must have been at this point that I felt a blinding light come over me, and I must have collapsed. They carried me to the river and we all went into the water together to cleanse ourselves. I floated in the silty warmth feeling drained and at the same time strangely fulfilled.

When I arrived home, of course I looked a state. Amin had been worried out of his mind. He had not slept, thinking the worst; that I had been caught in the curfew, stopped at a checkpoint. The guards are notoriously trigger-happy these days, their nerves being in shreds, never knowing what might appear out of the surrounding darkness, and also from drinking, so it was said. So when I appeared, standing by the back gate, hair hanging in damp matted locks, clothes bedraggled, wet, muddy, feet covered in henna and soil, a bloody red rag attached to my wrist, he looked at me in silence. I do believe that in that moment he was convinced that my mind had finally snapped, for instead of ranting and raving as he might normally have done, he opened the gates and simply put his arms around me without saying a word. There in the street where anyone could see us. It was the most tender gesture I could recall him making towards me in longer than I would care to admit.

17

Water has no memory, no regrets, no sense of its own history. Ernst Frager might have once come from the sea, but he was not made of water. Here, finally, in this city, of all places, he had found the antidote to that vacuum inside him.

They walked through the city together, leaning on one another, telling each other the stories that had brought them to this place. He talked of history and science. Miranda talked of jazz.

You can't make music without pain, she said. You only have to listen to Billie Holiday to know that. It was the pain of leaving home. They took people from Africa to the New World and it was like a voyage between past and future. It was in that dark ditch of history, that silent beat, where jazz began. A moan of loss, crying back across leagues and centuries, trying to reach what they had left behind. Things don't change just like that. The old African medicine men, the Griots, they call them. Their charms were shaken loose by that journey. No palm wine, no ancient traditions to keep them safe and warm. Gospel, blues, and jazz. It all came out of that feeling of loss. They lost their language, their history, so they had to make it up. That's where it comes from, from trying to make yourself understood. You don't have great buildings and libraries, all you have is the story you tell. That's who you are. It is in the telling of the tale. It's the old world letting go and the new refusing to listen. With each generation the continent of Africa drifted further away. Out of sight, over the horizon, beyond the reach of memory. The language of improvisation. Jazz was the dislocation of the soul.

Ernst was impressed by her understanding. Ismail Bilal had explained it all to her, she said. He taught her how to listen.

He envied her the ease with which life delivered up its secrets. He felt as though he had had to struggle for everything that he had learned, working in solitude, poring over books and manuals. The two exceptions being his apprenticeship with August Popinal and his time in the U-boats.

Trapped at the bottom of the Irish Sea that night listening to Scott Joplin. He remembered that. The silence all around when the record finished and the needle went on scratching away until Captain Usher reached forward and lifted it up. And not one of those superstitious men spoke a word. As though that tinkling piano was a last fading farewell from life up there on the surface. But something inside told Ernst they wouldn't perish. He had felt alive then, as he had never done before, as though this experience in itself was sufficient to have known life. A mere child warrior, barely fifteen years old. Why had he felt sure that somehow they would live? The music evoked a feeling of euphoria in him from that day on. The sense of defiance ringing in that irreverent little tune, like a white rose in full bloom on a rainy day.

That same bright flower was with him in Berlin between the wars, when everyone was so desperate and sad and people lived as though each day was their last. Jazz was a part of that madness. Sidney Bechet was there, he told her, in 1930 with his band, the New Yorkers. Josephine Baker, too, dancing with bananas around her waist. What they called jazz then was just another name for a far-way place, so exotic and bizarre it liberated them from the dark turmoil around them. Miranda took his face in her hands and kissed him. They walked the long afternoons away, hand in hand, oblivious to the strange looks that came their way. Down there by the waterfront there were fewer people to stare.

Herman Melville came here once, he told her. By that time the slave trade was officially over and the little Negro boys who stood watch upon the raised stoops of the big mansions on the hill were not weighed down by chains, but were scrubbed and shiny with abolition, freedom and the blessings of the Church. Their dark eyes swam in the sooty flame of burning torches. Trophies, with their little white gloves and fine dress coats. A living token, a reminder of the iron circle of wealth that ringed the world and spun blood and brine into money. African blood, sweat and tears made this city. They lent the city an element of legend.

Miranda let him talk, enthralled by this strange man more than twice her age, with his fascination for worldly things. She had the wisdom not to fight, not to try and block him, but to let it flow as it so obviously, urgently, needed to do. She squeezed his hand and leaned back against him on the bench, closing her eyes against the autumn sunlight to listen. He was obsessed for a time with the whole business of the slave trade. So much so that she fretted that this was what had brought him to her, crawling into her bed to find forgiveness for ancient crimes visited upon her African virtue by his European ancestors. He whirled her through the pages of his reading.

They walked on. The rain blew in their faces, slashing horizontally across the crumpled muddy blanket of the Mersey, while Ernst described the unfinished stories slumbering in the carved elephants and pygmies adorning the Town Hall at the top of Castle Street. Bubble-headed caricatures carved into the stone: the past inscribed indelibly on the skin of this city, just waiting for him to find it. Similar ghosts went clattering through the litany of street names: places like Goree that were once everyday currency in the mouths of the privateers and wealthy merchants who mingled in the marble lobbies of the banks and chambers of commerce. They lingered in the log books and ledgers that describe what made this city rich.

Miranda wondered about his wife and children down there in London. Perhaps she knew that her husband was away wrestling with his own personal demons, but did she also know he was seeking solace in another woman's arms? She trusted Ernst, believed him when he turned his grey-blue eyes to hers and said he adored her and wanted to spend whatever was left of his life with her. And she was smart enough to suspect she believed him because she wanted to believe him.

The question that was never spoken, not yet at least, was the one which hung between them, like the absent shoreline to their sea.

What was he really doing there? What had brought him to her?

'Tell me about the jazz again,' he asked, suddenly short of breath.

'What are you trying to avoid?' she teased.

But he didn't smile. For a brief moment he was back there, running through the trees, his lungs grasping at the thin mountain air. He couldn't put it into words. That sense of the evil we are capable of, the guilty feeling that he was not immune. He didn't quite understand what it all meant. The years with Edith and the children. What did his life add up to but these solitary fragments? His son Matthew, who would always despise him for making him go through life with a Hun for a father. The Royal Air Force turned him down for that simple fact. And Matthew was now turning this burden into his life, lolling drunk in the armchair every night. Edith encouraged this self-pity, seeing in his resentment a reflection of her own unhappiness. She should never have married Ernst. He was too unreliable, too unconventional, too unpredictable, and too smart. Yes, even that irked her, that Ernst had the capacity to immerse himself in his work, so fully that he needed nothing and nobody, not even her. Edith had always been possessive. Now she mocked his silly inventions for they had become a reminder of what she could never have, that part of him which was free. That left Rachel, the one closest in temperament to Ernst, devoted to her schoolwork, her books, searching for a way out, already distancing herself from the family, like a survivor swimming away from a shipwreck with steady, even strokes, never looking back.

Ernst had begun to understand that every man has his age, and that twilight was beginning to fall on his. He could invent typewriters, cleaning instruments, open-and-shut toilet cases with pop-up shaving mirrors and spring drawers that slid out with a clean razor blade, only nobody wanted such gadgets any more. Time had passed him by. The Americans were building rockets to the moon and clever little electronic circuits that hummed and whirred and left him looking like a plodding pack-horse sinking into a muddy field on the Somme.

When Ernst lay sleeping peacefully in the circumference of her arms, lodged as a ship in the curled eyelid of a sheltered cove, Miranda wondered how long he would remain there, a loose bud of raw cotton caught on a spiny twig.

They went shopping and he bought a Philips gramophone for his room and then sat down to listen. A screeching, thumping number: 'Haitian Fight Song', recorded by Charlie Mingus with Shafi Hadi on alto saxophone and Jimmy Knepper providing the trombone that squeals and bellows around the steady upward climb of the double bass.

'Can you hear it?' Ernst asked.

Miranda laughed, 'All I can hear is your landlady coming up here asking you to turn it down.' He made her feel like a film star, the glamorous creature she had always dreamed she would become. And he? He felt alive, floating out there where dreams are free to drift, with no desire to find the shoreline.

When they were taken away from their homelands, he said, resuming his narrative, by slavers who came down on them like demons who lived in floating wooden caves hollowed out between sea and sky, they believed they would be lost for eternity: if they died out of sight of the shore their souls would never find their way home and they would be condemned to wander for ever, out there in the blue.

It took four hundred years to travel from the shores of West Africa, from the old kingdoms of Benin, Dahomey, Ghana, the deserts of Niger and Mali, across the Green Sea of Darkness to the coasts of Florida, there to tangle itself in the mangroves and lacustrine waters of swampy littoral basins. The sound rose up the languorous bends of the Mississippi, sinuous as a century of Sundays, moving from cotton field to church, lingering there to ferment before sliding north along the underground railway to find freedom in the big city.

All that pain, she said, as she counted his fingers, the soft wind tugging at her clothes, running up her side like a revenant hand. We are two sides of the same coin, she whispered, restlessly moving her hand over his, needing to feel the touch of him, to remind herself that this was real. The sea wraps you in coils of spume, drags you into uncharted waters. People have always been afraid of liberty, for who can live without boundaries? Miranda raised his hand and kissed the palm, digging her teeth into the soft flesh.

18

When Ernst disappeared from their lives, Miranda retreated at first beneath the hard carapace of isolated independence. To pay the bills they took in lodgers and so Jade grew used to sharing her home with strangers who lasted a term or two, sometimes a year. Miranda, fiercely proud, rejected sister and family that had turned their backs on her for having a child with a white man twice her age. 'A German?' Lillie had exclaimed. 'Are you crazy, girl, or what? They already hate us as it is. Where is your child going to show its face around here?'

Lillie always teased her sister for living what she called 'a charmed life'. It was Miranda, the lighter-skinned of the two, who always came through. Lillie had a series of hit-and-run affairs with men, one less reliable than another. She did not age gracefully, liked to dress herself up and go out on the town long after it would have been advisable not to. She ran the hairdresser's salon like a pimping school. When Jade was fifteen, Aunt Lillie was pressing her into padded push-up bras. She would imprison her in the chair and cover her face in powder and glossy lipsticks. Jade recalled it as a strange time, a time when she realised that the love of grown-ups is not unconditional. Lillie never had any children. God, she said, didn't want me to. But there were rumours of abortions and men who had run away to sea to get out of her clutches. Lillie's love was a plea for acceptance, she wanted to convert Jade into an ally. And for a while this rebellious conspiracy worked in tandem with Jade's desire to liberate herself from her mother. It was Jade who made peace with her aunt, without telling her mother. Aunt Lillie was Jade's first alibi. She spent so much time at the salon people forgot she was Miranda's daughter. A broom grew into her hands as she learned to sweep away the fallen locks and clipped tresses. She rolled the dryers into position, huge noisy metal stands with glass visors. They looked like something you might wear on the moon. She found a sympathetic ear for her teenage complaints, a willing accomplice ready to listen to her problems. In return, Jade learned that sympathy was about give and take. What she took was plenty of abuse for her father, which rested awkwardly, working itself inwards like a tiny splinter of dissent under her skin.

Now Miranda sighed. 'I can understand you're curious about him, being your father and all, but no good comes from it. Leave well enough alone is what I say.'

'I thought he was good to you,' said Jade quietly.

Her mother's face softened. 'He *was* good to me. He was. To both of us, he was good, except when he wasn't, when he couldn't be.' Her hand reached to cover her daughter's. 'When he wasn't there.' The stories came in unpredictable cloudbursts. Other times she remembered nothing at all. 'The doctor says it will come at times of stress. He says I will get confused. Have trouble working out the bills and things.' She gave a light snort of laughter. 'I've always had trouble with the bills.' Then silent again. Miranda leaned her head on her daughter's shoulder.

'They have medicine, Mum,' Jade said, stroking her mother's hair. 'They have all kinds of things. It doesn't have to be bad.' Miranda gave a long sigh. 'I feel as though I am disappearing through a tiny hole in the world. A doorway in a great big wall that I never noticed before.'

'You're not disappearing,' soothed Jade. Miranda was clutching her hand, but gradually her grip loosened.

'Nobody told me. He just never came up that day. I waited and waited. I lay on the carpet by the fire. The glowing coal. It was like watching a planet burn. I curled up on the floor. When I woke it was cold and damp and you were standing over me. You must have been about six at the time. You just looked at me. And I started to cry. I don't know why. We just sat there together, the two of us. All day the sky had that grey whiteness to it, and sure enough in the afternoon it began to snow. Big damp flakes plastered themselves to the window. And we sat here, you and I, as the hours passed and the light in the room changed. Then the telephone rang. At first I thought there was nobody there. And then I realised it was her, his wife. That was when it hit me. Something bad had happened. The two of us were attached to one another by this line, this cord running through the earth, listening to the dark silence between us, into which he had just vanished. After a long time, she said, "He's gone." That's all. The line clicked and it was over.'

The memories bobbed to the surface like leaves in the rain outside her window. Miranda recalled the draughty hall behind the stage of the Blue Nile, with barely enough room to turn around in, equipped with a shabby curtain to drape across the end of it when it became a changing room. It took a week for him to fall in love and she peered through that curtain every evening to see if he was there. Everything was against them. All the odds. No takers. The whole world did not want that man and this singer to get together. Every law of race and class and age. They went against them all.

'My own sister turned against me. What good is family if it won't stick by you in difficult times? No damn good at all, is what. She got all puffed up. She said it was beneath me, said I could never take a man like that home, said I was betraying four hundred years of chains and suffering. And she called herself a woman of God, too, would you believe that?'

'Easy, Mum. Calm down now.' She soothed Miranda's brow, held a glass of water to her lips. 'Drink,' she said, and her mother drank. Jade put her ear close to her mother's ear. Miranda's head rocked from side to side, eyeballs twitching beneath her lids. 'In the beginning he said he would stay for ever, you know. Oh, I knew . . .' Her voice tailed off into a sigh. 'The books he had read, you know, make your head spin. But he didn't just read them. Ben reads books. He picks them up, turns the pages and he puts them down again. Ernie wasn't like that. He argued with books, he wrote little scribbles in them. What are you going to do, I asked him once, send it back and tell them they made a mistake? We laughed together, but he had so many ideas coming out of his head it made me tired just thinking about it. Everyone said I was too young, didn't know what I was doing. A black girl and a white man more than twice her age. He is slumming it, they said, he'll scoot off back to London, they said. You wait and see. He'll leave you high and dry with that mixed up Allsorts child of yours. I wanted to prove it could work. I knew they were all wrong and we were right.' With a gasp she clutched a hand to her mouth. Then they were both laughing and crying at the same time. Jade put her arms around her mother and they sat there like that for a while in silence. Miranda wiped her eyes and sniffed. 'You never stop dreaming, child. It never goes away. You forget a little, but it never leaves you, not completely, not ever.'

Jade led her mother up to her room. They sat on the bed together. The burnt halo of the hall light picked out her soft round features, no longer unassailable, immutable, but frail and vulnerable as a child. Jade stroked her mother's hair. Miranda fluttered in her dream like a moth. She fell in and out of sleep. Jade folded her into her arms to shield her from the light. She woke with a start to find her mother speaking. Her lips were moving but Jade could not make out the words. Holding her close, she felt the sound coursing through Miranda's body like a fever: a strange purling guttural chant, part spiritual, part blues, that might have been spoken in Wolof, Hausa, or Nubian.

Rachel

The boy's name was Djibreel, Gabriel to you; a Coptic boy. I had never seen him before. He simply appeared one afternoon while I was watering the plants. Slight in build, he had startling grey eyes and brown wavy hair that was combed sideways. It looked as though he had put some kind of oil in it and this had now accumulated a thick layer of dust the same colour as his skin, which had the effect of making him look as though he was sculpted entirely out of sand. His face looked old, timeless, like a prophet who had just stepped from the pages of the Old Testament.

At first I thought I was imagining him, my angel Gabriel, my messenger. He just stood there outside the house gripping the handlebars of his big old bicycle. He was looking at me in a strange way and it took me a while to realise what he was seeing: an old European woman whose skin had become as thick and hard as camel leather in the sun. I don't know what he expected to find, but I don't think it was me.

He was loitering, shall we say, when I first spotted him. Standing in the street, watching the house. I saw him through the railings, moving up and down shiftily, obviously believing the tamarind hedge concealed him. When I stepped out into the street to confront him he looked startled. 'What is it you want?' I demanded, probably a little more harshly than I might have done. 'Why are you spying on me?' He made no attempt to move off. He remained where he was, holding the bicycle. I could see he was around the same age as my son, perhaps a little older. He had a stringy look about him, but his clothes were clean and presentable. When I stepped closer he stood his ground, not moving, but without saying a word. From the way he was toying with his bicycle I sensed that he was considering making a quick escape.

That was when it came to me.

How many times I had tried to imagine such a meeting. At night when sleep refused to come. All the endless images tumbling around in my head.

I had mud on my hands. I rubbed them together and the loamy soil flaked from my skin and crumbled to the dust. I knew who he was. I had known he would come, eventually.

'You were with him,' I said. He nodded. It was like seeing a cautious, elusive bird alight on a tree, knowing that any sudden movement or sound would send him off again into the blue. I didn't want anything to scare him away.

'Tell me,' I said. 'Tell me what happened.'

And so he told me.

It was in a place called Bahr al-Zeraf. They were a small group of twenty or so inexperienced recruits who had become separated from their unit. Their radio turned out to be broken and so they had no means of contacting their command post. Their orders had been to reconnoitre an area west of the river and meet up with the rest of the battalion at a designated point. They were exhausted and fed up. They had nothing to eat. They were all raw conscripts, all from the north. None of them knew this land. Their officer had been killed a week earlier and no replacement had been found. Djibreel, a lance-corporal, was in charge. The others didn't show him much respect, partly because he was the only Christian. Between my son and this boy an alliance, a friendship of sorts, had formed. Djibreel was the only professional soldier among them, having enlisted as soon as he left school, not for ideological reasons, but because he needed a job.

It was a nice afternoon, he recalled; there was a steady breeze which made the leaves rustle in a frantic manner. And then suddenly, rather miraculously, someone spotted a small gazelle through the bushes. It was a magical moment. Ignoring Djibreel's commands they broke ranks, the tension dissolving as they began shrugging off their packs, shedding their ammunition pouches and rifles and what have you, dropping them to the ground to play a game of catch.

I can envisage them like that, suddenly children again, playing in the sparse forest. They spread out, leaving Djibreel and a couple of others behind, yelling at them to get back. But they didn't want to come back. As he talked, I could see my boy, crouching down, the harsh burden of war and fear lifted from his shoulders. Barely recognisable in his big boots and with the wispy beard that adorned his chin. I could see him rushing through the undergrowth, the silvery leaves fluttering at his side. The gazelle turning in tight darting movements between them, trying to find a way out. Its limbs tensing and flexing, springing loose in ripples of muscle and arched tendon. Its hooves digging deeply into the soil as it leaned its body over and turned sharply aside, leaving the boys panting and laughing, falling on their faces in a heap. And then the impossible happens: my boy is standing in just the right place, and moving in the right direction, his feet skidding around him, when the gazelle turns into him. He dives, hands spread wide and they collide. For an instant he has the wild creature beating fiercely in his arms, warm and alive, clutched to his chest as they fall together, tumbling towards the ground. But as they go something snaps. A tiny little stalk, a plastic needle protruding from the grey ashen earth. As simple as that. It snaps like a brittle twig, and the world comes apart at the seams.

His leg was ripped from his body above the knee. He lay shaking on the ground, covered in a hot wetness, the entrails of the dead gazelle mixed with his own torn flesh. He lay there while his blood seeped away into the sweet leafy earth. Between the beetle eggs and the ants' nests and the dropped feathers of passing birds his blood pumped sweetly away.

He called for me then. My boy called for me but I did not come. I could not hear him. I imagine he called to Allah, too, but there was no help from that quarter either. There was panic all around. The others were crying in disbelief, in shock. One of their own mines. He was shaking all over. He could not see his wound, but he could feel the place where moments before there had been firm flesh and now there was nothing but pain. There was no help for miles around. They had no medic, no radio, no way of evacuating the wounded. He was scared, and when he looked up he saw his friend, Djibreel, his own private angel, sink down beside him. My son pleaded, begged him to end his pain. How easy is it? To put a gun to a friend's head and pull the trigger? I had the answer looking at me; a boy grown suddenly old.

We just stood there in silence, Djibreel and I. There wasn't much for me to say. I knew now why he had come to see me in that strange way of his; hanging around the back door, ready to bolt. Now that I looked at him I could see that his face was more drawn than I had first thought. His features seemed not to quite match. His eyes were not the same size. One ear was slightly folded. His left cheek was pockmarked with brown spots. The gaze levelled at me was more desperate than I had at first realised. He had been compelled to come. I looked into Djibreel's tormented eyes and wished he truly were an archangel, so he could fly off to heaven and bring my boy back to me. But he had not come to perform miracles. He had come to ask for the impossible. It was written plainly in his face, in the rims of his eyes, in the clank of the chain, in the spinning reel of the bicycle spokes as he turned and pedalled away head down along the broken road into the ebbing flare of sunset. God will forgive you, I said. I cannot, but maybe God will. Those were the harshest words I ever spoke in my life.

19

In November 1945 the world was in another kind of disarray. On arrival in Berlin, Ernst was warned that he would be expected to be flexible, that due to the unusual nature of the circumstances he would be called on to adapt himself to a variety of tasks as they came up. The war had withdrawn leaving behind a tide of human flotsam; millions of refugees trying to find their way back to homes that no longer existed. People were starving. In the face of this chaos it seemed almost absurd to be devoting one's time to the task of going over old documents from the fallen regime, but this is exactly what they brought Ernst to Berlin for: files, communiqués, correspondence, strategy reviews, the minutes of high-level meetings, banquet menus, any written material that had managed to evade destruction by incendiary bombs, arsonists, and people just trying to keep warm. What survived had to be evaluated, redistributed, analysed, filed away. That was part of his job, helping them decide what to do with it. There were military logbooks, intelligence bulletins, surveillance reports, morale assessments of troops, as well as personal accounts, diaries, confessions, letters home – officers telling their wives how proud they were of what they had done, or alternatively, how much they despised their seniors, their duties, the war, themselves. It read like a record of humanity in turmoil. Most of the material that passed through his hands was of low-level importance. Anything relating to the Soviets, to the concentration camps, to torture, to scientific projects, industrial hardware, weapons development, hydrogen fusion, jet propulsion, rockets, chemical and biological research, was to be passed on immediately to another officer. They didn't really trust him. He accepted that, though there were times when he asked himself what he was doing there.

What Ernst knew of the war before he went to Berlin was

what everyone else knew, what he gleaned from the press, radio, the newsreels at the cinema in Hampstead. Images that remained with him. Soviet troops on the roof of the burning Reichstag, raising the hammer and sickle. Jerky newsreel footage of army vehicles picking their way over the charred rubble. The war for him in London was sandbags and barrage balloons; they sprouted from the ground, swelled up in the sky. Buildings which were there one day fell down overnight. Streets burst into flames. Life went on. Children ran to school with gas masks flapping at their sides. The mesmerising beauty of searchlight beams criss-crossing the sky, like giant cobwebs of light in search of an errant spider. The pounding of anti-aircraft guns, the grave judder of engines far away in the sky. Mrs Morris, who lived on the corner went down to her garden shed one evening to retrieve an oil lamp. She was fumbling around the cluttered interior, cursing as she bumped into walls, tables, deckchairs, when suddenly everything was illuminated in white light. With a gasp of delight she picked up the lamp she had been looking for, which was right in front of her, and turned. That was when the blast hit her. She was blown some thirty feet down the garden with the shed on top of her. When she picked herself out of the pile of matchwood she realised that her house was completely gone, along with her father, her housekeeper, and Mr Wright the dog. Her mind went and she was taken away, into care, they said. And thirty-eight years of reliable service ended for Henry the butcher one morning when a stray bomb landed in his path, leaving nothing of him or his cart but a greasy hole smoking in the road. Mrs Stevenson found several horse's teeth embedded in her front door she told Edith when she called round on Thursday with the eggs.

Curfews, blackout curtains, ration books, the All Clear whistle, the dull smoky trail of aircraft across the sky, that awful moment when the fuel ran out and the engine of a V2 would stutter into silence as it began its terrible arc towards the earth. The wireless spouted out names which soon became strange and familiar, charting the web of conflict snaking out across the world at a dizzy pace, snaring far-off places and peoples who had never imagined that they would have to share in the insanity that gripped Europe. Through the feverish jungles of Malaya and Sumatra to the Pacific, the war hurled onwards, spitefully disregarding boundaries and borderlines like a virulent fever. El Alamein, Tobruk, Rangoon. People became experts in the geography of an empire they had almost forgotten existed.

Edith's mother developed an obsession with reporting Ernst to the Home Guard. She called the military police and then she called the local constabulary. She called the navy and the air force. She wrote urgent letters; 'I have a German spy living under my very roof,' scribbled plaintively in her spidery, arthritic handwriting. She took to signalling from an upstairs window with a flashlight in rather jittery Morse code, which never failed to draw the blackout watch.

Her efforts finally came to fruition in the spring of 1943. Ernst arrived home one evening to find the front door of the house standing open and military vehicles parked in his drive. The neighbours craning their necks and whispering. Immediately imagining the worst, an unexploded bomb, perhaps, he rushed inside to discover the house had been ransacked, stripped from top to bottom. What they had been looking for, the officer in charge explained with all the authority of a waxed moustache, was a radio transmitter, maps, mysterious files hidden under the floorboards covered in secret codes, that kind of thing. They descended on his workshop gleefully. A veritable Cave of Wonders to their eyes, crammed as it was from top to bottom with all manner of curious treasures: scavenged instruments, wire recorders, electric valves, reels of fishing line, carburettors, copper cables, and even kitchen forks, bent into strange contortions or rooted like alien plants in pools of hardened glue. It all looked very suspicious. With their boots and gaiters the soldiers clumsily dug their way through, tipping their batons into every cupboard, peering under benches, finding things that whirred and purred, ratchets and cogs, boxes of wooden bobbins that resembled mortar shells, drawers filled with rivets and screws, buckets of clockwork springs, nuts and bolts of a thousand various sizes. Ernst felt sickened and scared: this, he suspected rightly, was the end. They took him off the Class B list and despatched him to a safer place. Edith's mother was delighted.

Of the internment camp, Ernst recalled waterlogged fields and the stench of the damp straw mattresses they slept on. A shortage of blankets. There was a war on they were reminded, with sneering irony. The voices of the guards swollen with smug confidence at being on the side of the good. No distinction was made between sympathisers and those who had fled the Third Reich. In late 1943 Ernst found himself penned in alongside men from every walk of life: butlers, domestic servants, merchant seamen, shopkeepers, a glovemaker from Tübingen, and a priest from Heide who clutched his fists to his temples all day and night, groaning about divine retribution. Ernst was locked on that windy estate alongside progressives, intellectuals, composers, writers, actors. The kind of people you might think would come in handy in defeating fascism. A virtual war ensued between sympathisers and their opponents. International Brigaders who had fought in Spain on the one hand and a man who was rumoured to be a member of the Gestapo on the other. Gangs of his men went around questioning people about their ancestry, their beliefs, their political allegiances. People walked into doors, on days when there wasn't a puff of wind. They fell down in the showers completely sober. The guards turned a blind eye to the whole thing. General despair welled up in the internment camp when the SS *Arandora Star* was torpedoed and sunk while carrying refugees to Canada. The internees whispered of conspiracies: a neat way of shaking off the refugee problem; feed them to the sharks.

'They would never do this thing, believe me.'

'That's what you people said in Germany, comrade: only agitators and troublemakers are being taken away. Then it was "only" the Jews, and then they came for the Bolsheviks, then the trade unionists, then the teachers, until suddenly there was no one left to fight.'

'Why King George himself is one of us. He only changed his name to Windsor during the last war.'

'Why don't you write to him then, and see if he'll come down and join us for a bit.' There was laughter at this, the absurd humour of the desperate.

The threatened deportation never came, but the arguments went on. He remembered that. The daily concerns were physical comfort and safety. The hard beds, the cold water. The wind rattling the huts at night. By the spring it was over and he was released. He went home, and found that home was no longer the same. It was how a man might feel after having been imprisoned for a crime he did not commit. The rest of his life becomes a mission, forever devoted to proving his innocence. The stain of the accusing finger never leaves him.

So Ernst spent long hours walking through Berlin, mulling over the circumstances that had compelled him to volunteer his services. The smoking void that was left of the ruined city seemed oddly appropriate, for the past was no longer there for him, except in hollow memories. He watched the children playing on the heaps of rubble, their imagination already reconstructing castles and kingdoms, propelling them away from the past. He saw people emerging from underground, from subterranean shelters, basement stoops, the tunnels of the underground railway, abandoned bunkers, like curious nocturnal creatures. Whole families climbing out of charred craters, their faces as weary as miners', their eyes showing white against the barren landscape. All that he recalled, of laughter spilling out through doorways, the shadows of luxuriant trees, brass bands, sunlit pavilions, was now unimaginable. There was only an eerie silence, disturbed by the fluttery grumble of diesel engines, and punctuated by the steady report of walls tottering to the ground, keeling over like gritty ice tipping slowly into a blackened arctic sea.

Finally plucking up the courage to do what he should have done a long time ago, Ernst went to Hamburg to try and find his mother. It wasn't just that the house was missing, the whole street was gone. The Allied bombing of April 1943 had been so intense people had been found buried alive, cooked in the molten asphalt. Someone said they thought she had moved away before the war when her husband died, but no one had a clue as to where she might have gone. One woman said she had been stabbed to death by a maniac, years ago. Impossible to make any sense of it. Ernst felt a strange sense of relief, realising that the last string had been cut years ago. As if he had always known that what he remembered of the past was unreliable.

'You came back to find that part of yourself you left here all those years ago,' ventured Werner Birnbaum confidently.

Werner was a colleague who had worked as an archaeologist in the years before the war. One afternoon he took Ernst through the maze of debris heaped up in the street, past the headless statue of a horse and into a darkened building. This was where he had spent the happiest days of his life, Werner said, as he led the way inside. In England, he had worked as a waiter, eventually fleeing to Dublin where he spent the war happily repairing barrels in a distillery.

Out of the darkness a golden creature floated into the eye of his flashlight. A dragon? A hybrid goddess. It had tiny wings on the back of its head. 'Nebuchadnezzar was rumoured to have kept a pet dragon inside the temple,' Werner breathed. The roving beam painted the long, slim body, neck and tail, illuminating the forked tongue and wings. It glowed in the dark, the image burning itself into his mind. Werner whistled to himself as he guided Ernst through the museum. Part of the roof was missing. Water dripped through a leaky tarpaulin onto the ancient wonders. 'They kept all fixed objects in place for the duration of the war. The fools believed their own propaganda and actually thought they would win. Of course, when the Russians arrived they made off with every piece they could carry.' The two men stood and looked up at the walls of Nebuchadnezzar. 'The Pergammon was the greatest museum in the world. You know why?' asked Werner. 'The Arabs were too busy worrying about their future, they didn't have time to care about what was under their feet. So we stole everything, and now we are the heirs. Civilisation is all about who steals the best stuff.' Listening to his friend's voice, Ernst picked his way over the fallen timbers and hasty scaffolds, following the beam of light that led deeper and deeper into the building. 'The awful and lovely goddess Ishtar. Queen of heaven and the goddess of love and war.' Werner's voice dropped to a hushed whisper. The yellow flashlight arc played over the upper serrations. The major part of the wall had been covered with plaster to protect it. Where it had fallen away it was like looking through the mundane surface of reality into a universe vivid with colour. Werner pulled away the plaster with his hands. Ernst held the torch steady on the expanding circle of deep blue as the glazed bricks emerged; 'A vast city in the form of a square, four-teen miles long and fifty-six miles in perimeter. According to Herodotus, the splendour of Babylon surpassed that of any city in the world. There were one hundred gates made of bronze. Inside there was another wall, smaller, which guarded the temple of Ishtar. This was the gate.' Both men were numbed into silent contemplation. Werner's voice came out of the shadows, telling the story of the Gilgamesh epic, how Enkidu lost his powers when seduced away from his natural life and entering Babylon. The animals no longer obeyed him so he turned to hunting them for food and skins.

'He was the first real nomad to be lost in the city,' declared Werner.

The word for the Sumerian underworld was *Kur*. The same word used to signify a foreign land. To go beyond the limits of the known world was to risk meeting such terrifying creatures. To leave home was to take the road of no-return.

How, thought Ernst, could a vision of such exquisite beauty have been waiting for him in this stark and decimated city?

In February 1946, as his time was drawing to an end, Ernst was put forward for a special mission: to accompany a certain Major Campbell to the south to interview a prisoner. The Americans had captured a German posing as a certain Captain Darwin of the Royal Engineers trying to cross the mountains into Austria on foot.

Campbell's doughy features hardened into a rigid expression of unhappiness when they met. 'I distinctly recall requesting a non-native interpreter,' he said. 'You're not Dutch, are you?'

'No, but I've lived in England for years,' Ernst replied. 'My wife is English.'

'I don't quite see how that changes anything.'

But Campbell had no choice; Ernst was the only interpreter available.

The roads were clogged with wanderers. There were reputed to be twenty million refugees on the move: returning, leaving, trying to find their families, or just pulling their belongings in circles, on horse carts, trolleys, prams. Where were they going? Ernst wondered. What did they hope to find? He was grateful for the khaki uniform he was wearing, for the privilege it gave him, for the ticket it promised him out of this hell.

They passed through villages that had been razed and looted by retreating Soviet troops. The abandoned paraphernalia of war was everywhere to be seen: tanks, artillery, burnt-out half-tracks, upturned cars and lorries. Scrap iron, picked over by the wandering hordes looking for something to eat, dressed in scavenged uniforms. A family of four trying to push a piano down the street; a man with two iron poles for legs and a cat on his shoulder, cheering, one hand held straight out in front of him in obscene salute. In a roadside pension where they slept, a young, reclusive woman cried all night in the next room. The landlord whispered the next morning that she kept the baked corpse of a child in a suitcase, shrunken to a purple mummy by exploding phosphorus. He didn't have the nerve to ask her to leave. When Ernst told him, Campbell snorted disbelief, tucking into his breakfast. The landlord turned his eyes to Ernst and said in German, 'A man would not lie about a thing like that.'

They swung around the outskirts of Munich, hemmed in by the dark slag heaps left by industry and bombs. As they rose up into the mountains, the vehicle slewed about the road as cold tyres skated on furred patches of ice. Water clattered through gleaming rock, an enchanted seam glittering in the mulch. Cloying diesel fumes, soft and enticingly warm, curled up from under the chassis.

He was thinking about the third law of thermodynamics: zero entropy, the way in which the cold and altitude thinned the mountain air, reducing all life signs to almost nothing. Reaching towards a sublime purity. Yet purity was an illusion. Everything is in perpetual contention; rising and falling, growing, dying. The trees were crisply laden with a dendritic frozen armour. The pine needles, bristling on trees like feathery spines, were fleeting seconds of frozen time. He was floating down the twisted course of his life, moving down the periodic table, to helium, to hydrogen. Becoming simplified, elementary. Time stripping him down as he passed through the familiar country like a foreign object, a metal splinter sinking through grease. Travelling as a stranger through his own land.

The warm putter of the jeep engine was muffled by heavy trees on either side. In the deep shadows at the end of the valley the vehicle began rising steadily, switching back and forth through the blur of straight, even trunks, the light semaphoring through the trees.

20

When they found him, the Rangers' seargant explained, the man was frozen in the foetal position like a relic preserved from the last ice age. Crouched beneath a hooded peak of gleaming black shale at an altitude of just under 2,300 metres and wrapped in ice, save for a pair of apertures around his nostrils. A modern-day Rip Van Winkle, complete with icicles dangling from his hair. The sergeant was a Negro tenor. He delivered his report standing straight as a tall pine, legs apart, hands behind his back. He had been decorated at Anzio, Lieutenant Burdon told them, when his platoon had been wiped out. For the last year he had been temporarily assigned to the Counter Intelligence Corps because of his skills as a first-class scout. Normally, the army had a strict policy of racially segregated units. 'To avoid trouble,' Burdon explained. Campbell nodded knowingly, unsure what to make of this black man. The sergeant figured that the patrol must have traversed the spot on an earlier sweep, but had been unable to distinguish the prisoner from his surroundings. The man had been poised on a narrow ledge, a hand's-width from a precipitous drop into a lifeless cleft of violet stone and diamond-hard blue ice. 'It looked like he was thinking of jumping and then just kind of waited too long.'

The village was silent. Nothing moved but the patrolling American GIs who shuffled morosely along snowbound streets, their gaiters damp, woollen hats poking out from under helmets giving them a strangely Quixotic appearance. In the closing months of the war a stray Dornier on its way back from trying to slow the Russian advance had shed its payload; an after-thought on the part of the pilot, to lighten the aircraft, increase his speed and get away. The three bombs had punched a knuckle-shaped row of holes into the earth. The fourth shell had bounced for some reason and careered away across the hillside to detonate itself against the thick outer wall of the monastery. The damage was relatively slight, but a crack had appeared, running like a miracle vine up the south-western wall of the chapel where the Rangers were installed. It snaked across the dome, causing chunks of the fifteenth-century frieze to fall away in floury, petrified flakes. The innocent cherubs, plump faces and buttocks, feathered tips on fiery wings, gleaming trumpets, horns, open hands raised in greeting, all suddenly lost their ability to remain suspended halfway to heaven, plunging earthward to explode in a cloudburst of plaster and fragments. A large tooth of stone had fallen away, leaving a hole in the painted sky through which the rain and the stars ate their way.

At the back of the chapel a spiral staircase in a recessed alcove led to an upper gallery that overlooked the inner court-yard of the monastery. The prisoner was being held in one of the rooms off this. The uniform he was wearing was standard British army issue, marked with the insignia and flashes of the Royal Engineers. The motto read, *Honi Soit Qui Mal y Pense*: 'Shamed be he who thinks evil of it'. The name Captain R. F. Darwin was impressed upon an identification bracelet and on the rather mangled papers found in the breast pocket of the tunic along with a diary. There was also a pair of dice and a fake Swiss watch which had stopped. The man didn't speak a word of English.

The Rangers had called in the Counter Intelligence Corps, whose main task was capturing and debriefing Nazi officers who had gone missing when the war ended. They were still being rounded up all over the place, some lying low, others trying to flee country and continent. The American officer, Lieutenant Burdon, was convinced that the man posing as Captain Darwin was unimportant. 'A time-waster,' he snarled. He was eager to get back to the 'Dustbin' – a secret interrogation centre located somewhere near Frankfurt. 'What matters right now is catching a hold of the people who were *responsible*. We owe that to humanity.' Burdon was swollen with righteous indignation. 'If I had my way, I'd shoot the son of a bitch and be done with it. He's guilty of something all right. No one runs away for no reason. Just a matter of finding out what he did.'

The fact was he had no real idea about the uncooperative man's identity, which was why he had involved the British. But Campbell made little headway. After little under an hour of interrogation he concluded that the suspect could not be the double agent he was looking for.

Burdon was not dismayed. 'We'll drag it out of him one way or another,' he said confidently. He suggested they adjourn for lunch. He was keen to hear more about the counter-espionage work Campbell was engaged in and had organised something of a feast, including some excellent Italian wine the Rangers had dug up out of a cellar. Officers only, as they would be discussing confidential information. Ernst was not invited to join them. Campbell suggested that Ernst stay and chat informally with the prisoner to see if that might trick him into giving something away. Ernst was relieved at not having to spend a long lunch listening to Campbell.

Left alone with the prisoner, however, Ernst wondered if perhaps they hadn't missed something. The broken, pathetic figure was hunched over the table. The frostbite to his face, fingers and toes had caused permanent damage. The bowed man resembled a photograph Ernst had once seen of a mummified Inca king discovered in a cave high up in the Peruvian highlands. The blackened tip of his nose and the ends of his fingers, the livid patches of red and leaves of dead skin which hung in white sheets from his chin and cheeks.

'My hands feel strange.'

'Gangrene. Your hands are infected from the frostbite.'

The heavy-lidded eyes flickered upwards to study Ernst for a time. 'What did you do during the war?'

'I was in England,' said Ernst.

'Are you Jewish?' the man frowned.

'No. I was just living there. My wife is English.'

'I'll never understand why they went after the Jews. What was the point?'

Dressed in bandages with a high, bitter reek about him, like gunpowder or brimstone, the smell that comes off igneous rocks when you strike them together, the man spoke a high

Prussian North German. A minor aristocrat and landowner, his story contradicted itself. He claimed to have remained a civilian throughout the war, opposed to the Nazis.

'I was questioned by the Gestapo, you know, several times. They wanted my land. Ignorant savages, ill-mannered city boys, led by that tram conductor.' The man looked at his hands. 'The country changed. What did you do, what profession?'

'I am an engineer.'

'A man of science, of reason, like me.'

The bandaged man appeared oblivious to his surroundings, as though this were a discussion around a familiar table in a bar. 'That fool, with the manners of a head waiter looking for a tip. He was nothing, a corporal with a grudge. He destroyed society. We turned over the country to a bunch of *Bierkeller* louts. Patriots. You know what's funny? The first thing they did was to give themselves titles, coats of arms. Envy was what drove them. They wanted to be like us. They destroyed the country to do it. Maggots. He bewitched them. That jumped-up little scamp. Women worshipped him. They would scoop up the earth he walked on and pushed it into their mouths, swallowed handfuls of it. Explain that to me.'

'You worked for them.'

'In the end, everyone worked for them.'

'You are a scientist?'

The man seemed no longer aware that there was anyone else in the room with him. In the midst of all this madness, perhaps only a clearly deranged man could speak the truth. 'We thought we had replaced God with machines, with science . . .' He broke off into a chuckle. 'But we needed him, didn't we? Our little Satan in an oversized hat . . .' his voice tailed off.

'Why were you going to jump off that ledge?'

The man stiffened for a moment. Then he put a hand to his face and tugged free a scrap of flaky skin. Rubbed it between his fingers. 'I thought they would shoot me. But they are too soft-hearted for that. What do you think?' he mused. 'Will they let me go? I can help. I can name people, officers. The experiments . . . great advances were made. At a cost, of course, at a terrible cost . . . to our souls.'

Ernst backed away from the table, the wasted man slumped over it. It was like looking into a mirror of possibility and seeing the evil we are capable of. You could rationalise madness. Here was the proof. Could he have become this repulsive, pathetic figure? Why not? What would have prevented him from becoming so?

The cathedrals would rise up again from the rubble, shiny and new. The streets would be repaved and would buzz once more with industrial impatience. All of this was just a moment in the course of history. Everything would be as it was before, better even. But the trees would know, rising out of the charred earth, they would understand what it meant to grow again.

And he, Ernst Frager, no longer had a country, no longer had a home.

He knocked urgently for the guard, impatient to get out, the room suddenly stifling. As he was walking quickly along the silent gallery above the courtyard, he heard the sound. It drew him to the narrow staircase, winding down through the old stone like a key through a lock. It drew him out, towards the entrance to the chapel, the doorway of light and the mountains of glassy ice beyond.

'Just that mad nigger again,' one of the American soldiers said, winking at Ernst as he passed. 'Pay him no heed and he'll likely shut up and go about his business.'

The cracked chapel resonated to the booming voice which made the old walls tremble. A man was standing in the open archway facing the hillside. Beyond his silhouette the steeples of rock and ice stretched their fingers towards the sky. The black sergeant had a serene look on his face. It was not a song that Ernst recognised, though he guessed rightly that it was a spiritual. When the voice ceased and the echo floated away across the hillside, the sergeant lowered his powerful chest and let his chin drop. After a silent moment he looked over and their eyes met. Ernst would remember that gaze for many years. It seemed to resonate through him. Although there was no menace in it, Ernst could sense naked defiance. Then the sergeant turned to go inside without a word.

To gaze upon nothing, no trace of human existence, just the rock, the trees, the stone, the precipice and the snow. Out beyond the medieval arch, above the cold clear air, the sky was hidden by soft clouds. Ernst gazed down the hill. The world was silent but for the sound of his boots crunching into the snow. He set off slowly, but soon found himself running; away from the heavy walls of the monastery, along the trees, out towards the rim of the white valley and the serrated peaks of ice and snow that rose beyond it. His breath came in stabs, his feet lost their purchase and slid, but each time he managed to regain his balance, still running. The earth felt slippery and unsteady, slipping away from beneath him. His entire life had been dedicated to striving for perfection, clean, shiny, irrefutable perfection. But now he saw there was beauty in incompleteness, a sublime grace, a gritty, human kind of imperfection that was a splendour which did not aspire to anything. It eluded him; the words needed to express what he felt at that moment would not come. Instead it floated through his mind as a sound. Scott Joplin; the evenings in Berlin spent in the American zone listening to jazz; Sidney Bechet's 1939 recording of Gershwin's 'Summertime'. The notes leapt from the soprano saxophone out into the unknown, bending and changing all that lay before them, lifting Ernst up, blowing him backwards into the future, down centuries, over ruined cities, carrying him out over the frozen valley, the clouded peaks, out to the blue ribbon of sky beyond. He did not look back. He put his head down and ran.

21

'Memory is an odd thing,' Waldo Schmidt mused. 'Facts remain buried in the mind like a ghostly shadow. After years of getting on with your life, just when you think you've put it all behind you, is exactly when they make themselves plain.'

'So why did he wait so long to finally leave Edith?' asked Jade.

'I can only speculate. Divorce wasn't as common as it is today, and besides, he wasn't the type to just walk out. The children were small. And don't forget that he grew up in a broken home, never knew his father and lost contact with his mother early on. Losing Edith and the children was the last thing he wanted.'

Jade was using a dictaphone machine nowadays to record their conversations. She wasn't sure why, it just seemed prudent. 'What happened? What made him leave home that first time?'

'Who knows? It happens all the time, doesn't it? One day it all looks like an absurd farce. The marriage. The little stamp machines, fixing bits of rubber onto wooden bobbins.'

So that was it? In 1957 Ernst Frager just stood up and walked out. The first step. The beginning of a twelve-year odyssey, shuttling back and forth from one world to another. That was where she came from, that restless devotion.

Ma petite métisse, Etienne used to call her. Jade hated him for that stupid endearment. Patronising. The nerve he had touched, leaving that lingering burn, making her wonder why, deep down, she felt inferior in some way. Unconsciously putting his finger on a tiny flaw, a line of weakness in their love, when he called her that. Why did such minor tics always have to blow up to Himalayan proportions? She found herself bowing with it, going with the flow, taking the path of least resistance. All in the name of love. For love she would be his little half-caste. Was love not about surrender? And if this tiny submission was the sacrifice required for the greater good of marital harmony could she not forgive him? Was that why her father stayed with Edith for so long?

Ernst Frager returned from Germany in the late spring of 1946 and went back to his old life, trying to restart the business, but something had changed. Ideas still began with that thrilling sense of infinite potential lying within his grasp, but it no longer lasted for more than a couple of days, perhaps a week at the most. He found himself struggling as never before to complete anything. It was, as he sometimes thought, late at night, when the house was quiet and the world around him was silent, as if he had stared at the sun for too long and been blinded. He seemed to have lost his faith in machines. Was it this loss of faith that led him to despise himself, his pathetic inventions, his loveless marriage? He was trapped in the wake of the decisions some former Ernst Frager had taken.

'He threw himself back into his work,' said Schmidt. 'He worked like a fury, night and day. But nothing came out of it.'

There were days when he would sit for hours on end staring at the inanimate objects around him in his workshop trying to remember what they were meant for, how to bring them back to life. The grubby benches, broken drill bits, steel shavings spiralled into silver hairs. All of this decay seemed to describe the course of his life, his dreams, reduced to a heap of worthless tools. The thread which had kept it all buzzing, hope, aspiration, vision, had evaporated. The magical incantation was gone. The eye of the savant, obsessed with precision, was now robbed of its secret spell. Once mad with purpose, now just mad. He idly spun the handle of a metal vice on the table. Ernst Frager, submarine machinist, inventor, stuck his fingers in the clamp one morning and squeezed until the blood seeped out from under his nails.

'I didn't realise how unhappy he was until I saw that.'

Schmidt lapsed into one of his silences. 'After he returned from Germany we were no longer as close as we had been. Oh, we still saw each other from time to time, but it wasn't the same. He wasn't the same. He didn't like me coming to the house. After I saw what he did with his hand . . . it got more difficult.'

It didn't quite add up. Was she imagining it, or was Schmidt being evasive again. Jade shook her head. 'That's not enough. There was something else, wasn't there? Something you haven't told me.'

He remained silent, his hands in his lap.

'You had something to do with it?'

Waldo Schmidt chewed his lip.

'You had an affair with her, with Edith? While Ernst was in Germany?'

Finally, he lifted his face to look her in the eyes. 'You still don't get it, do you? I was never interested in women. It was your father I was in love with.' The room had filled with the deep light of sunset. A soft purple glow painted his face. He had not shaved that day and the bristles on his chin glowed a luminous white. 'He remained oblivious to my feelings, but nevertheless . . . I suppose I had always been infatuated,' he sighed. 'Edith could be an adorable creature, but then she got it into her head to seduce me. When I turned her down she took it badly. She told Ernst she had been having an affair with me for years.' Waldo Schmidt's eyes were red and strained. In the strange light they began to swell with tears. 'You devote your life to protecting yourself, to keeping that part of you safe. You understand? I was a bachelor. No questions were asked. And when the time finally comes to reveal all, you can't, not for love or money. It was her word against mine, but it pushed him away from both of us, further into his work.' A stifled sob escaped him.

So for twelve years Ernst and Edith lived in misery. It was hard to fathom. But where would he go? Everything was in Edith's name. The house, the company. Instead, he travelled up and down the country, looking for new customers, trying to hold on to old ones. He lived in boarding houses, bed-and-breakfasts, small hotels in foggy Northern towns. Ernst preferred to be on the road than to stay at home.

Jade saw him then, her father, rising up and trying to walk out of his life. The car she remembered so vividly, speeding away from London. Until one day early in 1957 he drove to Merseyside and walked into the Blue Nile. He was fifty-three years old. His children no longer needed him. He turned his back on everything he had built for himself, apparently for good.

A dozen years went by with Ernst bouncing between the two halves of himself like an echo. The trip from London to Merseyside became a part of his life. Edith knew he had another woman, but she never admitted it to anyone. More importantly, she would never let him go. She would rather have died than consent to a divorce. Perhaps she always expected Ernst to come to his senses, to drop Miranda like a fad and just come back to her. He didn't.

Ernst enjoyed the drive. He took his time, tapping his finger on the wheel to the music they played on the light radio. He knew all the places along the way; the petrol stations, the attendants who were friendly, the ones who were not. The roadside tea shops and cafés where he liked to linger, savouring that feeling of rootlessness which had become a kind of solace to him. And that was how he would have stayed, in perpetual motion from one world to the other, until the day a dark landscape descended upon him. An unfamiliar country spread through his mind. A dark stain leaking over the contours of his brain.

In the watery light from the bedside lamp, her eyelashes flickering in half-sleep, Miranda's downturned face seemed at once strange and unfamiliar. Her chin had become peppered with small grey spirals of hair. She had been confined to that hospital bed for almost a week. At times lucid, and at others not. As if she were in the possession of another Miranda that would only allow her into the present for short periods. Jade made a note to remember to get some tweezers or depilatory cream. Her mother would not be thankful for being left to go to seed. She would try to fix her hair a little bit, too.

Steady deterioration, Jade had come to realise, was not steady or continuous at all. It went in leaps and bounds, like a stone rolling down a pebbly beach towards the sea. It jumped and bounced. It changed direction without warning. Time slowed.

Ben was in the hallway making an overseas call. He was assuring someone that this was not the end, speaking as discreetly as he could while trying to make himself heard across three thousand-odd miles of space. There was the question of what they were to do if this became a long-term invalidity.

'We'll take her home and I'll look after her there.'

Jade looked at him and saw a man struggling with a triptych of demons suddenly gathered around him: pride, loneliness and the prospect of loss. It all added up to bewilderment. This was not the time to think how much work was involved in taking care of somebody, how much effort, how much emotional energy was required. How much love. She looked at him and knew that Ben was not ready for such a decision. He was still not fully convinced that one more bunch of flowers and one more night of rest would not do the trick. Jade rested her hand on his arm. He smiled stoically and patted her hand. They sat in the waiting room, drinking milky tea in silence. Someone somewhere was singing a hymn. An organ was playing out of tune.

When she was a small child, Jade's great hero was Lieutenant Uhuru of the starship *Enterprise*. Whatever the universe threw at them, Uhuru, with her short red uniform and pointy bust, would give it a long sideways look with those unswerving Cleopatra eyes of hers, remaining cool and collected while hell broke loose around them. She resembled an Egyptian goddess, but actually was more like an oracle, because it was Uhuru alone, one hand cupped to her radio earpiece, who could hear the mysteries of the cosmos whispering. The stars and the planets sang to her, or so it seemed to this little girl. She was six years old and slept with her thumb in her mouth and a teddy bear under one arm. Lieutenant Uhuru cupped a hand to her ear. Captain, I'm picking up something, a signal.

Uhuru was her guiding light, her winking goddess, the woman she admired most in all the universe, well, almost – the woman she admired most was her mother. Even at the worst of times, when they could not speak but shout, when it seemed as if they would never survive one another, Jade and her mother were a team. They had always depended on one another, even when they weren't on speaking terms, and now she was vanishing, withdrawing into her own enclosed world, slipping through her fingers and disappearing for ever.

Miranda's eyelashes stirred, trying to brush aside the darkness.

The map of an unfamiliar country spread through Ernst's mind. The dark stain like an ink blot spilled over the contours of his brain. He knew what was happening to him. A stroke. Like a light that snapped quickly on and off in his head. A brief, blinding flash. He felt no pain though, which was strange. He had the sense of being suspended far above the useless contraption that was his body. He felt himself flying apart, as though his physical form were no longer able to contain his spirit.

A matter of seconds, this watershed between life and not life. One minute the car, the road and the next this. The familiar smells of benzine, engine oil and shaved metal were to accompany him. He saw himself smile. His hat, with a dent in the top which he dearly wanted to push out but could not, lay beside him on a bed of crystal granules like crushed ice. He was incapable of moving anything, his left arm was numb, one eye saw only blackness, and nothing but a nagging twitch far off in the region of his right leg. His head still tumbling, flying, bouncing across fields, sky-blue and green snapping back and forth as it rolled and rolled again.

As he lay there, Ernst tried to avoid thinking about what was to follow, about the consequences for those around him, about pain and separation. The road was a taut thread that ran through his heart, from the past which lay behind him in London to the windy port and the future, and the little girl who waited impatiently.

His mind, seeking a way out, took him back, to the first time he saw Miranda, that first night at the club. The winking lights over the doorway: a long-limbed bird moving one leg at a time, strutting down the stairs, a nod to the conventions of glamour to which the Blue Nile club aspired. Standing at the front of the stage wearing a long sequinned dress, she seemed a little out of place. It took him a long time to realise that the sound he was listening to was her singing. People were on their feet applauding but Ernst's mind was numb. Like light passing through a strip of celluloid film, what was black became white, and vice versa. The big man, Ismail Bilal, moving through, clapping shoulders, shaking hands.

'Still having a good time?'

'Yes, thanks.'

Ernst pronounced the words carefully. He actually felt as if he might be sobering up. Strange how he felt completely at ease in this place, as though it had been waiting here for him to find all his life. He felt relieved, in a way he could not recall feeling in a long time. This was a different kind of familiarity, of the present, not the past.

'Who is that girl?' he asked, nodding towards the small stage.

The big man lowered his chin and then raised it again in a slow dip of a nod, like a horse drinking from a trough. 'That,' he said, swinging round to lean his elbows against the bar and look up at the stage, 'is Miranda.'

A dark flower bloomed deep inside that labyrinth of nerves and corpuscles. A tiny spot no larger than a full stop grew to envelop his entire world. He imagined the stain swallowing him. He tried to focus on the facts, to concentrate on the details: It was 1969. The Americans were about to land on the moon, with a German scientist leading them: Wernher Von Braun's Saturn rockets thrusting the Apollo mission into space. He, Ernst Frager, was on earth, driving a Ford Consul Classic 315. Five years old. Pragmatic decision. No longer able to afford the luxury of the Jaguar, he had traded it in for an automobile first produced in 1961 and upgraded in the following years. Sharp and finny, rather like a snub-nosed dolphin. The wide front seat was one unbroken sweep of smooth upholstery. The gear lever fixed to the steering column. There was a lot of chrome, headlights and grille, along the interior trim and dashboard. The lines were soft arches. The engine emitted a sound like hot percolating gravel. Facts blurred. The road spun into the sky. The sky became ocean. He was on fire. He was extinguished. He was swallowed. Jonah in the belly of the leviathan.

Ernst did not want to think about the strange place he was stranded in, did not want to think of the little girl who was fighting off sleep in anticipation of his arrival, refusing to go to bed, waiting on the chequered porch, for him, the one-eyed man, the one-armed bandit. Then he was floating backwards, away from the scene, back down the road. He saw himself rise up from the table, pull on his hat and coat, wave a cheery hello to the surly woman behind the counter and, with a glance at the sky, saw himself step out and stride backwards towards his beloved vehicle, glazed with drops of blue water winking like mercury in the quickening dusk. Raindrops lifting upwards into the sky. Hallelujah. A miracle. Time moving backwards.

22

Looking out over the thin whistle of grey water that stretched towards the dorsal swell of Birkenhead and Tranmere, Jade saw copper-sheathed vessels emerging from the early morning mist in a bright hard, mineral glint. Three sides of a fateful triangle led back here. The old trading ships would nestle here like migrating birds, resting momentarily upon the marshy flats. There, where the kingfishers stepped cautiously at low tide, the plump hulls and tilted prows once leaned upon the tongue of glistening mud, waiting for a miracle hand to lift their sails and carry them a thousand leagues, flying south past coasts of gold and ivory to where ebony men and women could be bought for the price of a cheap pair of looking-glasses, bronze trinkets, woollen caps or glass beads, their fate sealed with a handshake, a jug of gin or hogshead of English cider. Then west they would blow, bobbing over the heaving troughs of the Atlantic to exchange their human cargo for sugarloaf and peppercorn, cotton and ginger root, before returning here to sleep, to dream, to rest belly down in the blue mud, letting the acetic tide wash away the residual moral grit of their nefarious travelogues. The estuary mud was riddled with shaved fragments, the crumbled remnants of wood, pewter, bone and iron, scattered by the waves, awaiting an archaeologist and an appreciative age to dig them out. Stories that remain untold until their weight is lifted from the mud.

It was time to let go, to allow it all to fall away. The history, the memories, the sense of responsibility. Jade wasn't sure she had found the end of her story, but that was no longer necessary, she had found something else. It seemed that making sense of her life was more about accepting that she would always be incomplete.

She no longer dreamed of building great towers in the sky. It seemed as though in her haste to reach the top she had forgotten why she had wanted to become an architect in the first place. But she no longer wished to put up great big buildings for corporations and multinationals. She wanted to get back to an architecture that was about how people inhabit cities. She wasn't sure how or where she would begin this, but she felt an excitement that she had not experienced for years and that was enough for her to go on with. Trust your instincts, she said to herself, and all else will fall into place. And already it was happening. Waldo Schmidt had told her that he wanted her to have the big house. It was virtually hers anyway, he said. Ernst had designed most of it and he couldn't bear the thought of selling it to one of those dreaded property developers. 'I want you to have it when I go,' he explained. 'And don't worry, I won't take long,' he added. She needed to give it some thought, but she had a feeling there would never be a better moment to branch out, to start her own studio. She had enough ideas and there was plenty of space in the house for her and Maya to live as well. Sell the old place, shake off the final residue of Etienne, the site of their failure which she had tried so hard to transform.

That was what had brought her walking up the hill from the waterfront to this wasteland on a small deserted street. She peered into the angry hollow of what looked like a building that had been hit by a bomb. A tale of violence told by the charred and splintered debris that filled the crater. The woman at the records office explained that there had been a fire, blamed on faulty wiring that should have been replaced decades ago. 'No one ever bothers,' she shrugged. She had seen this enough times to know it would not be the last.

Starry diamonds of glass sparkled in the black soil. Cracked wooden beams. An iron frame, the remains of a spiral staircase, hung in miraculous suspension like a butchered ribcage from the centre of a non-existent ceiling. Crude graffiti sprayed in luminous slashes evoked the palaeolithic rock paintings in the Lascaux caves. Weeds sprouted like dirty green ribbons from among the discarded bottles and rusted tins.

She had thought she knew where it was, half remembering

something from her childhood. But it had taken her a while to find it. She hadn't minded. Walking helped to take her mind off things. There were the gaps between visiting hours to fill. And Maya was spending time with Ben, consoling one another by going to the cinema to watch the latest offering from the gods. Their friendship was an unexpected development and Jade did not know exactly what to make of it. But it gave Maya a little more space, away from her mother. And perhaps it allowed her to spend time in the company of someone who to some degree might fill the absence of her father. In any case, there were less conflicts. And Miranda was now in full-time care, silent, withdrawn, waiting. This, Jade had come to understand, was the way things were going to be from now on.

She walked in a fever, in a blur, her mind unconsciously ticking off the landmarks as she went: Nelson's monument, his skeleton hand upon his heart forecasting his own death; Oriel Chambers, the most important cast-iron structure in the world, in its day; Hardiman Street where Aunt Lillie had her hair salon; Castle Street where Daniel Defoe once peered down pensively from his rooms; the mysterious planes and offset spires of the Swedish Seaman's Kyrka on Park Lane.

The Blue Nile club had been closed down years ago, when Ismail Bilal passed away. There was a son somewhere, but he appeared to have no interest in keeping the club open; it had outlived its age. A miracle that nothing else had been built on the site. An oversight in local planning, a gap in the economy. Whatever. Stepping closer, Jade thought she could make out the shape of the sign which once ran along the top, above a shiny blue and white awning. Miranda had a photograph of the club, showing the front entrance with the lights blinking on and off in succession, suggesting a flight of stairs and a long-legged stork in a top hat.

A carbonised fossil, a burnt-out ember: the fused key to a part of her life.

She took one final look before stepping back. As she turned, Jade caught sight of a man standing alone at the top of the street, on the next corner. A pencil silhouette marked against the skyline. A charcoal scratch. It was difficult to make anything of his features. A dark figure, wearing jacket and trousers, carrying a long bag slung over his shoulder. A musician, was her first thought. He seemed to be waiting for something. For a long time neither of them moved. There was no one else in sight. No cars, no people about this early on a Sunday morning. The man turned abruptly and stalked away, disappearing from view. Without hesitation, Jade walked quickly up towards the spot where he had been standing. She reached the top of the road just in time to catch sight of the man disappearing around another corner. She hurried down the hill, not quite sure why she was following him.

This was a lonely, derelict area, on the edge of an abandoned industrial zone overlooking the docks. An area marked by open tracts of land and old factories. When she reached the inter-section she was in time to observe the man in the dark suit crossing the street to vanish into a building. Jade strolled over to take a look.

The church was invisible until you were standing in front of it. Sandwiched as it was between two much larger build-ings, both derelict. It was once a place for women to pray for their husbands to come home safely from the sea. An old Anglican priory. A steepled grey butttress lodged in a wash of broken windows, neglected warehouses and obsolete factories. The church had gone through a series of transformations. Like Tibetan prayer flags, the ripped and frayed posters plastered over the weather-beaten noticeboard fluttered in the wind. From Taekwondo to bingo, through Gospel choirs and percussion, it had served as a Zen temple, a mosque, as well as a healing centre providing lessons in Shiatsu, Reiki, Tai Chi and some-thing called 'Astral voyaging'. Now a simple, hand-painted blue sign beside the recessed vestibule declared in uncertain red letters that its latest manifestation was as the Temple of the New Dawn.

Jade pushed open the big door and stepped inside. The inte-rior was a rather voluminous space that rose up into the shadowy recesses above the wooden rafters.

The place was deserted. She was just thinking of leaving when a door on the left opened and a man appeared. From his build and the way he walked, she recognised him as the man she had been following. A pile of folding chairs was stacked against one wall and he began to set them up in rows. When he was halfway through Jade stepped forwards. Without breaking off his work he looked up.

'Can I help you?'

'Could you tell me what this place is?'

'The Temple of the New Dawn.'

'That's what it says on the door. But what exactly do you do?'

'Oh . . . Well, you'd have to ask Pete about that.' The man straightened up, his hands on his hips. His dark forehead was covered with a light sheen of perspiration. He went back to setting out the rest of the chairs before exiting from the room.

There was something curious about a church that was no longer a church. The door on the left opened again and a white man appeared, his head completely shaven.

'Are you from the press?'

'No,' said Jade. 'I was passing, and I wondered. What exactly is this place?'

'The building, you mean? Oh, it's very special. It was built in the eighteenth century. Quite late, for the sailors, you know. During the war the entire street was razed to the ground by the German bombers, but this was left standing, not a scratch on it.'

'And now, who uses it?'

'Oh, we do.'

'What kind of a church is this, if you don't mind me asking?' He wore a scruffy polo shirt and patterned Chinese silk trousers. There was a tattoo of a seahorse on the back of one hand which spoke of an earlier, less salubrious existence.

'Oh, it's not a church. It's more of a spiritual centre? We are not affiliated with any particular denomination or faith?' He finished his sentences with an interrogative, upward inflexion. 'We provide spiritual comfort for people in need?'

A girl in pigtails and dungarees appeared pushing a trolley with a tea urn on it, along with a leaning tower of plastic cups, tea bags, instant coffee, milk.

'People come to us because they have no faith in the system.' The man smiled. 'A sad reflection of our country today, I'm afraid.' His voice had a nagging, earnest tone to it.

'When they come to us they have nothing. Most of them find their feet, or they get picked up. Either way, they disappear.'

She was still not clear about what kind of people he was referring to. Who needed this spiritual guidance? She wondered if he was being entirely honest with her.

The smile on his face was beginning to turn waxy. This was the circumference of his power, his means of holding on to the reins when the cart that was his England had gone crashing out of all control. The air of secrecy returned when the girl in pigtails came up to ask him about something. There was some whispering, after which the two of them disappeared through the door on the left.

Over by the main entrance Jade found a noticeboard displaying a meagre harvest of flyers, personal ads, handwritten notes, recommending vegan food clubs, tarot, palmistry, weekend retreats: Teahouse of the August Moon – spiritual retreat in Norfolk; there were others, further afield; names like Peloponnese, Sardinia, Irian Jaya jumped out at her. Distant islands seemed to be popular. Exotic places in the sun to contemplate one's navel, to discover one's inner self.

She strolled around the hall then, looking at the walls. It reminded her of a school gym. The wooden parquet floor, the black rubber skid marks marking the passage of furniture. The altar, placed beneath the high windows at the far end, was a fusion of various oriental styles. There were candles, rows of incense sticks, a smiling Buddha, plump with spirtual consiousness. There were also figures representing Ganesh, Hanuman, and pentagrams, I-Ching hexagons. Just then the big front door swung open behind her and she turned to watch a lone man enter. His clothes looked worn-out and rumpled, as though he had slept in them. His eyes darted left and right as he looked about the room, at the rows of chairs. Then he settled on a spot on the left-hand side of the room, close to the long table. Going over, he sat down quietly and waited. Shortly after that another arrived, and then another. As they started to file in, the big old priory door, dented and chipped, swung back and forth on its hinges with a resounding, irreverent wallop with each new arrival. They came in twos and threes. Young men for the most part, the occasional woman among them. People who had come a long way. Solitary characters filing past the assistant, who had reappeared wearing an orange robe of vaguely oriental style over her dungarees. They crossed the floor with their eyes to seek out a place in the rows of chairs set facing the altar. As they entered their heads inevitably turned towards to the long trestle table placed by the swing doors, covered now by a white cloth with stains on it. A pile of paper plates was stacked at one end, a hint of what was to come.

Jade found herself thinking of Thursday, if that was his name. She realised with a touch of guilt that she had not thought about the accident for some time. The detective she had engaged, Arthur Quail, had come up with little. Thursday had lived an almost invisible life. No fixed address and few friends, certainly none of whom were willing to pass on his real name, or where he came from, or how he got to London. But here, now, she sensed she was in the midst of that floating world, among people who lived their lives in the interstices, between margins, lost in the lines between shadows and light. Their stories remained untold. They would ally themselves with whoever could provide them with a slender foothold, anything to prevent them slipping back into the hazy zone from which they were trying to extricate themselves.

There were about fifteen people in all when the 'reverend' reappeared, wearing a white jacket of Chinese silk in place of the polo shirt. He sat cross-legged on a large, cushioned podium. He made a small speech welcoming them into the arms of their new spiritual family, describing the wonders that awaited them. To Jade, who had taken a seat at the back of the room, it seemed a cruel ritual to impose on hungry people. Today's little sermon consisted of focusing on the idea of light: 'I should like us to think about what light means to us.'

The room was silent. The reverend closed his eyes. There were a few furtive whispers around the room but most of them managed to remain silent. Then he began to emit a long, sonorous chant. When it was over he opened his eyes and said a bit more about the universe and harmony and suchlike. Jade wondered if he really believed anyone was interested, but her thoughts were arrested by the patience she saw on the faces around her. It was an old endurance, part of an ancient passage, of men and women crossing the seas against their will, leaving behind families, homelands. They learned how to listen, how to wait, this was what the world had taught them, what it was still teaching them.

Now they were on their feet, moving silently towards the trestle table upon which pans and bowls were spread out. They filed along, picking up plates and waiting to have them heaped with mashed potatoes and vegetable stew, a mug of soup and a few slices of bread. They retreated to find a place to sit and eat. They conducted themselves courteously. She overheard voices talking in what might have been Slavonic, others that sounded more African. Where did they all come from? Everywhere and nowhere. Elsewhere. She watched one of the men crouched over a plate shovelling food into his mouth with a plastic spoon.

I am Thursday, he seemed to say, for I was born on that day when I landed in this country. Before that, as far as you are concerned, I was nothing. The desert burns away memory. Salt water makes you choke with thirst. These things I know. To chant this song for a meal is nothing, to be buried alive below deck with a hundred and forty strangers. This I can do. I can chant the song this white man asks me to sing. I can clean away his shit, wash his windows, build his glass towers. It is the way of the world. You draw the arch which falls and kills me. You are free. You are not free.

Ernst Frager is running through the pines, beneath the crystal cathedrals of the icy alpine peaks. She sees him, feels the sound of his breath on her neck, his heart beating against hers. The air is cold. It is winter 1946 and Ernst Frager is running. Away from the stone walls of the monastery behind him, towards her. She sits there, alone in that unfamiliar place, long after everyone has gone, tears running silently down her face.

Rachel

Sometimes, when it is quiet and I am alone in the garden, just me and the earth and the leaves and the water, Sayf comes to me again. As time goes by I begin to see it from his point of view and I realise how much courage it must have taken for him to do what he did. Where did that conviction come from? I shall probably never know. I can only imagine what it was that he saw out there in the world; what he thought he was fighting for or against. I can barely glimpse the scale of it, the deep void upon which he felt bound to impose his beliefs – a chink of light in the darkness. He was wrong. I still believe that. But if he was, it was because we, too, were wrong. And so the son pays the price of his parents' failings. It has always been that way.

I walk barefoot through the yard leaving damp imprints drying on the ground behind me. I spray water over the tamarind bushes and the wind pushes it back into my face, it smells of life itself and I feel him there with me.

Once a month, if we are lucky, the mountain of waste that collects in the open square opposite the house is set alight. A government man comes along with a rake and a straw basket and heaps it all up and then officially sets fire to it. Most days, however, other people turn up unsolicited, appearing out of nowhere to sort through what we have deemed as being spent, worthless, looking for things they can use. They can see where we are blind, their eyes guided by a resourcefulness that we do not know. Through the iron whorls of the back gate I watch them scrabbling about, finding something, holding it up, turning it this way and that. I wonder what treasure they have discovered. I see dirt, soiled rinds and rotting peel. They see glittering gems. I wonder what or how. I imagine bits of wire that can be used to strengthen the frame of a shelter or hold down a roof, or slips of cardboard and plastic that can be bent, shaped and cut to a thousand purposes. Old tin cans become motor cars with which the children race excitedly along the street. Each object retrieved is a bead of life gained, another small victory in the struggle against diminishing resources, limited possibilities, the loss of rivers, homelands, herds and ultimately, of course, death. Our problems seem frivolous and insignificant in comparison.

I still see them coming through the smoke in the late afternoon. Tall ambling figures, moving with timeless grace through the heat haze that blurs the image, making them appear more spirit than flesh. They go slipping across my line of sight, harmless and out of reach, a wordless manifestation that speaks of the meaninglessness of the conflict which displaced them and which took my son's life. It binds me to them, this shared sense of futility. In a kind of daze I watch them until they vanish through the thin film of ochre dust beaten from the ground by the sun. I remain there long after they have gone, unable to shake off the spell of their presence.

When the rains fall on their homelands in the great marshlands to the south, the river swells, overflowing into a myriad of tributaries to flood an area as broad as England. It becomes a vast inland sea of bright water dotted with thick clumps of reeds and floating rafts of papyrus. In the last century numerous missionaries and intrepid explorers found themselves trapped there. They were determined to conquer the untamed, to make it theirs, to find the source of the Nile, to realise the foggy dream of a glorious empire stretching down from Cairo to the Cape. Their waxed moustaches wilted in the heat and their ambition evaporated in the frustrated humidity of despair. It was not easy finding a way through that maze. Ships ran aground, fatally lodged on obstinate humps of silt banks that shift unpredictably. Flat-bottomed steamers drifted in circles for weeks. There are tales of anguish and even cannibalism. People on board went insane, driven mad by the sun and their inability to distinguish one channel from another in that watery labyrinth. I wonder if they too might not have looked out in the last throes of their quinine-induced derangement, and glimpsed figures such as I do now, wandering across their field of vision, vanishing with ease into the horizon. They are here because their place in the world was taken from them. Their homes and villages burned and bombed, the earth scorched back to the time before God cut open the sky with his axe, as they believe, to give birth to man. I am not romanticising their life. I am glad for the iron gate which still stands, however symbolically, between my world and theirs, but I cannot shake off the conviction that they are the last obstinate survivors of an aspect of human dignity that we have lost or forgotten. They are moving through nothing towards nothing. There can be no more lonely place in the world. This I know.

The hosepipe has sprung a tiny leak and radiates a fine multicoloured peacock fan of moisture into the air. I stand there, lost in some reverie, the hiss of water escaping and I wonder if I really see them at all, or if a middle-aged Englishwoman peering through her gate might not imagine such things to herself. As I wander about tending the plants, spraying the big lime tree which fills the afternoon air with that acrid mix of dust and water, the world seems trapped in slumber. I find memories hidden there, fragments of a former life I thought lost, brief snippets from when the boys were young and used to chase one another round the garden. Amin calling to them grumpily to let him have some peace. That was life, I tell myself. I never realised it at the time, I was always too busy.

At that hour the light moves swiftly through the spectrum with the discipline of centuries. It feels as though I am watching time pass before my eyes. All the laws of the universe have been suspended, and all the lost ones come back to visit. When it is particularly hot and windless and I am standing there in the muggy humidity of radiant leaves, the frothy loam squeezing between my bare toes, I feel a strange comfort. I imagine that this is what it must have been like a hundred years ago, when those majestic old steamers used to lose their way in the great marshes down south and the travellers simply drifted in circles for weeks, unable to extricate themselves, going quietly but firmly out of their minds.

March 1999 – August 2005

202